THE DEVIL'S MISTRESS

THE DEVIL'S MISTRESS

The Diary of Eva Braun

The woman who lived and died with Hitler

10/23/97

ALISON LESLIE GOLD

To Josie —
Yours with
friendship —

[signature]

ff

Faber and Faber
Boston · London

Library of Congress Cataloging-in-Publication Data

Gold, Alison Leslie.
    The devil's mistress : the diary of Eva Braun, the woman who lived
and died with Hitler : a novel / Alison Leslie Gold.
        p.   cm.
    ISBN 0-571-19923-2 (cloth)
    1. Braun, Eva—Fiction.   2. World War, 1939–1945—Germany—
Fiction.   3. Hitler, Adolf, 1889–1945—Fiction.   4. Statesmen's
spouses—Germany—Fiction.   I. Title.
PS3557.03267D48   1997
813'.54—dc21   97-14169
                                                                              CIP

Printed in the United States of America

Dogs read the world through their noses
and write their history in urine.
J. R. ACKERLEY

BOOK I

The trail led me to Zell-am-See.

The instructions: Meet contact at café. Order Käsekuchen with coffee.

I didn't want Käsekuchen or coffee but, as instructed, ordered both. The boy who approached me had bulldozed hair, amber bristles pocking his skull. He was wearing a brown bomber jacket, bruised Doc Martens with steel toe-caps threaded by white laces that were untied. Both sides of his head had been tattooed in black and brown ink with double-bladed axes. The two helves crossed at the pink nape of his neck.

His right ear and the bridge of his nose were pierced. When he spoke his tongue lolled out, revealing that it too was pierced through the taste buds with a lightweight aluminum diaper pin, and that his teeth had been mended with gold. He told me to follow him, so I paid up.

Crossing the concrete parking structure, his attitude was belligerent. His footfalls slapped flatly. His right hand clutched at and kneaded his crotch. The lock on the rear door of the car rattled him into surly confusion until I popped the lock from the panel on the driver's side for him, so that he could open the door.

He sank into the leather back seat, cupped his hands between his legs, his fingers curling under his scrotum while I got into the front seat, inserted the key. So? I asked.

He mewled out driving instructions. These led us to a beaver-brown and buff-trimmed office block across from a square. A neo-classical-style monument stood at the center of the square. At first I thought that two columns of falling leaves had been cast in bronze but on second look I saw that it was a monument depicting the feet of an archaic unicorn. I locked the car, told the boy to wait.

I gave my name to the receptionist. I had barely admired the peach sepia etching behind her desk, when a voice called out with excessive *Gutmütigkeit*, Enter, please.

The man behind the desk in the office was quite fit, wore a

three-piece suit, stretched out his hand. He was splashed with an astringent aftershave that filled the office with the scent of wet dog. Before him, systematically laid out, were: a bridge of nine dentures in yellow metal, a cap with gold insignia, leather gloves, and a dog leash.

What currency? I asked, after a quick handshake.

Of your own choosing, he replied.

I mentioned a price. For the lot, I told him.

Ach.

For sure my pricing was on the money. I raised the offer, but not by much.

Ach.

Wirklich. I can go no higher without authorization.

From whom?

From the organization. I, of course, didn't say that the cap and gloves were too iffy.

How much for the bridge only? I enquired. Then for fun, I added, Throw in the dog leash.

He gave a price. In cash.

Cash is fine.

We closed the deal. He called in the receptionist who quickly wrapped the denture in bubble plastic, then wound the leash around her fist, threaded the collar through the bracelet of leather. She stuffed both pieces into a plastic shopping sack. We shook hands and left.

The entire transaction took less than five minutes. It left me rubbing my hands together with satisfaction. Two telephones were ringing at once when I closed the door.

The boy was beside the car, leaning back on his heels, slightly crouched, urinating up at the windshield. He directed the copious yellow stream back and forth with his hand. When he saw me looking at him with distaste, he rocked farther back and directed the stream onto the hood of the car. I know where are more souvenirs, he barked, thumping his stumpy penis against the rear view mirror in order to splash off the remaining drips, then he pushed it back inside his trousers.

He told me where to go. Shortly we were on the main road

speeding in fourth gear toward the border. I punched the Blaupunkt the whole time, not listening but surfing across various programs—in German, French, Polish, English, Russian, Swedish.

We skirted the mountains. Rivers threaded into the horizon, homey chalets with red-colored geraniums in window boxes dotted the terrain. At Chiemsee I was forced to slow. On the water, steamers crossed to Frauenchiemsee, decorated with flowers, and men in loden Bavarian hats stood with women dressed as brides, their veils waving in the wind.

We followed the A-11 east past Rosenheim then north until I could see the Olympic tower. After passing Siemens, BMW, and the Hellabrunn Zoo, he told me to veer into the outskirts of München where he directed me to a dingy wine bar.

I stood at the bar with the boy, my good Italian shoes sticking to the silvery floor, which seemed to be coated in decaying matter, wild garbage. The boy stalked the dance area, pulled open his pants, then lunged at a girl wearing nothing except wide straps crossed between her muscular breasts and buckled on the belly side. A third wide strap from the back of her waist went under her body and fastened up front.

The place smelled like carrion. The girl had a shaved head. The two circled around each other in play, then the boy began to throw tiny darts into the girl's cyclamen-colored genital opening until I couldn't distinguish whether they were dancing or copulating, and both their bodies were glistening wet.

When she walked toward me, I saw a snail ornately tattooed on both sides of her head. Her nostrils were pierced. Also her septum, nipples, and clithood. The latter was quite enlarged, stood up prominently as the surrounding area had also been shaved. On her pubis, another ornate snail. Radiating away from her pubis, whitish scars in the form of widening circles that gave her a kind of striping. The word Helix was branded across the back of each hand in ornate lettering.

When I left with her, he held a stein of beer in one hand, and was waving his erection at her with the other.

Outside, she draped a green bomber jacket across her shoulders and directed me to the center of München. She gave me instructions: Meet Grossmutter—Frau Monalisa Hochschmidt—across from the Richard Strauss fountain.

I followed the instructions: I parked the car and crossed over to look at the fountain, admired the dramatic scenes sculpted along the shaft and the veil of falling water that revealed—then hid—the operatic scenes depicted from *Salomé*. I crossed back and found a table in the Pschorr brewery beer hall opposite the fountain. Because I was watching for fatty foods, I ordered a plate of radish from the cold menu.

The waiter told me, The cutting of it by free hand depends on a stiletto, a good ability to judge by the eye, and a calm hand. It is better that you cut the radish before drinking your second mug of beer.

With this he unfolded a long list of beers. We have one-hundred forty to choose from, he said.

But I was happy with ordinary light beer.

The waiter attacked the large radish with the knifepoint, quickly turning one into a perfect rose, the other into a gnome's head.

She was quite prompt; a blond-haired woman, tall with the athletically fit body of a thirty year old, a raisin-shaped face of a seventy year old, the skin loose around her lips. She was unwilling to sit down but took me by VW Golf to a terraced housing development on the outskirts of München. Her yard had a gravel path, red geraniums in pots. It was fenced and protected by a growling mongrel of indeterminate origin at the end of a short chain. Black leaves were heaped in piles.

Over strong coffee, using my proven style of *Gutmütigkeit*, I drew her out: You have kept so fit through the years, Frau.

I didn't need to prod any more.

I stretch every day of my life for flexibility. I walk every day of my life. My feet impacting the ground has kept my bone density from decreasing. Every day I walk eight kilometers from when I was fifteen. I've walked over thirty-six thousand kilometers. I still wear weights for resistance . . .

She didn't notice my waning curiosity and spoke in a monotonous skip-a-long, . . . Ja, I go more slowly every year, I'm less agile, less flexible, but I'm consistent. I'm disciplined . . .

The granddaughter, Helix, in a hooded crimplene robe and looking her age—sixteen or seventeen years old—crossed the sitting room where we were drinking coffee. I hadn't heard her come in.

She spoke with contempt: Oma's talkativeness is like a bathtub that someone has forgotten to turn off. The water is cascading down the side, out the door, and soaking my shoes. You can't imagine how many times I've listened to those stories. Effie's stride position. Effie's musculature. The fire storm. Forty-five Mark for seven cigarettes.

Frau Hochschmidt wasn't offended. My granddaughter and her boyfriend use steroids. Yes, they're big as apes but their faces break out, they sweat. I never sweat.

I can bench ninety-nine kilos, Oma. I can eat six chicken breasts, gloated Helix.

But, no vegetables, no bread ever.

Quark? I asked, having just introduced quark into my diet.

Of course. Five hundred grams of quark with a half liter of milk. Sometimes with flaxseed, sometimes without. But I can only utilize thirty grams of protein at once, so at six I eat my muesli, at eight more quark. In the evening amino acids. I still coach a gymnast or two you know. A normal dinner. Six visits to the bathroom a day. I relieve two liters of urine daily, 37,441 liters since I started counting.

You'll live to be a thousand, I flattered her, becoming impatient. From another room an old short-legged, long-bodied dachshund with robust but aged muscular development and a confident carriage, walked toward his old mistress on stubby legs. He looked like a butcher's dog. Helix pushed his face with her foot. Dogs will one day be suppressed on the grounds of hygiene, she predicted, pushing the smelly old dog toward Grossmutter.

Enough small talk.

She didn't like seeing the tape recorder. Her look said, Who are you really? Where did you stand?

We pay, Frau. Our organization buys artifacts. We pay well. If you could start at the end.

She rubbed the tips of her fingers with her thumb. I jiggled the coins in my pocket.

She began: Even with the noise of enemy gunfire all around us we heard the shot. I was shaking like jelly but went closer, along the corridor, and there was the sick-making smell of gasoline.

The dachshund laid down at her feet.

Pressing his rifle across his groin, the Leader's bodyguard—his eyes rolling from side to side, his skin as shiny as patent leather—still guarded the Leader's door. From every corridor people were drawn toward the noise of the shot. The homely old secretary's lips were cracked, her shoulders were quivering with nerves. All our nerves were frogging and twitching in various parts of our bodies. Mine particularly up and down my flanks and legs. The cook, the one with close-set eyes, had prepared the Leader's potato purée and fried egg for the next meal as if he would be eating. A potato-coated whisk was clutched in her fist.

I kept my distance, not to annoy the ones in command. I didn't want to be guilty of pessimism—the penalty of which was death in those days—but what now? What now? The young secretary who Effie thought so pretty, had broken out in a rash. Her face was blotched like a python. The soldier nearby, a lieutenant-colonel decorated with three silver badges for wounds received in battles, had his hands across his eyes.

Frau Hochschmidt paused in the telling. More coffee?

With the second cup of strong coffee she sliced Apfelkuchen and distributed thin slices.

So?

The ones in charge waited ten minutes as ordered. The wife of the propaganda minister kept bringing a gold party badge that was fastened to her jacket up to her lips and kissing it. I saw that her face was suppurating. I was amazed how small and twisted-up her husband, the famous womanizing minister, looked up close. I was a head taller than he. He had a lame foot encased in a strange tall shoe and a deformed leg. His chin pointed toward the ceiling.

After consulting his gold watch, he jerked open the heavy study door and went in. The bodyguard, the party secretary, and head of the youth organization followed, stepping on each others' heels. A not unpleasant aroma of bitter almonds seeped back out, a smell reminding me of a particular tasty cake my Oma baked for us at Easter. Feeling faint, I began to back down the corridor in order to try to get some air when the party secretary stormed back out, looked across all the faces bunched in the corridor, and snarled my name. Frau Hochschmidt! Come here! *Schnell!*

I was only a few feet away. He needn't have shouted. I made myself known to him. He ordered, Come inside.

I did, the arteries in my temples suddenly pounding as if I might have an embolism at any instant. In the tiny, cold room, which was overstuffed with furnishings, I saw that Frau Effie's head was against the sofa. She had changed into a blue polka-dot dress with white collar and cuffs. Her goose blue eyes were open. Her face, white, unlined. Her hair was smartly combed. Her brown suede Ferragamo shoes stood side by side on the floor. A broken yellow metal phial was half under the sole of one of these costly, elegant shoes. On the table, a little pistol, a square of pink silk chiffon, and beside it a large, sacklike brown package wrapped in a brown satin pillowslip with a note pinned to it with a large safety pin. My name was scrawled across the note in wild letters. The party secretary pushed the sack into my arms, then slunk away. The propaganda minister was squatting on his haunches, looking closely at Effie's face.

I had never been so close to the Leader. I thought my legs would fold up under me. His head was hanging toward the floor, his hair unkempt, his mouth open revealing a dislodged bridge of dentures. Up close his body was not at all athletic or fit, but crumpled into accordion folds. Fresh blood was slowly rolling across his right temple, seeping onto the carpet. He was wearing the same uniform he wore in all the photographs I'd grown up with, the Iron Cross pinned to his chest, his mother's famous photograph propped against his ribs. I wanted to take a comb and comb his hair back down.

More coffee? Frau Hochschmidt asked.

I've had enough.

She continued speaking: On impulse I dabbed my handkerchief into the Leader's blood and brought the handkerchief quickly to my lips, licking the thick brown juice. Then I took Effie's little feet in my hands and squeezed them back into her shoes. Her face was beautiful but white as a rabbit. I touched her cheek with the back of my hand. Although it felt oily, it was cool like the room.

His bodyguard and valet wrapped the Leader's head in an army blanket, then lifted him up. One held the feet, the other his arms. The blood had stained the blue and white patterned fabric of the sofa. Then, the party secretary hoisted up Effie's corpse and followed the Leader's body up the steps to the garden. I noticed that the party secretary—the lout—was cupping Effie's breast in his hand.

The Leader's shoe brushed against my ribcage, and I felt a spasm run up and down my fingers. I got out of the way, caught my breath, and followed with my brown sack. Effie's body was too heavy and the bodyguard, who must have left the Leader's body upstairs, came back down and relieved the party secretary. He took Effie the rest of the way. His chauffeur and personal valet, and other helpers lugged many gallons of petrol in Jerry cans. Wrapped in dark blankets, the bodies were set side by side in a shallow crater near a broken cement mixer where the corpse of a dog or maybe a deformed man had already been burned until it was charred black. In there they appeared so small. But of course Effie was tiny, so short in fact she had been excluded by the organization from bearing children all these years. I noticed that the propaganda minister and his wife had joined us.

Petrol was poured over the bodies, soaking the blankets completely but when a match was put to it, the fire wouldn't light. Burning paper torches were thrown in, even the propaganda minister tried, but still the blankets didn't catch. Protruding from the blanket I could see the Leader's dark trousers, with military braid stripes at the side, his thick old soldier's shoes, and Effie's good gymnast's legs covered in nylon stockings in the brown suede shoes that I had returned to her feet.

Then—with the noise of an express train rushing through a tunnel—the fire flashed and leapt up at us. I jumped away. We all raised our arms in a salute. The wife of the propaganda minister gasped. Mustard-colored vomit shot out of her mouth and into the flames as she fell against her husband. A smell like burnt bacon rose up, then the smoke was sucked back into the bunker's air intake.

Feeling sick too, I leaned against the old cement mixer. The fire kept sputtering and more and more petrol was poured on. Until 5 o'clock Effie's figure remained taut and shapely, as though fireproof. The Leader's body smoked, smoldered, charred, stank, hissed, roasted, shrank, blackened, bit by bit.

At 6 o'clock it was quite gloomy because of the smoke hovering over the entire city. Rain began soaking everything. I felt like I'd caught a chill. I went back down into the bunker. By then the wife of the propaganda minister had given strychnine to her six children. She had then swallowed poison. She died wearing a plain black woolen dress decorated only with her gold organization emblem.

I tied a piece of cloth around my hair, a wet handkerchief across my mouth against the hot ash and phosphorus showering Berlin. Then I followed the little group that was leaving the bunker.

It took 45 Mark to buy seven cigarettes. Did you know that the pilot, carrying the Leader's favorite painting of Frederick the Great, was felled when a shell burst? He woke in a Russian hospital without the painting, and had lost a leg, but no one knew this for twenty years because he was put into prison by the Russians.

I knew this. I had listened long enough. The memorabilia, please.

Frau Hochschmidt was too wound up to stop. Her eyes were bright, her lips swollen up as though stung by an insect: You should have seen her! Tiny yes, but Effie looked like Brigitte Helm, the star of *Metropolis*, did you know that? She was my star pupil; I trained her in gymnastics. Did you know that? She could execute gravity-defying rolls, going round and round in rings. The armaments minister said that she was the only one in the bunker who displayed admirable and superior composure, that all the others were abnormal in some way. They were exaltedly heroic like the propaganda minister, saving their own skin like the party secretary, exhausted like the Leader, in total collapse like the propaganda minister's wife. But Effie radiated gay serenity, fitness. She . . . .

This time I asked more sharply: The memorabilia, please.

The dachshund gave a growl, his tail went up when Frau Hochschmidt—in a fit of pique—stormed out of the room. He growled at me until she returned with a big box, which she set on a chair.

She carefully lifted out a stiff, brown sack. From it she removed first a thick, folded fabric, which—when unfolded and laid out—was a pair of tattered black trousers that had been slit or ripped, and stained with blood or another dark substance. Then, a gray field coat with the insignia of the German Eagle, also stained. Beside them, she deposited a crusty blue album with cracked leatherette; then an off-ivory-colored leather album with the initials "E. B." in gold; then a blue silk nightdress, which she unfolded, removing a plain gold band. She placed the band on top of the silk nightdress. Finally she took out a broad leopard-skin belt.

Frau Hochschmidt crossed her arms and stood with her feet firmly apart. Her lips were no longer swollen and the skin around them was loose: General Chuikov, a Russian swine, was the first to hear of the double suicide. Are you aware that neither he nor anyone in the Soviet command knew anything about a Kanzlerbunker under Berlin? None of our countrymen knew that our Leader and his wife had been under our feet the entire time, she explained excitedly.

Nor had Chuikov or anyone else ever heard of your friend Fräulein Effie, I added with irony.

At the time, no one knew her. But now, everyone knows.

But it's not really written in stone. A few eyewitness reports, a few old photographs showing a blond girl who might have been almost anyone, a pretty German girl of the era.

But I was there!

Ja. I touched the nightdress. But you have an interest in her, wouldn't you say?

Why she's simply an established fact of the twentieth century.

Like the "facts" of gas chambers for extermination rather than for disinfecting clothing? Like the forged diaries of 1947?

Ach. She shook her head, irritated.

I had made my point. She was no fool. So, may I look at the notebooks?

I thumbed through the haphazard girlish entries with bits and pieces of dead flowers and papers stuck between the pages. The ornamental handwriting had gotten smaller with the passing of years, the entries had lengthened. A crushed yellow orchid slipped onto the table, stiff petals fell away, the edges crumbled off.

Just the other week a writer came all the way from New York to see these books . . . to see me, Grossmutter bragged.

And?

And spent hours drinking my good coffee and looking at me, at my artifacts, at my dog, at my granddaughter with intense hatred while scribbling notes.

Helix stood at the door. Oh Omi, here we go 'round the holly-holly-holly-caust again.

I stopped at a clutch of stiff blond, unnaturally colored hair stuck between the pages and mentioned a price. Her eyes darkened.

I fingered the jacket. And for the jacket? And the belt? I coiled the belt and placed it on top of the jacket.

I dropped the lock of stiff hair into an envelope, put a band around it twice, and placed it under the belt. Her entire expression had hardened but I knew she wouldn't refuse. People like Frau Hochschmidt had heard about the Fort Worth deal or the Lyons deal. And if they hadn't, without fail, they'd all heard about Phoenix—$153,000 paid in cash in 1973 when $153,000 went a long way. What they didn't realize was that the organization had paid for five tons of armored steel and glass—the Leader's Mercedes touring car—worth ten times that now in the ever growing market, not a handful of stiff hair.

From a drawer beside the telephone she removed a small cellophane envelope. Inside, a white hankie blotched with a brown stain, which she held under my nose to sniff. It gave off a fecal odor that was mixed with the smell of autumn leaves.

I didn't want to leave on a sour note so I doubled the offer, tried to take the hankie. She refused to give it. I chatted for a few more moments: Did you know that Niklas Frank, the son of Hans Frank, Governor General of Poland, believed that his father had been reincarnated as a dachshund?

She looked straight ahead, not forgiving me my irony. The old dog so like a butcher's dog put his head down on his forepaws and elevated his posterior in a most undignified manner.

Herr Niklas Frank lived in hope that his dead father would speak to him through the dog. He fed the dog with special sausage and beefsteak. He cajoled and petted and caressed the dog, but when it refused to speak to him he attached fifty firecrackers to its ears. He lit the fuse. The dog blew sky high, into a thousand bits, and rained down on his head and the heads of his neighbors. Funny?

Fräulein Helix thought I was very funny. Omi, it's funny!

A flustered look crossed Frau Hochschmidt's face. She stammered, You think everything's funny. We were sentimental then. We loved children and dogs. Did you know that Effie's Scottish terrier, little Stasi, who had been at the Obersalzberg during the bombing, had somehow managed to run the eighty kilometers that separated the Berghof from Effie's house on the Wasserburgerstrasse in München?

I didn't know this.

Ja. When I returned to München the war was over. My mother had lost her legs. When I went to Effie's villa, American soldiers and neighbors were pillaging, taking clothes, shoes, intimate things like underpants and brassieres. Inferiors in rags roamed freely once again. For years I had not seen these people except in work details. I assumed that they had been erased entirely by special treatment. But—like hearty weeds—I saw that a few had sprung back up once again.

Stasi—her little Scottie—in a terrible state of dehydration, was whimpering at Effie's door, crying for Effie who'd been like a mother to him. He must have run all the way from Obersalzberg, eighty kilometers. Eighty kilometers! I gave him water, a bit of food that one of our former *Scheissekommando* immediately stole and ate.

Frau Hochschmidt gave a deep sigh. But then a neighbor threw a stone at Stasi and chased him away. And suddenly he was gone, never to return.

Ach. Eighty kilometers. Quite a loyal little creature.

I handed her an envelope. Bid her, Good Day!

When I left, Frau Hochschmidt and Fräulein Helix were counting the bank notes with little rubber thimbles attached to the ends of their fingertips. The mongrel guarding their gate was rattling its heavy chain, and left a frothing wet margin of mustard paste for me to pass across.

BOOK II

It will be helpful to the reader to note that Adolf Hitler used affectionate nicknames for Eva Braun, especially Fräulein Effie, and Patscherl (pet). Early on he used the names Herr Wolf and Herr Schneider as assumed names.

The codes used by Fräulein Effie in the text of the diary to denote individuals of authority are as follows: Herr H. is Heinrich Hoffman, Hitler's personal photographer, who was Effie's boss. Herr B., who was also called the Brown Eminence by Effie, was the Nazi Party secretary, Martin Bormann. His brother Albrecht was Hitler's personal adjutant. The other Herr H., whom Effie referred to as Chicken Farmer, is Heinrich Himmler, head of Special Police or Schutzstaffel. Herr G., or the Flying Clown, is Hermann Goering, Commander in Chief of the Luftwaffe and eventually head of the State Secret Police (Gestapo). Dr. M. is Dr. Theodor Morell, a venereal disease specialist who rose to be Hitler's personal physician and has often been called a quack and accused of injecting Hitler with drugs. Dr. G., or Acid Tongue, is Dr. Joseph Goebbels, Hitler's propaganda minister. His wife was named Magda.

The armaments minister is Albert Speer, the personal pilot is Hans Baur, the personal chauffeur is Erich Kempka, the adjutant/bodyguard is Otto Gunsche, the head of Hitler Youth is Artur Axmann, the secretaries are Traudl Junge, Gerda Daranowski, Johanna Wolf, and Christa Schroeder, the cook, Fräulein Manzialy. Waffen-SS General Hermann Fegelein married Eva Braun's sister.

München

1 MÄRZ, 1929

This winter I have been wearing brown, a matching suit and beret. My braids are pinned and flattened in a coil which covers my ears.

My stomach clenches and unclenches because I've nothing to eat except Tyrolean apples. It's just as well as I need to slim down. My goal, even though I'm much shorter, is to duplicate the shape of my older sister, Oische, to be athletically distinguished like she is; also to beget at least five athletic children.

That or end it all!

Each day on arrival at my job—my first—as receptionist at the doctor's surgery—I hang up my brown suit and put on the uniform that includes a stiff cap. Then I sit all day at a desk in the reception-room, tapping my fingernail on the table, while my stomach cramps and thoughts of Brotzeit make my mouth water.

I must say: Good Morning, in the morning; Good Afternoon, after I've munched my apple.

At night I shall render an account of myself in this blue leatherette album. It's my second purchase from my first pay envelope.

My first purchase, a secret: this tube of lipstick that I grip in my fist but dare not touch to my lips though I'm 17 years old.

9 MÄRZ 1929

In the afternoon when the nearby school let out, the neighborhood children shouted and threw snowballs at each other in the street below us. The noise disturbed us all so I leaned out the window and shouted at them, Be silent!

One threw his gnome hat up at me, the rest threw snowballs toward my head, so I shut the window. They went on with their shouting until well after dark.

When I helped Herr Doktor on with his coat I sensed that he was fed up with me. I handed him his hat, which he took without

19

a word of thanks. Not only does my doctor despise me, but his surgery is in a shabby neighborhood.

A receptionist like me, my sister Oische works for a famous laryngologist in the best part of town. This doctor holds her in high esteem. Oische is our champion, an amateur ballroom dancer, who has won a Pan-European competition. I was the young ice skater, always skating round and round Starnberg Lake in circles with my arms folded in front of me. But that's where it ended.

Mutti once excelled also. She was a ski champion and an excellent swimmer who saved a drowning boy's life in a boating accident. But now Mutti keeps the house spotlessly clean, beginning with the wooden toilet seat, which makes the entire house smell of ammonia. In her free time she embroiders yellow covers for the arms of our chairs and worries about how to feed us during these hard times.

When our soup pot is full, Oische and Mutti can eat all they wish and never gain weight.

Not so me. Nor have I ever excelled in anything. Just "obstinacy" Vati would say.

15 MÄRZ, 1929

Still no break in the raw weather.

I sit all day at the doctor's surgery beside the bird's claw lamp.

All I seem to be able to think about is food.

I've knelt down and kissed the floor. Repeatedly, each time I give in and munch on my apple before lunch hour, I renew my resolve with my lips pressed against the old carpet.

Again, late in the day, those unruly children began shouting and throwing snowballs at each other in the street. Once more the noise disturbed the doctor and he ordered, Silence!

I looked to his old nurse for help but she turned away.

She has made it obvious that she doesn't like me, doesn't like the way I sit, even though my back is straight and my hands are folded on my lap.

So when the noise started again I didn't shout at the children, didn't look to the old bovine nurse for assistance. I simply heated a pot of water until it reached a roaring boil. Then I quietly lifted the window, and doused their heads with scalding water!

17 MÄRZ 1929

I've left the doctor's surgery because the doctor found another girl to do my job. She is extremely pretty and was wearing lipstick, rouge, and had plucked out her eyebrow hair.

The doctor had the old bovine tell me the news and hand over my pay envelope. What was inside barely paid for the streetcar and this box of cigarettes. My first. The remainder I must put into Vati's hand.

The streetcar was so crowded that when a worker ground his dirty fat thumb against my vaginal bone I could do nothing but stiffen my spine and look right through him with superiority.

I cried all night.

26 MÄRZ 1929

Weeks go by with no jobs anywhere in München. I pray that some little job comes my way.

27 MÄRZ 1929

Vati has urged that I take a job as a housemaid for a rich family. I dare not refuse but have begged him to allow me a few more weeks to find something in München so that I can live at home.

Last night I lost myself in my beads. Decade by decade I sought God's grace.

When Mutti and Vati went to their sleeping room I smoked a forbidden cigarette. Oische declined to join me but has promised not to tell.

1 APRIL 1929

At last! I have gotten another position as a typist.

5 APRIL 1929

How quickly this work becomes as monotonous as a beehive. I'm like a cat on hot bricks.

Though both hands are busy now rather than only one, it means much sitting and thinking of what Mutti might have put in my sack for lunch while I suck furiously on a fruit drop.

Most days I've already emptied the sack by midmorning.

8 APRIL 1929

My typing was too poor. I've been asked to leave the new job.

How can I face Vati? I know he'll shout about how much they need my earnings!

I'm so broke I cannot afford 20 Pfennig for the streetcar and must walk everywhere in the slush. My shoes are worn down but Vati cannot pay for new soles either. He can't pay to buy coal for our stove these days and has taken on extra work at night. And my fruit drop melted in my coat pocket.

Leisure is a dream compared with the tedium of work.

If only I played the accordion!

9 APRIL 1929

Once again dressed in matching brown suit and beret, I answered an ad for employment that appeared in the *Münchner Neueste Nachrichten*.

I was just one of a hoard of desperate women and girls packed into the reception rooms waiting my turn to be interviewed. I didn't have a chance.

If only I weren't all at sea.

16 APRIL 1929

No ads for weeks again so I thumb through the marriage, birth, and death lists. With over a million of us Volk unemployed, there's little hope that a dim girl, just out of convent, can find employment.

Worry makes me even hungrier though there's less and less in Mutti's soup pot. I'm mortally unhappy.

Vati growled, Find some kind of work or I will go to an agency for domestic workers and sign you up!

*Aller Anfang ist schwer.**

10 MAI 1929

I have cut off my braids.

I've saved them as a keepsake for my children. They took seventeen years to grow and five minutes to cut off.

11 MAI 1929

Today I left so early that the grocer was just opening the metal shutters of his shop with his long hook.

When I got far enough from home, I put on a thick smear of greasy lipstick. I was so scared that someone we know would see me that I held my hand over my mouth the whole day.

If the abbess at convent had seen me, I'd have been made to lie on the floor spread out like an X.

24 MAI 1929

I renewed my determination not to give in to hunger, but my sack was empty—my bread and apple eaten—even before morning coffee.

I'm racking my brain for conviction! I used the mirror to apply my lipstick. I had to draw my upper lip down over my teeth.

28 MAI 1929

Though hordes of München girls like me need work, for once, the others were ignored while I have been hired!

It is nothing I would have imagined doing but I'm a clerk at Herr H.'s photographic studio on Schellingstrasse.

I'm in terror that I'll be too stupid to accomplish my tasks. I've never seen a camera.

---

* (Every new beginning is hard.)

30 MAI 1929

My fears were ill-founded. As it has turned out my daily tasks are:
  Taking inventory
  Looking pleasingly into the customers' eyes
  Dreaded errands
  I'm marvelously happy.

2 JUNI 1929

In a moment of rashness I bought a brown moon-shaped hat with
my pay. How can I explain it to Vati? I can see his legs get stiff and
feel his belt against the back of my legs, but it's worth it.

6 JUNI 1929

This afternoon as I climbed the ladder to get new film stock, Herr
H., his face like not yet baked bread, was fawning over a rumpled
old man with a flabby face who was wearing a black slouch hat
and a long black coat.

The old man carried a thick whip with a large handle.

When I glanced down I saw that the old man was looking up at
my legs with bright blue eyes.

I climbed another step higher, which caused my skirt to hike
up, my thighs to part with a popping noise as the sweat had made
them stick together. When I presented the old man with my Hol-
bein smile—my blue goose eyes—his ears became stiff and erect.

He looked away, which made me think that I'd offended him.

A moment of terrible dread that he might report me to my
boss for flirtation.

When I was again in the stockroom Herr H. growled, Fräulein!
Go fetch beer and Leberkäs for Herr Wolf. He threw a handful of
money into my hand. So much, my hand began to sweat.

So, in my work smock, I dashed between green streetcars to
the butcher, and—after wild spending—ran back with delicious
Brotzeit.

Good appetite, I wished them, and piled a garland of small
pale Weisswursts, also Leberkäs, Lüngerl, and bread onto a plate,
feeling my own stomach clench with hunger.

How old are you? asked the old one without tact, examining me closely with ice blue eyes while breaking through the tough skin of the sausage with his teeth.

Seventeen, I told him. He put down the sausage and pinched my hand with his salty fingertips. Then he pressed my hand to his lips, "drinking me" in with his dominating eyes.

When the old man had gone my boss's face got mawkish. Don't you know him?

Herr Wolf?

That's not his real name he spat out, spat with glee. I am his exclusive photographer!

To know what I do not know gives Herr H. joy. And I am stupid indeed. He shook his head and walked away muttering *die blöde Kuh** which of course I heard. Which, I have to admit, is true. I am stupid, as the nuns and priests and Vati drummed into me.

An athletic, lean body and not a fat brain is my goal. A pretty pair of shoes with good strong leather heels and soles, also a basset puppy, and five boys and girls with Mutti's pretty face to play with the basset puppy is what I covet.

My boss has another studio in Berlin; he has made portraits of Caruso, the King of England, the Kaiser. He knows who is important and who is not. Perhaps the old man is a businessman though he looks like a letter carrier to me.

But all things considered, why kowtow to a letter carrier?

Herr H. growled at me before I left: If need be, your duties include "entertaining" any of my "important" clients. Also you must learn to be discreet. Do you understand? I do, I told him cooperatively. He waved his arms toward the plate containing the leftover Brotzeit. What joy to eat my fill and wrap the rest in butcher paper as a surprise for Mutti.

---

* (The stupid cow)

7 JUNI 1929

I was alone in the file room long enough to locate the "Herr Wolf" file:

In it, dozens of photographs of him. In some he wears a uniform and shined boots. In others a high hat. I discovered a batch of a parade that shows rapturous women trying to push aside guard lines to get to him. Women both young and old throw flowers in his path as he rides by standing stiffly in a Benz. Why? He's at least forty and stiff as an ironing board.

Nor is he athletic. I discovered this from a photo of him wearing leather shorts while he was relaxing in a meadow.

Later:

I asked as Mutti was bringing the meatless soup, Vati, do you know this man? and showed him a photo of Wolf I'd borrowed.

Vati's ears became red at the lobes.

He's "fanatic," of dubious origins. He's on the fringe of Bavarian politics. The church would do well to speak against his kind, against the beatings he and his followers dish out to people who don't join his cause. I would cross the street to avoid him.

Vati gave me the look of disgust he reserves only for me, and pushed the photo away, as Mutti served his bowl of soup with a breadroll and then mine.

I pushed my bread away.

I'm too fat and my face looks like a potato, I told Mutti, which made her cluck her tongue and shove it back at me, made Vati's face "freeze up," soup dripping from the ends of his fat mustache.

Eat it! Vati growled.

In a silent war of wills with Vati, Vati wins out. I ate the day-old bread.

Yes of course, now I recall who he is. His organization sponsors clubs for groups of girls who wear blue skirts, brown blouses with white collars, neckerchiefs with armbands showing crooked crosses, and unfeminine socks and shoes. My friend Mitzi had once been a member. What boy would look at a girl wearing those heavy shoes?

Not for me, those shapeless skirts, marching shoes. No rouge or lipstick. Eight years of convent—"contrition, purification"—was plenty.

After the soup, a half-stale poppyseed Kaisersemmel, a great treat. We had vanilla crème in a mold, which I never can resist. So much for will power!

After dinner Vati was determined to explain the various political groups in München to me, but I was quickly restless. Politics bore me. Yes Vati, I responded in my most servile voice, I too have been fanatic as a white clad girl at my first Holy Communion. But it's men like you, Vati, who hold the "reins," are the gods on earth. I leave these matters in your capable hands.

Instead of cuffing me for being cheeky, he puffed up.

Yes, men, and not clerks with new hairdos to curl. I excused myself, and went inside to work on my hair.

29 JUNI 1929

I'm all at sea since Herr H. told me that the old man has asked that "the young clerk with the good legs" join him at Herr H.'s apartment on Schnorrstrasse for an evening of "repose and relaxation" tomorrow night.

How grand! How it makes me want to scratch my face with both hands from "nerves."

Can it be that my star might climb a little higher? I doubt I'll be able to sleep at all tonight.

30 JUNI 1929

The evening was a success. I think.

When I arrived my boss was not at his own home. Herr Wolf was gayly dressed in a light-blue linen sports coat and a yellow tie.

Rather than offer refreshments, he walked me around the flat and examined photographic awards. When he walks, his knees turn slightly, he seems knock-kneed. At great length he explained the significance of the shiny Silver Medal, caressing it with stiff fingers.

His talk was a monologue. He uses a hundred words where Vati would use two.

While he talked I saw that his tongue was ham-pink, his teeth had been mended with gold. From his hands and clothes I picked up his fresh meaty scent.

I willed myself not to twist a strand of my new hairdo until we were seated again.

Seated, he clutched me around the waist and painted my mouth with his pink tongue, which dangled from the corner of his mouth.

After he'd wetted me, he sat back. But, when I lit a cigarette to hide my nerves his light-blue penetrating orbs changed in an instant from warm and kind to billiard-ball hard that shot fear through me and told me—of course I should have known—that he disapproved of women smoking cigarettes.

I crushed the cigarette out, then when he forgot our kisses and began to talk once again I willed myself to neither yawn nor drift off. I hoped to avoid his angry look, prayed that my hair hadn't gotten mussed.

I'm too tired to write more. It was like a dream. I tremble at the thought of his long tongue across my mouth.

1 JULI 1929

I saw Herr Wolf lunching with my boss through the window of the Café Heck, the place with plain wooden chairs and iron tables. I studied his face.

8 JULI 1929

Herr H. telephoned from the café to inform me that after 4 o'clock tea Herr Wolf would be stopping at the shop to see me.

Comb your hair! Wash your hands!

Quickly I "crumbled" two handkerchiefs and positioned one within each saucer of my brassiere.

9 JULI 1929

Herr Wolf invited me to attend the opera!

Two bodyguards with close-shaved heads arrived to fetch me.

Imagine that! A boy my own age couldn't do much more than take me for a walk in the park.

Though I do not like opera at all, I sat obediently through all three acts of *Lohengrin* by Richard Wagner. (Although none of our family has ever attended one, I've listened to opera on the radio with Vati and Mutti. We're not entirely uncultured!) It went on for almost four hours.

When, in Act I, Elsa sang "Elsa's Dream" all in white, I had to suppress tears. She is so innocent and good like I tried and tried to be. But otherwise all the action was impossible, it doesn't make sense. A colossal bore!

In the interval, he "gazed" at me over his shoulder and stroked my hand, pulling me until my thigh was pushed against the back of his out-turned knee. I was overwhelmed with self-consciousness at the thought of my little pig thighs, and I could not take my eyes off my knuckles.

Afterward the bodyguard took me directly home. I was alone in the back of the car so no one could stop me from smoking, which I did. And out of spite, I ground the end out on the floor of the car.

I dreamed all night that I was playing the accordion until it went out of tune and I fell ill.

10 JULI 1929
A yellow orchid and a signed photograph of "HIM" in uniform was delivered to me at work. I've placed the orchid in a bowl of water in the stockroom.

Here in the sleeping room that I share with Oische I've hidden the stolen photo between the bedding and mattress. Should I dare to hope?

14 JULI 1929
Again he took me to the opera.

This time we saw *Salomé* by Richard Strauss. Though only one act, it is tiresome. I found it dull and brutal at once when Salomé is killed by soldiers and crushed with shields. He especially liked the "Dance of Seven Veils."

Afterward he told me, I should so much like to be seen at the Osteria this evening with a "pretty woman."

My first meal at a restaurant ever!

A splendid tureen of soup was ceremoniously placed at the center of the table by a waiter in uniform. The most delicious smell floated my way. Königinsuppe! the waiter announced.

I'm too fat, I told him, but he gave me one piercing look and my big spoon dipped into by far the most delicious soup I've ever tasted.

I devoured the soup. Herr Wolf stroked and pinched my left hand while he spoke without interruption to a moon-faced man with cocked ears wearing silver pince-nez. This mild man told me that he was a rabbit breeder as well as a chicken farmer. He's Herr H.

After that, the waiter dished out my plate of Pichelsteiner, then he poured heavy cream over the top of the stew. Also delicious. Like a fairy tale.

Another of his coterie sat in brooding silence all evening. This man looks like an unhappy mole with cold eyes and turned-out feet. Herr B.

Again the bodyguard drove me home in a separate car.

Oh that someone had seen me sitting alone in the back of such a car, my stomach full, with a cigarette raised up between my colored lips! Oh if the old abbess at my convent had!

His flatteries have lifted my head. Of all the pretty girls in München, diminutive and dim as I am, he has singled out me!

16 JULI 1929

I was too gloating not to talk freely to Mitzi about these recent adventures. Mitzi also is enthralled. She told me that Wolf is publicly linked with a society lady.

Are they engaged? I asked, very, very curious to know more, fearful that he belongs to someone else.

She shook her head. The society lady is not his only one, your boss's daughter Henrietta also keeps company with him. Haven't you seen the photographs of him in the company of beautiful and wealthy woman in the newspaper? He is known to prefer *auffall-ende** women.

No, because I never touch a newspaper unless I'm looking for employment. But yes, I do know Henrietta, she's seventeen, the same age as me.

A shock. Henrietta has a "bad" reputation with men.

Before we parted, I made Mitzi promise to keep everything I've told her to herself. I'm sure she'll be as discreet as I am, even when I write in my diary.

18 JULI 1929

A day of repose.

For reasons of my weight, I've taken an intense interest in gym-nastics—especially work on the uneven parallel bars.

Vati would be pleased if I competed nationally like my sister does. I have begun training with this secretly in mind. Perhaps I can win Vati's admiration?

My first exercise acquainted me with suspension and swinging movements. Static stunts are discouraged. First the grips:

Regular grip. (I prefer it with thumbs around the bar.)

Reverse grip.

Overgrip.

Undergrip.

Mixed grip.

Crossed mixed grip, and finally

reversed, when the turn is in the opposite direction.

7 AUGUST 1929

Word leaked out to Oische about my "evenings" with "him." She does not approve of my "association" with a "ruffian" twenty-three years older than me. But then again, I do not approve of her "attachment" to her doctor/boss/amour who—though famous in München—is "older" and "Jewish" on top of that. I asked her, What kind of "ruffian" has a big car, a driver, a bodyguard?

Oische bragged haughtily, You are naive, all München knows

---

* (noticeable)

Herr Wolf is in love with his half-sister's daughter. Her eyes slid from side to side when she talked.

She's the one who is naive. All of München doesn't include me, who has never—except by him—been kissed by a man.

Tell more, I begged, shocked, yes, but curious too.

She told me that his niece is twenty-two years old. Though the niece lives in a separate wing of his very grand Prinzregentenplatz flat, it is well known that the niece actually sleeps in a room that adjoins his bedroom.

I felt bubbles in my stomach. I asked, Is there more?

They are seen everywhere together—the Heck, the Carlton for tea, the Prinzregenten Café near Brown House, the Stephanie after lunch, and the Osteria after opera.

What does this "niece" look like? Perhaps I have seen her through the window at the Heck?

She looks like you, Effie, but dark and five years older. Imagine that!

8 AUGUST 1929

I've begun setting-up exercises before bedtime prayers. Tonight a summer thunderstorm blew the chestnut tree against the window making eerie scraping noises.

9 AUGUST 1929

A surprise! Herr B. invited me to Fasching. I discovered that Herr B. is the party secretary. We sat at a small table in the most lively beer tent drinking and eating.

I suffered from a terrible case of tongue-tie, I couldn't take my eyes off the mustard under his fingernails. He ate Weisswursts and sweet mustard while I nibbled on a giant white radish cut into spirals, and a plate of bright red Mettwurst. Like Vati does, I dipped the radish into salt.

Shaven-headed waiters are so strong they carry large trays with at least twelve steins overflowing with brown foam. The frothing steins are like miniature cathedrals.

Across the tent I saw Herr Wolf arrive with a girl older than me.

Who is that monkey-faced girl? I asked, suddenly moist under my arms.

You know perfectly well, he quipped.

Herr H., who I just learned is head of his special police, skulked by and tipped his hat to us. And who is this fresh-faced Fräulein? he barked. (Obviously he doesn't remember me.)

My niece.

My escort burst out laughing at his own joke. Rude, like a chicken farmer laughs. I'm sure I went red. Through the crowd I could see nothing more of Wolf and his niece.

31 AUGUST 1929

Again his "visits" to the shop have ceased. His tongue no longer paints across my lips and cheeks. So much for my mad interlude! So much for my new flouncy hairstyle.

So much for dreams of playing the accordion, of keeping company with a high personage in politics rather than a poor, blunt Catholic boy.

Today to keep busy I waited for Mitzi after work. Two "working boys" asked to walk us home. The one who chose me had fuzz on his upper lip, a limp excuse for a mustache.

6 SEPTEMBER 1929

Just when I thought that surely he had forgotten me, the telephone rang at the studio. My boss handed me the telephone.

Dispensing with salutations, he exhorted in a gruff voice, I don't like eating alone. I'll send someone to fetch you *gnädiges* Fräulein.

Before I was seated he clasped me tightly by the elbow and pressed his palm against my rump.

Glad that he had not forgotten me, I pressed back while he studied my new hairstyle with a critical eye.

He barked, pressing more. How would I look if I changed the way I comb my hair?

Perhaps no one would recognize you, I ventured. The thought made me want to laugh.

At Herr H.'s I had seen him comb his dark brown hair by bending forward and combing it straight over his eyes. I'd seen how carefully he parted it, then combed back the left side, then, how he had jerked his head so that a lock fell across his forehead.

I heard that his mustache was clipped always the same too. Mitzi told me it was forbidden for any of his staff to have such a mustache as his.

After our meal—crispy Kartoffelpfannkuchen, simmered Kalbs-haxe with potato salad—he walked me to the car. The air was quite cold. I cursed the girl—the crouching ape—who'd cut my hair this way. I'd make sure she was sorry. Beside the car he gazed down at me, his body thrust forward. I heard his breath come in pants. He reached under my coat and dress, and clasped my woolen stockings.

His blue orbs narrowed, causing me to roll my pupils back, to also show him my very wet, lolling tongue.

14 SEPTEMBER 1929

I've heard nothing from him once again but now I always know his whereabouts because they are reported in the *Völkischer Beobachter*, which I buy and scan for news of him. Vati curses if I leave this newspaper in the sitting room, so at work I skim the paper for his activities.

On the streetcar I push this forbidden newspaper under my seat.

Just now I wrote an amorous letter to him. Why not? Tomor-row—first thing, before I get cold feet—I'll put it in the mail.

19 SEPTEMBER 1929

With glee Oische pushed a copy of yesterday's newspaper under my nose. I sat with Vati and Mogerl. Yes, our baby sister is home from convent for good. I read every word and my palms got boil-ing hot: . . . *his niece, age 23, shot herself through the heart with his Walter 6.35 revolver near midnight on September 18 and shortly there-after died locked in her room.*

He had been in Nürnberg at the time delivering a speech to his organization.

Later:

After Vati had gone to bed, I stole a few Pfennig from Mutti's household purse, and ran out into the rain to purchase today's evening newspaper. I held it up under a streetlamp and read: *The suicide resulted from a violent argument between him and his niece over her desire to leave his apartment and settle in Vienna where she intended to marry a young Viennese. An unmailed letter to a girlfriend in Vienna was found in the apartment that said she hoped to leave soon. When the body was found, the doctor observed extensive bruises and the bridge of her nose was broken.*

He has gone to stay with friends in a villa overlooking the Tegern Lake. He is said to be prostrate with grief. Why are the police not making a formal investigation? Why has no inquest been ordered?

But I could not read the rest because the rain had soaked the pages of the newspaper onto the sleeve of my coat. All the way home the muscles up and down my flank quivered and jiggled from the cold.

22 SEPTEMBER 1929

I could barely wait for the Sunday supplement.

Quickly I read lurid descriptions of wild parties at his Prinzregentenplatz flat. Dare I believe them? Oh that I could go to him in Tegern Lake . . . offer my "lap" for his head.

I'm nervous and anxious. I dread having to stay calm and just plain do my work.

24 SEPTEMBER 1929

After work I met Mitzi. We've opened our ears to every bit and string-end of rumor because it is all too exciting.

The café gossip is that the niece was killed by the head of the special police at Herr Wolf's orders. Also that Herr Wolf often beat her with a riding crop made of bull-hippopotamus skin and also with another made of hide.

The niece had supposedly once told a friend, You would never believe the things he makes me do. My uncle is a monster.

What could she have meant? Remember, I know him too, have

had his tongue across my entire face. But, maybe there's more that I don't yet know? I couldn't help but think of the photo of him on the meadow, his belly-colored white legs gawking stiffly out of leather shorts. Calumny is cruel. Murder less so. My opinion only.

I'm not sorry that she's dead. The drama is too too exciting and I am longing to know every dot and dash!

Of course it was suicide. That's what I'd have done. My theory.

22 NOVEMBER 1929
I have heard nothing from him. It has been weeks and weeks. Am woebegone. Took a sleeping tablet for the first time, which I "borrowed" from my boss's tin left on his desk.

24 NOVEMBER 1929
Yes, I finally slept well after two nights of sleeping tablets but I felt heavy-headed all day long. Unfortunately, I'll also need a pill tonight.

Late at night in bed, like now, I can't help but think about the drama of his niece, Geli. Murder or suicide, just like Rudolf and Maria! Had I been a boy, Vati would have chosen the name Rudolf for me, for Archduke Rudolf of Hapsburg, who died dramatically with his "mistress," Baroness Maria Vetsera at Mayerling, his hunting lodge. There are two endings of the story just like there was for his niece: One that both had been murdered. The other that they died by suicide.

I never doubted that it was suicide. More romantic. Though in the unfolding drama, he has forgotten me.

I'm not surprised.

I'm too plump. I'm also too short.

27 NOVEMBER 1929
Mundane days blend together. I have so little to write about.

15 FEBRUAR 1930
After 158 days of silence, he has just sent a note inviting me to an evening of "relaxation and repose." Should I be hurt that he ne-

glected me for so long? Or should I accept? Should I let him know that a handsome, young clerk with thick hair and a stiff mustache has been leaving love notes under my door?

Perhaps he will remember my recent birthday? Perhaps a little "remembrance" from the only person I know who still has money in his pockets since the Depression; the first and only person in my entire life who has taken me to a restaurant for Königinsuppe; the first man who ever kissed me.

Or, should I see if Mitzi is free for gossip and a cup of coffee?

Ha. As though I could resist his invitation!

München, Berchtesgaden:

4 MÄRZ 1932

A day off today. How lovely to be without obligation though it has been drizzling non-stop for days.

Nineteen weeks of silence. Almost a record. In these three years—our scattered evenings of "relaxation and repose," of kisses and tonguings—HE has often forgotten me but rarely for such a length of time. Yes, I'm very used to being forgotten and always elated to be remembered once again.

These days with not just us but all of Europe on the brink of starvation and bankruptcy—with four million of us unemployed, and money worth nothing—there are so many battles in the streets between his organization and the Communists. So it's unlikely I'll forget about HIM.

His fame has spread far beyond München, in fact, the whole country follows his comings and goings while I grow old sorting film stock, dreaming of Brotzeit, and smiling lavishly each time any one of two dozen customers walks into the shop, hoping that one with "position" will single me out. When Mutti was my age, she already had two children.

No need for diets these days, I'm as slim as I'd like to stay forever.

11 MÄRZ 1932

I was paid today and snuck away with Mogerl to see *Der Blaue Engel*. We were shocked that Lola Lola wore high heels, underwear, a silk top hat when she sang while standing with one leg resting on a chair, and when she made the "old" professor crow like a cock, I had to laugh. How sad for the professor, when his canary died. The theatre was packed. I'm not alone when I use my pay to go to the cinema instead of bringing groceries home to Mutti. What Vati doesn't know can't . . .

38

1 APRIL 1932

I'm still trembling and can barely write.

Today with no warning a car was sent to fetch me.

For the first time in all three years since I've "known" him I was invited up to the second floor at 16 Prinzregentenplatz, the famous five-story apartment house he lives in.

Never before have I been to such a grand place.

After I'd taken off my coat, he showed me around his private rooms. He pointed out moody paintings on the walls. These I painted, he told me, I am an artist as well, you see.

I hadn't known this.

Also there are other oil paintings in ornate gold frames.

Then he guided me over to a long red sofa. Sit down! he barked.

Apprehension caused my mouth to fill with saliva, my tongue felt fat. The back of the sofa was covered in lace. I wished he'd offer an aperitif to quiet my hunger and nerves, but he didn't.

Without offering refreshments he demanded, Aren't you too hot in your clothes?

He was telling rather then asking. This was the invitation!

Boldly I removed my clothes as if I'd done it before. I held my breath to keep from whimpering. It was easier than I could ever have imagined. It was as easy as flicking a dead fly off the window-sill.

When my—why does it have to be so?—plump bare bottom rested on the red plush, in haste, he removed his clothes, except for his boots. I stood up stiffly before him, my eyes unable to look at his loose skin.

While he mounted me I stood quietly with my thighs apart and my tailbone arched.

He clutched me around the waist, his boots firmly on the carpet. My palm closed over the ruff of coarse hair at the back of his head. But . . . his lunging did not quite penetrate. His eyes bore into mine. I dropped my head, flattened down my ears, smelled his meaty scent. Then he arched forward. I opened and closed my mouth, gave a piercing utterance, which caused him to stab at me again.

Again again again. I gave him many tries and realized I was panting from being frictioned. I broke away because I needed to urinate. That stopped it.

Then, he took me to the Osteria where his entourage awaited him and though I longed for a "splendid" meal he ordered tomato Ravioli for the entire table.

After sweets, his driver appeared to escort me home. When I rose to depart he pressed an envelope into my hand. I looked up to thank him, but he was talking to someone else so I just left.

In the closed Mercedes I opened the envelope. Inside, a 100-Mark note! The first I've ever touched.

This day has opened my eyes and my only regret is that I don't know more. Of course this all must remain my secret. I daren't tell Oische or Mitzi anymore of this.

Mutti would tell me that dogs and money were not hygienic, if she knew.

Of course Vati would put a bullet through both of our hearts if he knew.

29 APRIL 1932

Repeatedly I have been brought to his private apartment at Prinz-regentenplatz, to the red plush sofa, for raving talk and thrusts.

Afterward an envelope with 100 Mark is given. If I'm lucky he takes me to a restaurant for a (longed for) meal. If I'm not in luck, he sends me directly home with an empty stomach, sometimes no envelope at all.

How much I need his cash and food, he'll never know.

Vati has taken to sweeping snow and selling bootlaces to put bread on our table, has demanded that each payday I give him my entire salary. No longer may I hold onto a few coins. When I give him my pay envelope, he puts the money deep down into his pocket. Then coin by coin he counts out the exact fare I'll need to ride the streetcar during the coming week.

Exact to the Pfennig. Not a Pfennig more for cigarettes.

Even if I wanted to, I'd have no way to explain these 100-mark notes to Vati. They're my secret. I keep them at the tip of my shoe against my toes. I can feel them crimping my toes when I walk.

The thought of my "savings"—of what treasures they can buy "me"—bolsters me up as I lie here, my bed heaped with blankets, but my face frozen from the cold, my stomach still aching after Mutti's evening meal of watery soup.

28 OKTOBER 1932

I was driven to his Obersalzberg house above the town of Berchtesgaden, two hours drive from München. With the snowy Alps in the distance, the car drove past a vast tent camp I'd never seen but of course had heard about.

None too friendly looking riff-raff and unemployed were standing idly at fires, warming their blue hands. A woman from the country was wearing onions around her neck like a necklace.

It was wise that the driver picked up speed and left the "unfortunate" victims of these hard times behind. Thank God, "modest" though our earnings, our family is not among them.

As the car wound up the road I could see his chalet tucked against the mountainside. The chalet is built of stone on the ground floor. Wood on the second floor. It has painted shutters and bright red geraniums growing out of the window boxes like a Bavarian dream.

It is a dream.

He showed me the reception room stopping at a full length portrait of his dead niece. Yes, it was her! I commissioned Adolf Ziegler to paint this, he explained.

Not that pretty, I thought, elated. I'm much prettier though not as tall. He paused and studied the painting. Beneath the portrait was a table with a bowl of fresh flowers.

Who is Adolf Ziegler? I dare not ask.

He guided me to the window to point at the sharp peak of the Kehlstein behind the house and said, Eagles nest above the summit of Kehlstein . . .

Here I could not avoid meeting his housekeeper, his half-sister, and the mother of the dead niece. I hated her on sight, and she disregarded me.

He immediately ordered her, Leave the room.

I looked to see if "refreshments" had been left on the table but saw none.

Liebelei,* he addressed me—then a cross between a stab and a caress. His hands were trembling on his hips. Aren't you too hot in your clothes?

At first I was fearful, but then I vaulted around, grazing against him. He wanted to quiet me down when I stood up, my shoulders twisted sideways. He moved around and mounted me while I pressed at him with my pelvis and hips. I pressed very hard, and suddenly I squirted urine across the room.

When I urinated he grew still, then he sniffed the furniture, his hands, the discarded clothing. Then he sniffed my genitals . . . professed "mad love."

After the car dropped me at my parents' home, I came to earth. The Föhn had given me a headache. Also I had eaten nothing all day.

It was late. I could smell "it" still.

Because my parents were away overnight bringing flowers to the family vault in Geijelhoering, Oische had also taken the opportunity to stay out late. So the house was deserted, ice cold because we have no coal these days.

The smell didn't wash off. I—no longer a humble postulant—knelt down but no matter how many times I kissed the floor, I imagined that I could smell it still. What had I done? Who would marry me? What if HE, like Christ, wants nothing more to do with me?

The Holy Spirit didn't come to me. I should have known all along that my prayers would never be answered. Around midnight, I went to Vati's night table and removed his 6.35 mm pistol. I rehearsed this scene in secret with Vati's old pistol many times.

Then I got into Mutti's bed, under the cornflower blue eiderdown.

Stalwart Vati had hoped I would become a dressmaker when I grew up, not a clerk who got by on good looks, a round rump, trivial work for a drunken photographer.

* (flirt)

Mutti wouldn't have minded seeing me become a nun, a cross on my chest, Christ's ring on. . . .

Then my heart made rings around my chest and I aimed the revolver at it and fired. *Die grosse Entscheidung!**

When Oische returned home near dawn, the damp chill of the house must have sobered her. I heard her gasp when she saw me lying in the bed, the embroidered duvet soaked with blood. She observed the gun on a pink cushion, the broken water glass on the bedside table, the 100-Mark note soaking in water.

Had I had been attacked with our father's gun? She saw a wet hole in my throat as fresh blood continued to well up and seep out. She must have been thinking of the great artery in my neck because she ran toward the telephone but turned back when she heard me call her name.

I stood tottering at the side of the bed. I told her, I've already telephoned my boss, he's coming here right now.

But he'll report to you-know-who! She was in a panic, so fearful of "him" she didn't even want to say his name out loud.

My knees were buckling. She held out her hand and led me back into the bed.

O. understood now. There had been no intruder. She began stripping the bed. Vati would go into a horrible rage. What punishment would he find to inflict since I was too old to be send back to the nuns?

A memory: In 1917 when Vati had returned from the Great War, he'd said to me, Put your slice of bread under the light and if it shines, it means it's buttered. I had done what he told me to do and had seen clear through the bread. Because it did not shine I refused to eat it. To persuade me to eat it, Vati had forced my entire face and head into a basin of freezing water. I'd still refused, and further, would not touch Mutti's rutabaga puree. Since that day "obstinacy," according to Vati, has been my middle name. Mind, Vati had warned me, You'll turn out like the Hunger Artist I saw in Berlin in 1926, living under a glass bell!

Might he force my face into a bowl of freezing water once again?

* (The final decision!)

My boss did not arrive but instead sent an ambulance that did not turn on its Klaxon as I lay inside. I couldn't tell if I'd truly ended it all as blood oozed and the sound of the nurse speaking grew fat and thin.

The ambulance took me to a private clinic where quickly the bullet was removed from my neck.

O. told our parents a story about an intruder, which they believed.

Quite frankly I deeply regret that my shot missed its mark.

1 NOVEMBER 1932

Herr Wolf just returned to München and visited me at the clinic.

When the nurse brought him to my room I felt ashamed that my visitor wore such a shabby gabardine trench coat, that his bearing was so common, or as Vati had said, "from the gutter."

At that moment he looked exactly like the famous sex-murderer in Hannover whose case had made headlines in the Sunday supplements. The same mustache, the same eyes, the same coarse nose . . .

He began a monologue on obstinacy: On the front in 1917, I was a dispatch runner. While the others slept, I aimed my flashlight into the mud at the bottom of the trench and speared rat after rat with my bayonet. A soldier shouted at me, *Halts Maul! Ich will schlafen!** But I continued to spit rats.

He "bayonetted" me with his eyes. Did he think of me like a rat? Why did he speak of his soldiering days long ago in the Great War with so much sharpness?

When he presented me with a pearl necklace that would conceal the scar on my neck, he became a "leader" once again. "He" stood with his hands on his hips. His legs were wide apart and he gazed down at me, which caused my legs to twitch under the blanket.

---

* (Shut up! I'm sleeping!)

3 JANUAR 1933

I was released from the clinic today. I mooned around, restlessly.
He telephoned at 10.

I knew better than to ask where he was. Naturally he didn't
utter a word about his political activities, his way with women. Of
course he couldn't know that I read the newspaper that is always
full of news of him, his 230 seats in the Reichstag!

16 JANUAR 1933

Nightly, I wait in hearing distance of the telephone in case the call
comes.

Sometimes I think I will explode with "our" secret. A man
known by the entire country, a man as obstinate as me no less, has
professed mad love for me!

Yes, mad love, but then I hear nothing from him.

30 JANUAR 1933

I read today's installment of "Mail Order Bride" by Margarete
Zowada-Schiller. Thrilling. Romantic.

His call did not reach me until almost midnight. Imagine, all
things considered, that our "Chancellor" had to speak with me!

All of München is overjoyed, except Vati, who to my mind is
bullheaded and narrow minded. Also out of touch with us Volk.
Vati says that he will quickly be disgraced, will fall. Vati votes
strictly with the Catholic Center Party.

31 JANUAR 1933

Herr H. was "sick." His fat hands were quivering, his eyes were
red. He left me alone in the shop all afternoon.

Vati is furious about the telephoning at night. Against Vati's
wishes Herr B. arranged to have a telephone line installed in my
shared bedroom. Vati assumed that "the fat drunkard" to whom I
am employed has organized the telephone and is to blame for "my
daughter's defiance."

Vati no longer screams: Bend over, pull your pants down. Nor
does he throw me into the chest full of dirty clothes when I'm too
stubborn. Instead, he turns off my electricity at 10 sharp.

A dog in our quarter began to foam at the mouth. It was Vati that took his gun and shot it.

6 FEBRUAR 1933

I am twenty-one today!

An ordinary day in München, the smell of brewing beer in the air. Saw lucky idlers with skis on their backs as I trudged all the way to work because I'm down to my last Pfennig and need cigarettes. No little envelopes stuffed into my hand this month so far, no wedding ring, no prospects.

Mutti cooked a special meal of roast goose ringed with small baked apples and Vati toasted my health with his dark beer. From Oische a box of Cat's Tongue chocolates.

No congratulations from "HIM." No hullabaloo.

Everything is horribly bleak! Horribly ordinary! Mutti had three children when she was my age.

28 FEBRUAR 1933

Constant marching and singing in the streets, flags and bunting decorate simply everything since the Reichstag fire in Berlin. But love has been struck off his schedule.

Borrowed money from O. I treated myself to a brooch in the shape of a flower. Also a pair of "soft" underwear.

6 MÄRZ 1933

He ordered: Wait for a car on Saturday. Bring a change of clothes.

I told Vati and Mutti that I was visiting Mitzi for the weekend. I took the little green suitcase with me to work, and after work, I walked to Turkenstrasse intersection and stood case in hand like a lost traveler until a black and silver Mercedes-Benz drove up to fetch me.

On arrival at Haus Wachenfels I was shown to a bedroom. Immediately I took a bath, put on my new "soft" underwear. But it was no longer fresh after hours of anxious waiting and "anticipation." Every hour is like an eternity. The voice in my mind is not very good company. Hourly I sink.

When he finally came to me, I could contain myself no longer. Immediately my tongue lolled, dripped. He licked my genitals.

After folding his uniform, I licked his. Then I jumped up at him, whined, whimpered, rolled on my back in front of him like a dog in submission, not a clerk in a shop . . .

Oh, that I could howl and bark!

When he dressed, I sat on the side of the bed unclothed. Instead of an envelope, he handed me a box, explained, I must attend a state dinner.

Against the rule I asked him, Will you be back?

He ignored my question, kissed my hand and left.

I must not ask him questions!

In the box a short note offering his congratulations on my twenty-first birthday. Thank God, "he," who is generally recognized as a genius and savior, hasn't forgotten! Also inside the box, a set of tourmaline jewelry. I studied each stone in the light, admiring its transparency. Then, I adorned my neck and bare breasts with the necklace.

Even if it's not a wedding ring, how I love jewels.

7 MÄRZ 1933

A black Benz drove me back to München and dropped me at the intersection of Turkenstrasse, then drove immediately away just as it began to snow and I'd forgotten my woolen gloves. A lost traveler once again.

A gloomy curtain descended at the thought of waking tomorrow and going to work.

30 MÄRZ 1933

Work. More work. Humdrum life.

3 NOVEMBER 1933

Two seasons have passed with little to write except dreary work day after dull day in Herr H.'s studio.

11 NOVEMBER 1933

At last, an overnight trip to Haus Wachenfeld:

I told my parents a "story," an overnight with Mitzi. I explained that we would be visiting her sick Grossmutter. Quickly, before the car arrived, a "cat's wash." Also washed my new quiff hairdo, which—when brushed above my forehead—gives me extra height.

I put my quiff into curlers, tied a scarf around to allow it to dry during the motor trip to Berghof.

When the car dropped me—though I hadn't seen him in more time than I can barely stand—he was not waiting. He was at a meeting.

Telling my lonely mind to be silent, I walked the heavily wooded slope down toward the foot of the Kehlstein and back. The driver told me during the drive that in this area Obersalzberg is known as Upper Salt Mountain because of its hazelrock and salt from the ice age.

Still at "sea" I returned to my room. Two books beside my bed: A copy of *Mein Kampf* and a book called *Zwei Menschen*. Also, a box of marzipan candies shaped like piglets, flowers, and fruit. To pass the time, I nibbled orangewater-scented marzipan and sampled *Zwei Menschen*. The style is heavy like syrup, a book from my parents' youth by Richard Voss. It is tedious, but to make the time pass I read. I should know the story if he asks.

The story: Judith and Rochus, childhood friends; she is an orphan who must earn her living by managing a farm called the Platterhoff. He is an only son whom his mother has convinced to become a priest. On a summer afternoon Judith and Rochus take a boat ride and get caught in a violent thunderstorm. They're thrown upon an island. Staying on the island that night, they fall in love.

Ignoring his mother's wish that he become a priest, Rochus proposes to Judith. He puts a ring given by his mother on her finger. Then, though not explained, they "consummate." However, when they are rescued, and his mother sees the ring, she dies. So, Rochus breaks off his romance. He becomes a priest and when they see each other through the years they realize "love" has not dimmed. In the end, seeing no way out of her dilemma, Judith climbs the rocks of Obersalzberg and leaps to her death. The very same Obersalzberg I'm peering at now.

I felt dizzy. I gripped my breasts, my chin to the sky.

The walls of my room are gray.

His portrait in uniform, over my bed.

I went down on my haunches . . .

19 JANUAR 1934

I am "away" again. Little did I know that Mutti and Vati had decided to take a drive in a rattletrap car borrowed from Vati's supervisor and that they had driven south in the direction of Berchtesgaden, into the mountains for the day.

On the way back to München they must have stopped for afternoon coffee in Lambach, which was thick with Schutzstaffel troops. Of course they had no way of knowing that the road was tightly secured for our motorcade. They must have drunk coffee and ate their usual apple cake at the Lambacher Hof. It was filled with other Bavarians in green sugarloaf hats on their Sunday outings when the big black Mercedes-Benz in which I and the secretaries were riding stopped for coffee. As I jumped out with the other "staff," I saw them. Mutti and Vati were emerging from the Hof, an arm's length from me.

Mutti gasped, Effie. You?

Vati went leathery, his legs stiffened. He shouted, Where have you come from? What does this mean?

Protected from his anger, I smiled sheepishly. I have come from Haus Wachenfels.

Vati ordered, Come with me now!

But I threw my head back, brushed past him into the Lambacher Hof.

Mutti ran after me as Vati stood clenching his fist. Just then "his" very large Mercedes pulled up at the entrance and he stepped out followed by his bodyguard.

Vati told him, I am Effie's father!

Where is your Frau Gemahlin? he snapped and strode past poor Vati.

Shortly an adjutant went to find them. Sheepishly they followed the adjutant into the private dining room, where we—"secretaries" and entourage—were seated around "him."

"He" stood up and gestured for Mutti to sit beside him. Vati was put at the far end of the table.

"He" launched into a monologue about his new Euthanasia Program, the modern methods being introduced to eliminate the physically and mentally degenerate. What he says is so sensible and will no doubt improve life for us Volk.

When he talked, everyone listened. When we talked among ourselves, he sat silently.

Tea and coffee, nut-crusted Kuchen, Apfelkuchen heaped with whipped cream. I saw him squeeze Mutti's hand.

The whole time Vati sat, shabby, tongue-tied, leather-faced.

Then he and I—in a state of exhilaration—and his entourage, all rose and walked away.

Two hours later I was at home braced for their return. I was calm, but at the sight of Vati's slippers I almost fainted with fear.

Vati growled from the doorway, It is said that you are his mistress. Is this so?

If you wish, I'll leave, I replied coldly, backing away from the arm that was pulling off his belt. Vati's throat constricted. He rebuckled his belt and wiped his hands with his ironed handkerchief.

When he turned his back on me, walked out of the room, shut the door, my heart froze.

When I was a little girl home from my convent school for the holidays, I always helped Mutti by ironing laundry. I took pride with Vati's big handkerchiefs, ironing until they were stiff. Once taught how to fold a man's handkerchief, I folded them with care and pressed the hot iron one time only against each fold. As the door slammed I thought, Let them fold my handkerchiefs now! With not an iota of sentiment I slammed my door too, feeling a stab of guilt at the look on Mutti's face.

Later:

Mogerl told me just now that Vati and Mutti told her they had stood and watched us getting into our grand cars and watched as we drove off in a column; that "their Effie" didn't look back.

I asked her, What did Mutti say about him?

That he had the most incredible sweet tooth of any man, drank a bottle of Metternic's best *Gewürztraminer* and heaped caster-sugar into the glass.

Only his sweet tooth had impressed her.

10 JULI 1934

No more lies. When invited away now I simply pack my little green valise and go.

Renovations have begun on Haus Wachenfels. Painted Bavarian beer tankards and stuffed deer heads with large antlers that I so liked have been removed from the walls. Of course no one asked me what I thought.

Already a wing for overnight guests, a stone patio, and a car park have been added. Also an entirely new façade, along with a ceremonial staircase, sentry posts . . .

Neighboring chalets are being demolished to improve the view. From a window I can see buses and carloads of "Mädchen" parading in single file past the entrance wearing white blouses and dark skirts and sometimes "HE" stands and smiles as they file past him.

He has arranged a private performance for the "entourage."

He told me: I have seen *Die Lustige Witwe** one hundred times. It is my favorite light opera. I never tire of it.

Meekly I studied how his face changed color when the semi-nude maidens came on stage. I saw his cheeks go russet just the way they do in the sun—quickly sunburnt, and quickly pale again—when Dorothy did a backbend and the spotlight lit up her shape under the transparent costume that looks like butterfly wings.

I swell inside knowing that afterward our "sniffing" will begin. Perhaps I can truly "entice" him . . .

But sadly with old Hindenburg dead, he went right to Berlin. No "sniffing" tonight.

---

* (*The Merry Widow*)

2 AUGUST 1934
Every church bell tolled for fifteen minutes at noon.

9 AUGUST 1934
In the newspaper are photographs of him taken in Berlin. He is surrounded by beautiful screen actresses: Anny Ondra, the wife of boxer Max Schmehling, Jenny Jugo, Renate Müller. Also women of standing and prestige like Frau G., the wife of the propaganda minister, old Winifred Wagner, Frau von Dirksen, all photographed at his side.

In one photo he's posed with Gretl Slezak, the daughter of world-famous opera singer, Leo Slezak.

What can I do? Nothing. With unemployment dwindling and order everywhere restored, he's more popular than ever. Why would he want to be photographed or even seen with an unknown convent girl?

I worry most about Gretl Slezak and Henrietta because they are so bosomy. Henrietta's reputation is spotty while her bosom is big.

17 AUGUST 1934
He takes "me" nowhere. When I ask whether he'll ever marry he replies that he's married to Germany. With me he doesn't want to talk. My conversation is usually ignored. My breasts are minute no matter how much I pull at them. I'm so short!

At Haus Wachenfels he has finally allowed me to mix with his "intimate" circle. But *never* his "official" circle.

He has also allowed me—very occasionally—to ride in his car with him. If his mind is not elsewhere, I part my knees. We sit side by side on the plush leather seat. I sit straight but I shift my torso, part my pig thighs. Desperate for some sign of recognition, I lick at him, pant, peering into his face.

I pull at his arm until he drops his hand into my blouse and presses my narrow nipple. I breathe spasmodically while his hand caresses me. My ears droop, my head rests against the seat,

Then—contented—I watch the scenery rushing past. Our Bavaria!

When we arrive, officialdom once more. Every time the same play: Loudly enough for all to hear, he tells me, I wish you a good night's rest, Fräulein Effie.

Then I reply in a stage voice, Good night mein Kanzler. Sleep well.

After his chauffeur has put the car away, he walks back to the door where I timidly wait for him.

If he's so inclined he takes me to his bedroom. It contains a white metal bed decorated with ribbons, also, a painted chest of drawers, a straight chair. It's no different than his valet's room. Not the room of Kanzler, the greatest man in Bavaria and all of the country, certainly.

Then he reaches inside my clothes again . . . promises mad love. His tongue drips copiously.

20 AUGUST 1934

The half-sister refers to me as *die blöde Kuh*. She takes every opportunity to humiliate me at Haus Wachenfels. Usually when I arrive she claims that the guestrooms are all occupied.

She huffs, You will be lodged at the Platter Hof. And so I am.

When she went into the village I flung scalding water at her canary.

She said about me: The disgraceful blonde who chases the Chancellor. Worse than a common street walker.

I am hurt. My hurt is like her frantic canary.

24 AUGUST 1934

Again my weight is going up! And no 100 Mark, no envelopes.

I'm desperate. I need more money, but my boss refuses an advance on my salary. All day today despite the heat, he growled out errands for me to run or else kept me in the back room organizing his dusty stock. He must have drunk too much at lunch, he gave me a sharp nip on my arm for no reason at all.

26 AUGUST 1934

He was seen at the theatre with Olga Tschechowa and Lil Dagover!

Photos in the newspapers of him in Berlin with beautiful actresses.

I can do nothing.

Even my lottery tickets are Nieten.

All I can do is look pretty, go to work, run errands, smile "lavishly" at the customers, and then come home at the end of the day to listen to the radio tell of boring routes planned for our Autobahnen.

Nightly, I feel a burning in my stomach. Rather than responding to "invitations" by other men—young men, free men, virile men—I wait for "his" call.

On weekends I've begun to master positions on the parallel bars. In this order: Front support. Rear support. Stride support. Front lying support. Rear lying support. Long hang.

At night, if the telephone call does not come, I await the news that he has discarded me for someone else. If only I had never met him.

I long for this madness to let go of me.

München, Berchtesgaden
Zugspitze, Bad Tölz

6 DEZEMBER 1934

My confidants:

Mogerl. Herta S., with golden Gretchen plaits, is my new best friend replacing Mitzi, who has gone her separate way. Also Paul, the handsome waiter at the Carlton Hotel.

I told Paul, He can turn against a person. He can also be ruthless.

Paul assured me, He would never turn against a beautiful, young girl like you.

But this year—all summer and autumn—has brought only the occasional "secret" visit. Usually I wait for him at Herr H.'s, and then weeks of neglect, weeks of humdrum once again. God has left my prayers unanswered as usual.

When I see him he is unusually cold, devoid of ardor. If I reach over to stroke him, he "snaps" or "growls" until I withdraw my hand. I daren't complain. I daren't ask for an envelope if he leaves none or ask for supper if he's not hungry.

He has begun renovation on the Prinzregentenstrasse apartment that seems to interest him as much as politics do. When he's in München he stays at a hotel and I am not invited near it.

Perhaps the time has come to end it all?

10 DEZEMBER 1934

Finally! An invitation to Obersalzberg was delivered and just at this important moment, Vati locked my bedroom door with me inside.

Precisely because I've been afraid that Vati might lock me inside I've kept a spare key. I let myself out. When Vati saw me crossing the sitting room, overnight case in hand, he crushed a cigarette against my arm.

And, when I didn't bat an eye, instead stared him down with

ice-cold determination, he looked right through me pretending that I was invisible.

Once this look would have made me grovel before him, but now that childish disease of parental worship is gone.

And out I go, Mutti sobbing in the kitchen, the smell of seared flesh on my arm covered by a splash of cologne.

17 DEZEMBER 1934

The gossip is that he had singled out Renate Müller, the star at UFA, Germany's largest movie studio, but that he's also "smitten" by an Englishwoman with shining gold hair whose father is a lord.

Mutti didn't comment when she saw the brown scab on my arm.

In Herr H.'s archive, whenever I have time, I rifle through photos that show "him" with women. Though it torments me, I can't stop spying.

I was especially wounded by a photo of Frau Magda G.'s wedding party in which she wore a beautiful black silk dress, a white Brussels lace shawl. A crooked cross flag entwined elegantly with the standing crucifix at the altar. The Kanzler was a witness. He was wearing a plain suit, the soft hat I hate. How much more svelte I'd look in that black silk dress than Frau G. did. The arrogant look on her face taunts me. It looks as though her ears are transparent. My mind swirls with visions of "my" wedding dress, "my" shoes . . .

Later: I saw him with the Englishwoman at the Osteria eating "our" Ravioli.

6 FEBRUAR 1935

I have just happily reached the age of twenty-three, but whether this is really a cause for happiness is another matter. At the moment I am very far from feeling that way.

I probably expect too much from a day that should be so "important."

If only I had a "little dog" I would be less lonely. But that would be asking too much.

All things considered, I am ungrateful. But I did so want a basset puppy, and still no sign of one. Perhaps next year, or even later, it will go better with somebody who is approaching spinsterhood.

Above all, I must not despair. It's time I learned to be patient.

I bought two lottery tickets because I was convinced that it was a question of today or never, but they were Nieten.

This evening I am going to dine with Herta. What else can a very simple woman of twenty-three do? And so my birthday will end with guzzling and boozing.

11 FEBRUAR 1935

He was here just now. But no little dog, no cupboards stuffed with dresses. He didn't even ask me if I wanted anything for my birthday.

But I bought some jewelry on my own. A necklace, earrings, and a ring for fifty Mark—very pretty. Let's hope he likes them.

If not, he can find me something himself.

15 FEBRUAR 1935

It looks as though the Berlin idea is going to come off. But I shan't be-lieve it until I am in the Chancellery of the Reich.

18 FEBRUAR 1935

Yesterday he arrived quite unexpectedly and we spent a delightful evening. But the best thing is that he is considering the idea of taking me away from H.'s shop—but I prefer not to rejoice too soon—and pre-senting me with a little house. I dare not think of it, it would be just too wonderful. I would no longer have to open the door for so many "hon-orable clients" and be obliged to play the part of a shopgirl.

Dear God, please let this come true and let it happen in the near future.

There are times when He behaves in a vulgar fashion.

I am infinitely happy that He loves me so much and I pray that it may always remain so.

4 MÄRZ 1935

I am mortally unhappy again. And since I haven't permission to write to HIM, this book must record my lamentations.

He came on Saturday. Saturday evening there was the Nocturnal Ball.

I spent two marvelously beautiful hours with him until midnight and then with his permission, I went to the ball for another couple of hours.

He had promised that I would see him on Sunday. But although I telephoned and asked for him at the Osteria and left a message that I was waiting for news of him, he took the plane to Feldafing and even refused H.'s invitation to coffee and supper. I was waiting at H.'s like a cat on hot bricks. I imagined every moment that he was about to arrive.

We went to the train, because, on his return to München, he decided to go off again. We reached the station just in time to see the rear light of the last coach.

Perhaps I still take too gloomy a view of things. Let's hope this is the case, but he won't be back for a fortnight and until then I shall be miserable.

11 MÄRZ 1935

I only want one thing, to fall very ill and hear nothing of him for at least a week. Why has nothing arrived for me? Why do I have to bear all this? Oh, if only I had never met him. I'm desperate. Now I'm buying sleeping tablets again; then I fall into a state of semi-imbecility and no longer have to think so much about all this. Why doesn't the devil carry me off? Hell must be infinitely preferable to this.

I waited for three hours outside the Carlton and had to watch him buying flowers for Anny Ondra and inviting her to dinner.

He needs me for special reasons. It can't be otherwise.

When he says he loves me, he thinks it is only for the time being. The same with his promise, which he never keeps.

Why doesn't he have done with me instead of tormenting me?

16 MÄRZ 1935

He's in Berlin again. If only I weren't all at sea when I can't see him so often. Of course, it's normal that he wouldn't take a great interest in me at the moment with all that's going on in politics.

Today I'm going up to the Zugspitze with Mogerl and I imagine that my madness will calm down. Everything has ended well and this time too, all will be fine. I simply must wait patiently.

1 APRIL 1935

Yesterday, he invited us to dinner at the Vierjahreszeiten. I had to sit beside him for three hours without being able to say a single word to him. As a farewell gesture, he gave me an envelope with some money inside. How lovely it would have been if he had also written a line of greeting or a kind word. But he never thinks of such things.

29 APRIL 1935

I feel apathetic. About everything. I spend my time singing "Tout ira trés, Madame la Marquise," but it doesn't help much. The apartment is ready, but I can't visit him. Love has been struck off his schedule. Now that he's back in Berlin, I'm coming back to life a little. But there were days last week when I cried every night as I accepted my "duty." I had a bilious attack when I stayed at home alone on Easter day.

I've made desperate efforts to economize.

10 MAI 1935

Herr H. lovingly, and tactlessly, informs me that he has found a replacement for me. She is known as the Walküre and looks the part. Including her legs.

He really ought to know me well enough by now to realize that I wouldn't try to stop him if he suddenly lost his heart to somebody else. What happens to me must be a matter of indifference to him.

I shall wait until June 3, a quarter of a year since our our last meeting, and then demand an explanation. Let nobody say I'm not patient.

The weather is magnificent and I, the mistress of the greatest man in Germany and in the whole world, sit here waiting while the sun mocks me through the windowpanes.

But it's a pity that just now is spring.

28 MAI 1935

I have just sent him a decisive letter. Will he take it seriously?

Well, we'll see.

If I don't receive a reply before ten o'clock tonight, I'll simply take twenty-five tablets and fall asleep very gently. Is this the mad love he promised me, when he doesn't send me a single comforting line in three months? It's true that recently his head has been full of political problems, but there must be moments of relaxation. And what about last year? He had a lot of trouble with Röhm and Italy. But in spite of this he found time for me.

Perhaps another woman, not the Walküre girl, that would be really rather unlikely, but there are so many others.

What other reasons could there be? I can't think of any.

Later:

Oh God, I'm afraid there won't be a reply today.

If only somebody would help me. Everything is so horribly bleak. Perhaps my letter arrived at an inopportune moment. Perhaps I shouldn't have written to him.

I have decided on thirty-five tablets. This time I must make "dead" sure.

Later:

There was no reply at 10 o'clock.

I've left this diary open at the last entry, on my bedside table, and will take twenty tablets!

No "regrets." Nothing else I can do, no confessor to give me ten decades of the rosary for penance, as he has discarded me.

27 JUNI 1935

I was saved and all has changed!

Returning home late, O. found me. This time I was unconscious. She telephoned her doctor who came immediately and purged me with my sister's help.

Then Oische took a knife and cut out the last diary entries. She told me, I've put them away for safekeeping.

Imagine, my life saved by a doctor who is a Jew! I'd never have guessed he was a Jew by looking at him, but, all things considered, I know no other Jews except the proprietors of the best lingerie shop in town.

No letters came. No jewelry either. Instead, two Scottish terriers were delivered today. Just what I wanted all along!

I named one Stasi, the smaller one Negus. They are darlings.

He telephoned at 10 o'clock!

14 JULI 1935

An apartment in the Bogenhausen district on Wiedermeyerstrasse has been prepared and the key given to me. He ordered me to move in immediately. How can I refuse his orders when the entire country obeys his proclamation to rearm?

As it would not look right if I lived alone, I invited Oische to share it with me, but she refused. She'll be sorry she did one day.

Mogerl agreed. Dear doe-like Mogerl. Poor Mogerl, her blue eyes are flecked with amber. Her new "boyfriend" has been called into the newly restored military service and was sent away for training without even a farewell.

All our expenses are paid! Food is delivered.

The Bogenhausen district is at the edge of town. The building has an elevator and the flat has three rooms, also a small accommodation for a maid, which we do not have. And central heating! I have brought only a few of my old things, my stiff-necked doll with its gold-colored braids and flouncy dress. Of course on the day I left I never told Mutti and Vati a thing. I just went to work as usual—my doll and music box stuffed into my lunch sack—I simply didn't come home.

All night a dog howled outside my window. You'd think a dog would be clever enough to find food for itself.

16 JULI 1935

During dinner at the Osteria with Herta, Mogerl, and Oische, Mogerl draped herself across the table and told me: Renate Müller has leapt out of a window to her death.

Because of the Kanzler?

I saw my palms go bloody under the skin.

Yes, because he has dropped her, but also it's rumored that the head of the Special Police discovered on a trip to England, that in spite of our Nürnberg laws, Renate had been keeping company with a Jew of inferior status. When she returned to Germany she was blacklisted . . .

Was she?

Yes, for "race defilement."

Only blacklisted, not axed at dawn? A lame joke.

I leaned in to hear the rest.

There was talk that she would be put on trial. There was talk also that because she was no longer allowed to work she began to take morphine.

I wondered out loud, What were her last thoughts?

God knows, replied Oische, who has no job now that her Jewish doctor has left the country.

The newspaper acknowledged: *Renate Müller, age 30. Dead of heart attack.*

How strange not to be speaking with Mutti and Vati!

18 JULI 1935

I went to the theatre in Oliverplatz to see *Broadway Melody* with Mogerl, her new "friend," and Paul. Then we treated ourselves to drinks and a meal at a small restaurant. What fun!

20 JULI 1935

Nothing but telephone visits. I have no idea where he is. Lonely nights because Mogerl stays away with her new "friend." I dreamt that I was a young "wife" and my "husband" must work late. While I waited I steamed potatoes, then when they were soft I peeled them uniformly and cut them into thin slices. So they wouldn't stick together, I put each slice into oil, vinegar, parsley, chervil, tarragon, onion juice, sugar, salt, and mustard. But, when I stirred the lot together, they all stuck into a clump.

22 JULI 1935

The tenants in the building on Wiedermeyerstrasse are asking, Who is the man who arrives in such a big car at such a late hour? Why is our street filled with men wearing trench coats and trilby hats?

Fräulein Mogerl tells them she does not know.

I tell them that I do not know either.

3 AUGUST 1935

Herr H. was persuaded by one high in the organization to purchase a villa in a more exclusive section on the outskirts of München and donate it for "use" by the Kanzler.

Herr H. told me at work: It is better that you live beside the Isar.

H. was drunk since lunch so at first I didn't know if his eely sense of humor was at work or if it was true. Then Herr B. telephoned to explain the arrangements.

Just think! Me beside the Isar!

11 AUGUST 1935

Beside the Isar River stands the new "villa." His Prinzregentenstrasse home is just across the Isar.

Furnishing has been arranged by the United Workshops of München, though I would have preferred to choose "my" own pieces this once.

My doll stands on the vanity, clean as a whistle, alongside the music box that plays: "Ach, du lieber Augustin." This *is* the mad love he promised me!

The villa has six rooms, three on the ground floor—kitchen, dining room, sitting room—and three on the first floor—two bedrooms and a miniscule maid's quarters, this time complete with a part-time maid responsible for housework and some cooking. What joy! My own maid to clean my blue-tiled bathroom! Wouldn't Mutti—who scrubs and cleans all day—be envious if she could see this place! How sad that Mutti and I are not speaking.

Nightly now, after returning from work, I demand that the maid run my bath. Right afterward she must leave. She has prepared and left a cold supper covered with a cloth in the kitchen. Then—alone in the villa as Mogerl rarely "sleeps" there—I eat, then soak in Kamille and hot water in my new bathtub. I admire the blue tiles. Wrapped in my long wide nightgown with flounces at the neck and a hood, I make a fire in the fireplace and sit beside it, sad that no one is here to admire me.

Tonight as I write it is almost 10.

My telephone number is listed in the München directory—417. My telephone is ivory. Herr B. has listed me as: secretary. Would people laugh if they knew that this "secretary" can't really type or take dictation?

Yes, this "secretary" excelled at pranks in convent but not in grammar. Yes, when this "secretary" couldn't answer a question she was told to stand with her hands folded behind her back until she wet herself.

15 AUGUST 1935

Every night I wait for the telephone to ring. I smoke my Junos and sip my vermouth until the sound of the telephone silences the angry ache of waiting. Or until there is the sound of boots on gravel.

The advertisements say: We Juno smokers are optimists. I wish it were always so for me.

11:30 P.M.

Finally I heard the sound of boots on gravel. His key in the door. I walked forward to meet him.

He uttered, My Patscherl.

I took his hand and led him to the seat in front of the fire. Because—of course—the girl had gone for the day, I fetched him tea myself. Here is tea made of apple peels, I told him.

I have to be very careful what I give him now that he has become a fanatical, teetotaling vegetarian.

Tonight he drank three cups of my tea, his mind elsewhere. Yes, of course, it's very good, his voice stung me.

But it wasn't apple peels at all, it was black tea with a dollop or two of apple wine for flavor. I watched the tea relax and wake him at the same time. He stroked my hand. I was experiencing vaginal bleeding. I kept pressing against him and whimpering until he uttered, Aren't you too hot in your clothes?

Then I rolled on my back in front of him and pulled at his trousers. He followed me with his eyes and then leaned and licked my skin and then my genitals. Exuberant, I pulled him into the enclosed garden. We roamed the walled space, urinating on plants and trees. He took great interest in the spots on the earth where I had urinated. Pools of amber.

He sniffed also at the raspberry spots where blood had dripped, then stretched his nose over my head.

When I looked, his mouth was wide open, he was baring his teeth, his ears were laid back against his skull, and he began pressing my hindquarters with his whole weight while I crouched.

We went back inside. I let the firelight play on my athletic body when I lay by the fire and he sat in the easy chair. These days I let him do as he pleases, I even "squat" over his face when he asks. I let him snap his whip and stalk around the room. I urinate on demand: Over. Under. In squirts. In drips. Copious quantities when all is said and done.

Tonight he fell asleep after tea. I waited until he woke up to offer him chocolates and lemon buns with currants. When he stood up to depart I observed, You look more relaxed.

But I could see that his mind was already on other matters. Before he was even gone I could feel the letdown begin.

Yes, it is true. He always arrives tense and angry and he invariably departs relaxed and refreshed.

Pretty child, he kissed my hand.

When he was gone, I stepped out of my shoes, tucked my feet beneath me and listened to phonograph records, smoking once again but irritable because I saw in the firelight that my shoes are down at the heel and he has left no envelope.

Although I would be the envy of the entire country—if anyone knew about me—I feel like ending it all.

I so miss Mutti!

19 AUGUST 1935

Because I was not invited into München society, nor can I go home anymore, the villa suffices for my social life.

It has a garden with a high wall blocking it from view by any passerby. The wall goes entirely around, with a gate in front.

He has filled the sitting room with paintings from his private collections: by the artists Popp, Gallegos, Midgard, Tischbach, and Rosl. I must learn these names by heart!

Stasi and Negus help fill the hours. My little four-legged "children"!

When I try to correct them by snapping a rolled newspaper across their bottoms, they hide under the couch.

29 AUGUST 1935

What news!

A three-litre Mercedes-Benz was delivered to the villa, then a chauffeur put at my disposal!

Herta and I went for a breakneck drive to Bad Tölz.

A fully grown German shepherd has been delivered. I was told to keep him in the garden in case anyone takes it into their head to climb over the wall. The dog is trained to tear open the throat of an intruder. He is named Basko, but he does not get along at all with Negus who can be vicious and intimidating.

My nasty Negus, I love you!

Basko agitates the entire time I perform my rigorous exercise on the parallel bars that I've set up in the garden.

This afternoon I was perfecting my back hip pullover mount, which may be performed from either side of the low bar. With my hands in a regular grip, I stood facing the low bar. My elbows were bent and my chest was close to the bar. I swung one leg forward and upward as I pushed off with the opposite leg. Keeping both knees straight for the swing, I pulled with my arms to position my hips near the low bar. I rotated around the low bar and came to a front support position.

Again. Five times. Rest. Five again. Elation.

30 AUGUST 1935

He told me he would teach Basko obedience. When Basko agitated, he flogged him with his whip. Stung, Basko crept toward his feet. He lashed him again. The dog crouched down.

Come here! shouted the Kanzler. His tone frightened me too. It's the same tone of voice I heard at home when I didn't obey.

Basko crawled on his stomach toward the K. The lash snapped his rump.

He said, It is true that obedience is most needed during times of emergency. It's equally true that obedience—like insurance—must be obtained before you need it.

31 AUGUST 1935

The Kanzler just telephoned to say I no longer have to go to work at Herr H.'s studio! He told me that Herr H. would continue to pay my salary of 450 Reichmark a month, which pays for cosmetics but not for clothes or food. I could cry with joy though my heart pounds with the anxious feeling that I'll always be broke and at the mercy of the K. and Herr B. for pocket money.

9 SEPTEMBER 1935

My boss knocked at the door of the villa just as the maid was putting on her hat and coat. I was combing Stasi while Negus sat at my feet.

He growled, Your father has asked me to deliver this letter to the Kanzler.

I went to my writing table, took out my letter opener, and sliced open the letter he had put into my hand. He walked over to the decanter and poured out a glassful of claret.

As he drank, I went back to combing the black coat of my baby. After I put the comb down I stood with my arms folded. And, I asked, My salary?

He slowly counted out 450.

No longer must I kowtow to H. It was my chance to strut around the room showing off the dog.

But not too much. I need to be wary because Herr H. can be willful if he feels that a woman has been too smart.

8 SEPTEMBER 1935, MÜNCHEN

Your Excellency the Chancellor:

I find myself in the unhappy situation of having to contact you with a private problem. I know that you have a great many other problems and cares as Kanzler of the German nation.

*However, since the family is the smallest unit of the social struc-
ture, a unit that enables Germany to be strong, I think my letter
is justified and I am asking your help.*

*My family is now separated because two of my daughters,
Effie and Mogerl, have moved into an apartment that you have
put at their disposal. I was not consulted on this matter. For a
long time I have criticized Effie for coming home late, long after
office hours, because I did not believe she was getting the proper
rest needed for her health. Perhaps I am old-fashioned in this re-
spect. However, the parent's supervision and the children's duty
to live at home until they are married is an inviolable principle.
This is my code of honor. Besides, I miss my daughter enormously.*

*I would be very grateful if you would agree to help me. I ask
that you not encourage Effie's desire for freedom from her home.
Please advise her to return to her family!*

Yours respectfully,

10 SEPTEMBER 1935

Mogerl told me just now, Mutti also has written a letter to the
Kanzler.

I told her, I've not the slightest interest in what is *anständig** in
their little, pathetic circle.

But I couldn't resist asking, So, where is the letter? What's in it?

Mogerl said, In the letter Mutti asked what are his intentions
toward you? Mutti gave it to his housekeeper at Prinzregentenstrasse who has promised to give it to the Kanzler.

11 SEPTEMBER 1935

This afternoon I went to see Frau W., the housekeeper on Prinzregentenstrasse. She asked me to wait. I noticed that a large new
portrait of the dead niece hung on the wall of the living room. For
the first time I noticed that the niece's oval face had a touch of
subhuman, Slavic origin. She looked taller than me, and her eyes
mocked me, showed that she despised stupid blond Bavarian girls.

* (respectable, decent)

Fresh flowers were in a bowl on the table below the portrait. Five years have gone by since her death, not a day without fresh flowers.

Frau W. walked behind me, commented, It's a true resemblance.

You found her, yes you?

Frau W. answered, Ja. I took the newspaper to her every morning at ten. The apartment had not been remodeled at that time. I knocked on the bedroom door. There was no answer. My husband then broke open the door and she was lying on the floor. You know there was a letter from you to him, which he'd left in his jacket, on her bedside table?

I listened, enraptured. The Kanzler's Walther pistol was on the sofa. The niece was wearing her blue nightdress, embroidered with red roses. . . .

What brings you here? Frau W. asked me. The Kanzler is in Berlin.

My mother gave you a letter to give to him, did she not?

Frau W. folded her hands across her dirndl dress.

I want to make sure that you put it directly into his hands, I said.

It's too late, Fräulein.

Why?

Because I gave it to the party secretary. But I have no doubt he'll give it to the Kanzler.

I could happily scald her with boiling tea.

Herr B.—the K.'s "shadow"—is sneaky, snarling, secretive, slinking around. I've grown to hate him.

I asked, Did other women spend the night with him here?

You were the first, Fräulein, the very first to stay the entire night.

A jolt of joy. And after that, did others visit?

A man in his position knows many beautiful women.

Beautiful? How beautiful? I asked, but her lips remained silent.

Before I left I took a good look at the long red sofa where I gave up my innocence.

In the car my boldness increased. I asked the driver, Please detour to Rupoldingen.

Where is Rupoldingen, Fräulein?

Near Traunstein, I told him, feeling a wave of shame that his car should go to such a lackluster quarter of München, to a house with overstuffed furniture, threadbare rugs, petunias in the window boxes.

At the sight of me, Mutti wiped her eyes.

I noticed a pile of unpaid milk and coal bills on the table. I noticed that Mutti has lost four back teeth, that her skin has a dry look to it.

I told her harshly, You must not intrude in my life.

She blew her nose.

Where's Oische? I asked.

Oische is in a dance championship in Italy.

Your "husband"?

Your "father" has gone out.

Coffee and Apfelkuchen?

Yes, thank you Mutti.

She poured coffee into the cup and saucer she used for special people like the priest.

The door opened, and I saw Vati's downcast face. When he saw me sitting on his sofa he walked straight through. I looked through him too, with the same iced facade.

Our family has been investigated, Mutti whispered nervously, squeezing the satin pincushion beside the chair.

We have nothing to hide, I angrily replied. Indeed not, our *ahenpass** is Aryan without doubt!

Oische's mail is being delayed. Can you think of any reason for this?

I changed the direction of the conversation. Mutti, will you come to my villa for coffee and cake next Sunday?

I cannot go without my husband.

So there's nothing more to say.

---

* (Proof of ancestry)

I pushed the empty plate aside, ignored her pleas, shut the door behind me.

I had a date to meet Herta and her fiancé at the Osteria Bavaria and first had to change my clothes.

Later:

I arrived at the Osteria, walked through the garden to the statue of the god Bacchus under the niche designed to resemble a temple. The place was buzzing. I asked the maître d' for a table, and then noticed Schutzstaffel uniforms dotting the room. I saw Emma, the waitress I know.

I called her, Emma, is the Kanzler coming?

The Kanzler is already here with his party.

Then I saw Dr. G. and his Frau. How lovely the wife of the propaganda minister is.

Emma spoke excitedly. He ordered a sweet lettuce salad and sweet zabaglione for dessert.

Without Marsala wine! I reminded her. Are there women in his party?

Just one, the very tall girl.

How tall?

Two meters tall, the English girl, she's bosomy but otherwise like an Amazon.

I know very well who that girl is! The Kanzler calls her a "racial masterpiece." I saw them photographed together at Bayreuth at the festival. Also in Berlin.

I stood back. If I tried to enter the private room I would be lost. Then, striding across the room toward the private dining area, I saw a woman wearing a white waterproof coat with large pockets and large-brimmed matching white hat. This woman I also know and hate. She's the actress from *Das Blaue Licht*, who often wears tight, white dresses at night. Her father is a plumber, I said in my mind ten times; his hands are up to their elbows in *scheiss* every day of his life.

Berchtesgaden

4 OKTOBER 1935

The renovation of the Berghof at Obersalzberg is almost complete. I begged the Kanzler, Please, it would mean so much to me to have my own room there.

Yesterday when I sat beside "him" in the car, he did not utter a word. My new blue nightdress embroidered with red roses was starched and folded at the top of my overnight case.

Your housekeeper has said that I'm no worse than a common streetwalker chasing the Chancellor. Do you know that?

He did not comment. When we arrived he went directly to his half-sister. Frau, pack your belongings, you are to leave here by train in one hour.

He turned away, erased her.

A small triumph! And it was *my letter* beside *her* bed when she was found!

He pulled me by the arm to show me the results of the renovations. I felt like fresh air had been pumped into my lungs. I squeezed his soft upper arm.

A rustic chalet once, an immense chalet now. A sheet of five-meters-high glass covers what once was a small window that looked out on the mountain. Now it seems to be in the center of the room. The original house has not been destroyed but is lost within the new Berghof.

The living room was now twenty meters long, fifteen meters wide. Italian paintings were fixed to the wall where Gobelin tapestries hung. Oversize carved wooden chests housed his beloved collection of phonograph records.

He pulled me roughly toward the doorway and stood in front of a painting of an enormous bare-breasted woman. This is by Bordone, the pupil of Titian. Next to it another painting, this by Titian himself.

I could feel his skin prickle. Large women were what he

"really" liked. He led me to a bronze head of Richard Wagner. By Arno Brecker, he informed me.

Part of the floor space was sunken. It was necessary to walk three steps down to the patio and sitting area.

He gloated, I conceived of this myself.

The fireplace was close beside the sunken space. I stepped back and almost tripped into it. We walked down the steps into the patio. There were five heavy armchairs arranged around a circular table with a heavy glass top. The fireplace was faced with green faïence, which is not my idea of tasteful furniture.

You are hostess tonight, he barked.

He led me into the dining room, the floor covered in a thick Persian carpet. But we are alone, I observed, of course proud to have him to myself though wishing he were in a "friendlier" mood.

He seated me at the enormous oak table on a chair covered in red leather. He sat on my left at the center of the table facing the window. The dishes and cutlery bore his initials; the cutlery was solid gold. The china, hand-painted Rosenthal. These happened to be just the dishes I'd have made if . . .

He bragged, I have a new chef.

The servants brought a salad, then a dish he savors—baked potatoes flavored with cream cheese and doused with linseed oil. Because he has become a vegetarian, I try to follow his lead.

I asked, Do you know who the Fräulein from *Das Blaue Licht* has had an "interesting" long-term arrangement with?

He was silent, eating with relish.

Your "Flying Clown." I planted just the seed I wanted. If I could have put her at the top of the Euthanasia Program lists, I would gladly have done so.

He took a second helping of baked potatoes and called for more linseed oil. Not a word was spoken during the entire meal.

After dinner he pinched my elbow and guided me up the velvet-covered staircase to a corridor. The walls of the corridor are crowded with even more paintings and—on wall sconces—statuettes, vases, curios. He seemed now to be in a better mood.

At the first door he stopped. This is your apartment.

I felt the heat of triumph rising in my cheeks. My sharp finger-nails clawed into my wrist.

Inside a living room, a bedroom, and a door leading into a marble bath, quite luxurious, with gilded taps. In the living room, a sofa. The walls, silk covered. Above, a nude drawing . . . of "ME"! What joy!

Across from the nude, an imposing photograph of "HIM." Just his head. The bedroom was furnished exactly like the *chambres séparées* in the operetta *Die Lustige Witwe*. He explained, I must leave you for the moment. There is a matter which demands my attention, Patscherl.

He bent and kissed my hand. I shall return shortly. He clicked his heels together.

When he was gone I opened the door on the far side of the bath and entered his room. The iron-frame bed was as I remembered but covered by a brown quilt. Embroidered across its center, a hooked cross. His brown satin pajamas were folded across the brown pillowslip, a black hooked cross embroidered on the pocket on a red background.

The matching brown silk robe hung nearby. The telephone, beside his bed. His private number was marked on the phone.

His room opened onto the balcony. I stepped out into the night air and contemplated the stars. Methodically I memorized his private telephone number. The sisters had taught us to memorize by rote. 6. 0. 0. 600. 600.

I felt sweaty and unbuttoned my white, silk blouse—so as not to stain it—and let the breeze tickle my button breasts. The whiteness of my skin puts a rabbit to shame.

I felt my ears droop forward, I began to growl. I couldn't help it. I stood with crouched legs and produced urine. Then I crouched lower and squirted a small quantity of urine against the balcony. Then I pawed the ground, my tailbone coiled.

Berchtesgaden, München, Berlin, Bayreuth, Nürnberg, Godesberg, Stuttgart

1 NOVEMBER 1935

The rules at the Berghof were left on my bedside table in my room today. The same ones for all invited guests.

1. *Smoking is prohibited in this bedroom.*
2. *The guest must not talk to servants or carry any parcels or messages from the premises for any servant.*
3. *At all times the Kanzler must be addressed and spoken of as such and never as "Herr" or other titles.*
4. *Women guests are forbidden to use excessive cosmetics and must on no account use coloring material on their fingernails.*

I am not to be seen if dignitaries visit, or if there is a meeting or conference of any official nature. Keep out of sight was the dictate.

I waited all day for him today. I tried not to smoke but failed and have hidden my butt-ends one by one in an envelope. I hummed tunes to keep my mind silent, keep the voice in my mind from belittling me.

2 NOVEMBER 1935

He went off to München.

I discovered who his "proper" guests are by sweet-talking the girl that changed my bed, the girl that I've caught looking up at me with fascination, idolizing me.

All fourteen gray guest bedrooms, with scenes of German mythology hanging in frames on the walls, are filled with "official" guests. The baths are made from Carrara marble, and Bohemian stone. Of course beside each guest bed are the list of rules and an autographed copy of *Mein Kampf*. For men, a book—usually French—of soft pornography. The girl told me that the guests are important personalities and international dignitaries.

75

After waiting the entire day the administrator himself informed me that tonight I must spend that night at Bechstein Haus on the Obersalzberg until the guests have gone.

By whose order? I asked.

By the party secretary's orders.

My euphoria was dashed! I gathered my things and thought about a lonely meal of Erbsensuppe.

3 NOVEMBER 1935

The guests have gone. I may return to "my" room.

The instructions to employees at Berghof were left on my table while I was gone.

1. *Employees/guests cannot discuss, even with Schutzstaffel men, what they might see at the Berghof.*
2. *No discussion of politics is permitted.*
3. *Do not approach any part of the building or any other building you have not been ordered to approach.*
4. *No letter writing.*
5. *Guests are not permitted to keep a diary.*
6. *No whistling because the Kanzler dislikes whistling.*
7. *Never address the Kanzler unless he speaks first.*

I'm neither an employee nor a guest! Don't they know it? But I shan't complain. And, writing this, I'm breaking the law! I will ask HIM for special permission. Perhaps the two helmeted Schutz-staffel that stand guard at the foot of the steps night and day have noticed me? Whenever I pass they scrutinize my permanent pass. On it my status is listed as: *secretary.*

18 DEZEMBER 1935

Alone so much of the time here. Though it's against the rules to keep my diary, he has given me special permission to do so to fill my hours.

I asked him, Might Herta join me?

Ach, he replied, his thoughts elsewhere.

But he must have heard me because a small apartment was

made ready for Herta's disposal. Another one for Mogerl. Their passes state: *Guest of the Kanzler.*

18 JANUAR 1936

I go nowhere anymore without my precious "children"—Negus and Stasi. They are becoming more vicious the older they get. They are my badge.

Though I have made some feeble efforts to train them with stings across their little rumps, pushing their faces into basins of cold water, they continue to whine and make nuisances of themselves.

What can I do but adore them?

I've purchased a little camera and have begun to amuse myself by taking snapshots.

Finally I met his favorite Alsatian, Blondi. She was in a cage. When she saw him she became excited and leapt up against the wire partitions. He stood back, and watched her repeatedly leap against the partition, bark and whimper. When he released the catch on the door, and Blondi bounded out, my little black bundles threatened to tear her to bits. The viciousness of my dogs made me laugh.

Later:

A first! I was invited to join his "group" for dinner. There were fourteen for dinner. I was put next to a dark foreign man. Perhaps he's an Italian?

The K. began a harangue at dinner when he noticed that I had left a trace of lipstick on my napkin.

Do you know what a lipstick is made of?

A dinner guest spoke up, I once heard it was made of plant lice.

Several women gasped. My feelings were hurt. I bragged, My lipstick is French, surely made from the best materials.

"He" looked at me and said, Do you know that in France lipsticks are made of fat and sewage?

Because he demands that soup should only be served when it

is scalding hot, I, as well as the foreigner, burnt our tongues on the *Käsebouillon mit Ei* that his cook has festooned with chives.

Dinner finished, we sat in the chairs around the glass-topped round table. The tapestry was raised and the hidden movie projector was exposed. Though the blister had ulcerated on my tongue, I smiled up at him.

Blondi was led in and told to lay down in a corner of the room, but she immediately crawled over to her master and pressed her shining snout against his knee. Then we watched the film *La Jana*.

After the film, he demonstrated Blondi's tricks to the group. A ladder was brought. When the K. ordered her, Blondi climbed up to the top of the ladder to a platform set up for the purpose. In this position she sat up and begged.

We applauded but Herr B.'s mistress—an actress with lips like a sucking dove—keened as Blondi begged. You'd have thought the dog had turned cartwheels from the way she keened.

When the demonstration was complete, he decided that we should walk up to the teahouse in the moonlight. Herr B. hated this walk. The K. and I, with Blondi on her leather leash, led the way up the narrow path. To vex me, he wore his gray oilskin lumber jacket and the felt hat which I despise, which he affectionately calls *mein Schako*.

We assembled around the fireplace while he admired the twinkling Berchtesgaden valley from the window, then he lowered himself into the easy chair beside mine. Tea, also pastries, were served. He devoured an entire box of chocolates while he monopolized the talk.

Then he fell asleep.

For two hours he slept. The rest of us whispered with each other, always careful that our voices not disturb him. I took a few snapshots of him in "repose."

Finally he woke, took my arm, and we walked together to the area where several cars waited. In procession, the cars drove quickly back to the house.

It was 4 A.M. when he said good night to the guests. I had never been at his side like that and rather than puff up about it, I felt quite "normal." Of course my "hopes" began to soar once more.

When we were alone he told me that while he slept he had had a nightmare in which he was being suffocated.

By someone or something? I asked with tender concern, but when I had slipped the blue nightdress embroidered with red roses over my head his thoughts were elsewhere.

4 FEBRUAR 1936

The Winter Olympic is due to open at Garmisch-Partenkirchen in two days. But I am not invited to attend any of the "official" events.

9 FEBRUAR 1936

With discretion I parked my car three streets away at Marienplatz, then walked quickly to my friend Paul's little flat for lunch. Paul wanted to fix white gazpacho that he said he tasted in Andalusia in faraway Spain, but when I saw three large garlic cloves I begged off, so he fixed wild cherry soup with plenty of cream and brandy instead.

Time ran away from us. By the time I drove past, the little enameled copper figures of the Glockenspiel were moving in and out of the archway striking 5.

22 MÄRZ 1936

Am beside myself with nerves. I am to fly with him to Berlin.

27 MÄRZ 1936

Heavy rain beat down the entire way to the airport. I was so worried that my hair would frizz.

On the aircraft, through the little windows, I could see nothing because of the heavy rain. An adjutant took me to see the cockpit but by then it was dark and I could only see pale green lights on the panel.

We were about to fly up into the sky so I was shown to a seat. Because I'm so short, my feet didn't touch the floor. A very uncomfortable position.

As the airplane took off, I so wished that Mutti and I were on good terms again. How much I miss her.

When we swooped over the city of Berlin I saw the Spree River snaking through, also a vast network of railroad tracks. When we had landed and were driving through the town by car I was thunderstruck by the size of Berlin. How industrial, how sprawling. How sharp-tongued Berliners are, how sarcastic, insolent! I didn't dare to venture very far from my hotel, which is not in the best part of town. When all is said and done, he's still a pinch-penny.

I briefly met the tall American Herr Lindbergh. He arrived at the airport when we were leaving.

5 JULI 1936

I was not included in the "official" circle that accompanied him to Bayreuth for the Wagner Festival. I was stuck with "underlings."

Quickly, when the Festival ended, he was gone for high level discussions because of troubles in faraway Spain.

I took a batch of snapshots with my little camera.

17 AUGUST 1936

Where has the time gone? Yes, I'm at sea because he is so often busy. Yes, he takes me places, but then I spend the entire time painting my nails in dingy hotel rooms or putting my photographs into little books or bored "blue" with underlings and hangers-ons not in "official" circles.

Mutti told Mogerl privately (which Mogerl just related to me), All is not well. Your father was under consideration for promotion to assistant master at his trade school, but when the director discovered that he was not a member of the organization, he didn't get the promotion.

Mogerl said that she begged Mutti to visit me for Sunday coffee, but Mutti had replied, I could not go without my husband. Then she told Mutti that I had been in Berlin in March. Mutti was distressed. Effie, in Berlin? Berlin is a dangerous town. Has Effie been to confession?

Mogerl told me: I wished I had not brought up Berlin. Mutti had no idea that her "little Effie" went places with the Kanzler and his inner circle and has even stayed with him in hotels.

What does she think I do?

Poor Mutti. Yes, I'd been at the Victoria Hostel in Stuttgart, the German House in Nürnberg, the Hotel Dreesen in Godesberg. The only thing I was ashamed of was that these are not luxury hotels, to say the least, as the K. is so tight fisted with money. In these hotels I was kept out of sight, treated as an official secretary on the staff, and his visits to my rooms were sporadic. His amorous interest, nil.

Oh Mutti. Do you think of me fondly?

4 SEPTEMBER 1936

In Berlin again.

I roamed around K.D.W. but had no money in my pockets for purchases because I spent everything on a bracelet. Saw Dr. G. at K.D.W. with a young starlet, an armload of packages, his hands all over her.

I'm longing to return to Bavaria where things make sense.

7 SEPTEMBER 1936

The gossip is that there is something wrong with my family's *Ahnenpass*. To squelch the rumors I've decided that it's best that I get back in contact with my parents! I went at coffee time.

They could not believe their eyes! I was not the same little mealy-mouthed convent girl who'd walked out of their house with a doll and a music box. Instead two barking black dogs jiggled in my arms.

I was wearing a Nile-green dress of heavy wool with long sleeves. The upper part of the dress was low cut in front. My hair had been tinted a light blond. The jewelry was no longer cheap costume. My figure was trim, my legs strong as a horse. Mutti got soft. To my shock Vati did not leave the room. I've never known why, but Vati announced, I have applied for membership in the organization.

I looked at him carefully but he seemed the same as ever though his hair is no longer thick, and the skin on his neck has gone stringy.

He bragged, The Kanzler awarded me a special green membership card.

A leopard changes its spots.

When I heard the coffee mill grinding and smelled Mutti's strong coffee, I sank onto a chair. I couldn't stop the tears from filling my eyes.

9 SEPTEMBER 1936

Sunday get-togethers have resumed for my entire family, but it's not the same. They're so "provincial"!

I have seen Oische more often too, but it's not the same either. This "new Effie" can't forget that Oische once refused to share my flat.

11 SEPTEMBER 1936

Vati has been promoted to assistant master at his trade school. Any whispers about our *Ahnenpass* will surely stop now.

Herta has broken off her engagement.

My hairdresser told me that Frau Magda G. brushes her hair exactly forty-two times each night before bed.

12 OKTOBER 1936

My horror is that I will get fat and have to end it all as more and more he demands that I stay at the Berg where eating—huge five-course meals as well as sweets—occupies important places in our life. Often I simply drink vermouth to silence any pangs of hunger. I have become so hungry at moments that I could eat a fat string of sausage. But I don't.

Paul, the waiter at the Carlton, my friend from days gone by, rang to invite me to a party. I told him I didn't want to be seen with him any longer.

11 NOVEMBER 1936

So often now we are in Berlin. He arranged a room for me in the Adlon Hotel. I waited until the telephone rang and he said, Please accompany me. I have government business, but later it would be so nice to have your company.

I pray that he is not angry with me. These days on a moment's notice—as his daily itinerary is kept secret—I must prepare to depart. An official aircraft or a private sleeper train is awaiting me.

Oh how I now love to fly! Just like I came to love swimming and skiing and amorous forays with him. Because I am too short for the seats, I put my little overnight case on the floor and use it as a footstool. At my villa, I keep several suitcases ever-ready, but these are not sufficient because I have begun to change my clothes three or four times a day. I brush my hair exactly forty-two strokes each night.

I have started to have clothes made to order by Auracher in München and have begun to shop on the Kurfürstendamm in Berlin.

But every week I am getting more deeply in debt.

Oh, that I hear the words tonight: Aren't you too hot in your clothes!

18 NOVEMBER 1936

I asked if Mogerl would keep me company during this trip to Berlin. While shopping, I spied the perfect leather handbag in the window of Lederer, famous throughout Germany.

I pointed. That one.

The clerk looked me up and down. I'm sorry, Fräulein, but that handbag is much too expensive for a working girl. I can show you one less dear.

I held my tongue. Would you be so kind as to summon the manager.

The manager enquired. Ja, Fräulein?

I told him, I want to buy everything in the display window.

Of course Fräulein, he crooned sarcastically, and where shall I have these leather goods sent?

I want them delivered to the Chancellery this afternoon. I grabbed Mogerl's arm, and burning a hole through the center of his face, added, I want that clerk dismissed immediately!

My eyes seared hers. I meant what I said. I swept regally out of the shop, black bundles growling in my arms.

Out front the Mercedes-Benz, the driver—my Schutzstaffel—in uniform, opened the back door for us.

What is her name? I heard the manager ask the shopgirl and saw her shrug.

Let it be a lesson to her! I thought. But my spirits had sunk. Yes I'd made my point. Yes, I'll make sure she loses her job, but what's the use? The truth is that no one knows my name. Or ever will know it.

I tried to snap back. You see, I told Mogerl with false gaiety when we were driving to the next shop on my list, I rummaging though my bag, HE gave me a pass that entitles me to free travel on all the railways.

Yes, laughed Mogerl. And so do thousands of organization members enjoy that privilege!

Like a slap. Mogerl will be sorry one day that she makes me the butt of cruel jokes.

Go ahead, laugh now, I bragged. You'll see that one day he'll marry me. But who'll marry you?

Thinking over the day makes me need a sleeping tablet.

24 NOVEMBER 1936

I couldn't order lingerie at my old place because the shop bore a sign "Juden" smeared across the glass in white paint. The Jewish proprietor and his wife no doubt have been removed. I hope they will quickly be replaced by Aryan Volk so that business can resume again. If I can't get good lingerie, I'll surely have to end it all.

To make up for the inconvenience, I went on to the best sta-tioner, and ordered a supply of envelopes in a particular shade of blue. My initials are to be engraved on every flap. At my villa I now keep silver and linen with my monogram in my mahogany dining room. My monogram: E. B. inside a four-leaf clover.

22 JANUAR 1937

I spent the night at the Berg. I brought Mogerl for company. In the morning Mogerl told me: When I got up early today I saw that after a night together, when the Kanzler and you greeted each other, you did so like strangers meeting for the first time. Isn't this difficult? Doesn't it demoralize you that you're thought to be of the secretarial pool?

Why reply? She'd never understand.

6 FEBRUAR 1937

My twenty-fifth birthday. Not only have I approached—now I've arrived—at spinsterhood, and must rub my face with cucumber slices. My dream of five little "offspring" has been put off again.

Herr B. gave me a painting, the head of a little girl. When he presented it to me he called me "Fräulein Ewe" with mock affection. "Ewe" is the Jewish and also Polish form of my name.

I hung the painting across from my favorite, a watercolor by the K.—"The Asam Church"—on the wall of my villa. Herr B. never misses a chance to humiliate me, call me "Ewe," and I can do nothing but hatch cruel plots of revenge in my imagination when I'm alone. I imagine putting out my cigarette between his eyes. I imagine a clot of my spit hitting him squarely in the face!

Bad Schachen, München, Peacock Island, Berchtesgaden

6 AUGUST 1937

I have not seen him for weeks. I am in a deep fit of blues. Herta mewed at me, The Kanzler is old enough to be your father. Stop moping, wake up. I know you think otherwise, but open your eyes, he will never marry you. There are other men.

Instead of making me feel better she made me feel worse. But there never has been another man for me. You'll see, he WILL marry me someday. Dr. and Frau G. take separate holidays these days, yet they're devoted to each other.

Ha, she laughed, We all know about his many affairs.

To distract me, Herta has arranged for Mogerl and Mutti and I to make a journey to Bad Schachen, to stay in a castle on Lake Bodensee, near Lindau. I must prepare.

16 AUGUST 1937

On our lively holiday I grew "friendly" with an attractive business-man. His name, Herr Peter S., age thirty-two. He played the piano for me, elaborate playing. He announced to me with bright eyes, I play with Lisztian *fioritura* just for you.

What does he mean?

Later:

We danced. We walked together in the moonlight. I let him stroke me below my leopard-skin belt—only between my coat and dress—but not on my skin. How strangely he caressed me, never sniffed me, his ears never moved, his tongue never lolled out. His hair smelled like a baby's.

I asked him for 10 Mark for cigarettes, which he gladly put into my hand.

20 AUGUST 1937

Back in München, flowers arrived from Herr S. Herta told me: You make a fine couple. He'd make a fine husband, a fine father.

Yes, we would but when the telephone rang, I refused to speak with him.

Why? asked Herta.

There's already a man in my life.

Does she think I'm that dumb? Look at this villa. Look at my clothes. Look at the car in the garage. What about "love"?

29 AUGUST 1937

Again I'm feeling deserted. And to make matters worse Herta told me she will marry.

Who?

A regular army officer.

When?

In two weeks.

I must remember to telephone someone named Hanni to thank her for the charming earrings delivered to the villa today. Who is Hanni? Why would a stranger give me such a lovely gift?

13 SEPTEMBER 1937

Because I cannot be seen with the K., Herr H. took me to Venetian Night on Peacock Island on the way to Potsdam.

First we crossed a pontoon bridge to a path where Dr. and Frau G. and the K. waited to receive us. The sight of Frau Magda G. with the K., her many "social graces," put me in a bad temper. The moonlight had turned her transparent ears a soft ivory color. Though she shook my hand she looked right through me. Sad to say I think she doesn't know "who" I am. He treated me the same way.

Along the path, glowing lamps hung from the trees lighting the young faces of hundreds of pretty schoolgirls in their white silk breeches, blouses, stockings, white leather slippers. With white wands in their hands the schoolgirls bowed as we passed. Then I and all lady guests were presented with figurines from the Prussian State Porcelain Factory as keepsakes. Up close Dr. G. has a

club foot but is glib in spite of his ugly deformity. If he were anyone else he'd be first on the list for the Euthanasia Program and
would be exterminated for the purification of Aryans.

Frau G. left quite early as did the K. Herr. H. kept drinking
more and more. His bulbous eyes kept searching the figures of the
girls. I noticed that the schoolgirls had gone home and "chorus
girls" as Herr H. called them arrived, were mingling and dancing
with the respectable men. Herr H. sneered that Dr. G. should
have a tadpole as his coat of arms.

Too much drink went to my head. Herr H. put me in a car and
told the driver to take me home because I could not walk straight.

19 SEPTEMBER 1937

A watercolor of Venice and a landscape of Rimini have been
added to my walls. Also several rugs, a Samarkand and a Gobelin,
which I believe are real, but Mogerl thinks are imitations. I was so
lonesome today that I took photographs of these new acquisitions
with my little camera. At least here I can:

smoke
whistle
use "excessive" cosmetics and nail color
write letters
discuss politics if I so desire, which of course I never do.

11 OKTOBER 1937

Because the K. so fears assassination, Herr B. has ordered fences
built to protect him from the myriad of visitors to the Berghof—
5,000 or more daily. Still more renovations are started at the
Berg. Dust is ruining my clean hair. Detonations, to clear rock,
explode. As roads are also being built, sections of old forest are
dynamited too.

Herr B. has given himself a farm. It has 80 cows, 100 hogs, and
is meant to be an "example" of agricultural hygiene since tiles line
the pigpens. Daily the sows and piglets are hosed off. They are
cleaner than Herr B. The cows and hogs have better food than the
workers who sometimes steal the animals' food. Imagine grown
men stealing food from helpless animals.

14 OKTOBER 1937

The entire country calls Obersalzberg "Holy Mountain of the Germans." Herr B. has sneakily added land to his property until it extends from the 1,900-meter tall Kehlstein down to the valley below. When a farm ruins the view, Herr B. makes magic and the cottage vanishes, the farmers disappear. Who knows where.

Because bright light bothers the Kanzler's eyes, Herr B. moved a full grown linden tree from the forest and had it replanted outside the Berghof to shade him where the Kanzler often stands. So that the view from the drawing room was improved, a gigantic retractable window was installed providing excellent views of Untersberg, Berchtesgaden, as well as Salzburg.

Unfortunately, when the wind comes up, automobile fumes from the subterranean garage blow into the drawing room.

24 OKTOBER 1937

To my delight, a bowling alley is being constructed in the basement. My complaint—Herr B. is also building a wall around the K. Inside the wall with him is Herr B.

25 OKTOBER 1937

Herr B. now signs *all* my checks! Though the Kanzler occasionally puts money—in minute quantities—into envelopes and hands them to me, I am chronically short of money unless Herr B. slips a check under my door.

The K. gives me trinkets and worthless, semi-precious jewelry, petty-bourgeois necklaces. (Except for the gold clips.) But Herr B. approves my other expenditures, shoes, jewelry. I get trinkets! Herr B. gets a farm!

I must tread carefully around Herr B. I've "quietly" complained to the Kanzler that his staff has been investigating my family again. But how to get out of debt? The puzzle taunts me hourly.

29 OKTOBER 1937

Because I've learned that the investigation of my family has resumed, I went to see Herr B. earlier today. I asked him, Why does your staff continue to investigate the ancestry of me and my family?

Ach.

The Kanzler promised to put an end to it. He told me that he would speak with you.

Oh.

And has he?

Yes.

So why haven't you quit?

Obviously we have not been more discreet.

What can I do when he says one thing and does another? Nieten. Using this moment of frankness I asked him, Oh, and have you investigated a certain lady's "arrangement" with the Flying Clown?

We have, Fräulein Effie, since you personally imparted the information through—as you call the head of the special police—the "Chicken Farmer's" staff, suggesting the certain lady be put on the Euthanasia Program lists.

Who told him that I call this fearful man, "Chicken Farmer?" Does he know that we call Dr. G. "the tadpole?"

It would give me great pleasure to put out a cigarette between Herr B.'s sly eyes.

31 OKTOBER 1937

I would like to tear my arms off my body because I've been having so much trouble with my mixed-grip thigh-turn mount. From an oblique angle I stand behind my high bar. I jump to a long hang position using a mixed grip. Then I swing my inside leg upward.

This is when the trouble begins. My twist is awkward. Once more I have proved to Vati that I'm inept. And clumsy at that.

1 NOVEMBER 1937

The cook told me that Herr B. has given a direction to guests and staff: You are not to discuss Fräulein Effie, the secretary, who sits at the Kanzler's left hand.

Of course I would like to tell people: Discuss me! But they don't.

As though my wish had been heard, out of the blue a Czecho-slovakian magazine published a photograph of him and me taken at Berchtesgaden, though it is a crime to do so.

It said under the photo: "The Kanzler's Madame Pompadour." Who is Madame Pompadour? Is it a compliment or an insult? No check pushed under my door this week.

Herta and I spent the day bowling.

2 NOVEMBER 1937

Now that I am assured that "the lady's" arrangement with the "Flying Clown" had been passed along, I am worried once again about the Walküre. I saw her dining at a München restaurant while parked outside was her well-known Austin, which is deco-rated with the hooked cross and the union jack.

Oh, if only I could be an arch. Let these "ladies" pass under me!

5 NOVEMBER 1937

Herr B. calls me "the Kanzler's little clerk." Because I am forbid-den to become embroiled in or even discuss politics, he thinks I have no sway with the Kanzler, which well I might not.

Of course the "Brown Eminence," Herr B., can't keep his hands off any woman. He flaunts his affairs with actresses, secre-taries, housemaids.

A dull day, this. A little head cold. A long, lonely nap.

15 NOVEMBER 1937

The K. confided in me, I'm certain I have cancer. His stomach aches though the vegetarian diet was supposed to cure it. I myself have searched for cures that affect the stomach and also might cure his flatulence. How healthy he was long ago, that very first day I met him and watched his teeth bite into fat sausages.

The maid from the country told me that moles' blood is a cu-rative for flatulence. How so? I asked her.

You tear a mole in half, then apply the still warm parts to af-flicted areas of your body.

She thought it was *my* body. Just how stupid does she think I am?

Once again I've put in a good word for my friend Hanni's husband. Dr. M. Hanni keeps me company on lonely evenings and has showered me with presents—handbags, jewel cases, good jewelry. Her eyes are flecked with green spots. She asked, Call me "Pralinchen."

As I've never refused her expensive gifts, I'd like to find a way to return her favors.

16 NOVEMBER 1937

When I brought the subject of Dr. M. up, he snapped at me, This man is a specialist in skin and venereal disease.

(Everyone thought this because Dr. M. had so rapidly cured my boss, Herr H., of gonorrhea with sulfonamides rather than with the old electrical treatment which included painful cauterization of inflamed tissue. And with total discretion.)

Dr. M. is also a genius who discovered the powder used to rid German soldiers of fleas and other vermin.

This made no impression.

And, I added, He has been offered positions as the special physician at the court of the Shah of Persia and also for the King of Rumania.

He looks Jewish.

I explained as Hanni had explained to me, He is also a specialist in electrotherapy and diseases of the urinary system. But skin diseases as well. Think of your boots!

I'd touched a raw nerve! I may be the only one in the world who knows that he has eczema on his lower left leg and because of it he cannot wear his boots.

A sensitive subject indeed.

25 NOVEMBER 1937

He agreed to see Dr. M. and did!

After intensive fecal examination, Dr. M. decided that the eczema is connected to his digestion and the K. agreed to follow the doctor's plan.

Dr. M. boasted to me and Hanni during our celebration evening yesterday, I'll have him fit again within the year. I will replace the dysbacterial flora in his intestinal tract by emulsion of a strain of coli bacteria. I've prescribed capsules of mutaflor with his morning meal, which will relieve the accumulated gas in his intestines and stomach, and the resulting flatulence. I prescribe Dr. Koster's anti-gas pills, four taken with each meal.

Again tonight a jolly evening with Dr. and Hanni. Much wine. Pickled herring. A deep sleep from the wine.

7 DEZEMBER 1937

Gas and romance do not mix! He hasn't thrust at me in months. I'm out of my mind about it. Is my end . . .

14 DEZEMBER 1937,

This occasion makes me once more put pen to paper. He can wear his boots once more! He gave Dr. M. a fine house.

He told me, Rare is the man that lives up to his promises.

Three times in as many days I have caught him sniffing me in an amorous way. And his moods are so light. Not once has he made fun of me, even when I reminded him that it is *"reprehensible to withhold healthy children from the nation."*

Your idea not mine, I told him, then took his hand and put it on my breast.

20 DEZEMBER 1937

Sniffs, yes, but still no "activity." When I try to lock eyes with him he looks the other way.

He's gone. Everything is so horribly bleak. An afternoon of guzzling with Käthl, her boyfriend Georg, and Hanni discussing the scandal of Field Marshal von B., and his new wife/secretary who has just been exposed as a prostitute who posed for pornographic photos.

Saw the Austin with the hooked cross and union jack again, this time across from the shining white marble of the *Weisswurstpalast*.

Berlin, Berchtesgaden, Vienna, North Cape, Italy, München

8 JANUAR 1938

I have begun to experiment with my hair. I had my Berlin hairdresser bleach my hair until it is very light indeed. Then, in a fit of daring, I had her give a drastic cut and combed it into a new up-sweep.

After the hairdresser I was delayed on the street by a long succession of army automobiles, so I spent the entire afternoon with Hanni drinking wine and eating Vorspeisen in puff shells at the exclusive roof garden of the Hotel Leden. The Kanzler has been again—as he has been day after day—in meetings and conferences.

In point of fact, I have not seen him at all. Herr B. told me that he's gone to Berghof so this evening I went to the theatre with Hanni. When Hanni laughed she threw her head back, made a braying noise heard throughout the theatre. Afterward she tried to talk me into going to a nightclub but I dared not go.

11 JANUAR 1938

I've come to the Berg to surprise him, but it wasn't until quite late that he returned from his conference. I watched the arrival of the cars from the window above. When he emerged there was immediately a swarm of male bodies in brown uniforms around him.

Later:

To get a better look at my hair he turned on a bright light. He was distressed, You look completely strange, completely changed to me. You are a different woman.

My elation shattered when he went directly to bed after bidding me, Good night.

He wanted nothing to do with this "new" woman.

12 JANUAR 1938

I went back to the hair salon and demanded they restore my hair to the original style but leave the new color. And, I ordered, refund 10 percent of the fee.

6 FEBRUAR 1938

Again he is gone.

My birthday is forgotten because he is delivering a long speech at the Kroll Opera House.

12 MÄRZ 1938

Much excitement over Austria. Our troops sent to restore order. Even I was caught up. I rang Mutti: Mutti, I want to see what is going on. Will you come with me to the border?

Mutti asked, Since when does politics interest you?

You can't avoid it anymore, it's truly in the air.

She asked, Shall I bring overnight things?

No, we'll drive to Salzburg in the morning and then drive back. I'll send for the car, but I must first wash my hair.

13 MÄRZ 1938

We drove past the red and white poles at the Austrian frontier, then on to Salzburg. The city was ecstatic. I learned that the Kanzler had gone on to Linz to visit the grave of his parents. Are you willing to drive to Linz? I asked Mutti.

Yes, she replied. She was thrilled to be driven by a driver for the first time in her life. What a good sport, my old Mutti. Poor Mutti, an old woman has invaded her hair, her shape, her demeanor.

So we drove on past cream-washed churches to Linz then Leonding.

Again he was already gone, but for five sombre minutes I beheld the wreath laid against the headstone of his "saintly" mother. What would she have thought of a convent girl like me? Had she dreamt of grandchildren?

Later:

We were delayed because of parades of National Socialists from Linz. They wore knickerbockers and short pants and armbands. His armored Mercedes and motorcycle escort have gone on to Vienna.

Shall we try to catch up with him in Vienna? I asked Mutti but the tone of my voice was telling not asking.

As you like, she replied timidly.

(How life has changed! Nowadays "little" Mutti is afraid of "little" Effie.)

Later:

On the outskirts of Vienna, the door of our car was wrenched open. Mutti and I were dragged out. Who are you? we were asked by men with rubber tire necks.

The driver answered for us, They are from München.

Immediately they embraced us. Everywhere: flags, crowds, men in military uniforms, bronze eagles with spread pinions.

One look showed me that Vienna is a romantic city indeed though it smells of Gulasch.

Later:

Mutti was getting anxious because we had no money, no food, not even a toothbrush, so we found a hotel.

Your luggage? the manager asked.

It's coming in another car, I lied.

How easily you lie, observed Mutti, which made me laugh.

In the room Mutti rang the porter. If you would be so kind, bring soap and toothbrushes.

When they did there was plenty of soap but only one toothbrush. Disgusted at having to share such a personal item, I took it for myself. Never mind, let Mutti use her finger to clean her remaining teeth.

Later:

The porter told me that the Kanzler was at the Hotel Imperial, so I rang the Imperial, and told his adjutant where I was. A car arrived to bring me to the Imperial. I was put into a suite with a rococo bed. When I was settled I realized that I'd carelessly left Mutti with no money nor had I arranged a meal for Mutti, who never once complained of hunger.

All night, while I waited, the Viennese stood in front of the hotel and sang.

He finally joined me in my room and scolded me for following him. It's dangerous.

I stamped my feet, Don't scold me, I had Mutti with me.

She ought to have more sense than you.

I tried to entice him to bed. My vulva was becoming very pink and swollen. Finally he noticed it protruding from my clipped blond fur. I saw him looking at it. He hunkered down and began to prod it with his tongue. Under his licking it grew even more swollen and its pink color turned bright red.

Twisting around with longing, I lifted my rump up high. He dropped his fingertips around my little chestnut-colored nipple. When he hesitated, I grasped him with both legs and thrust against his uniform, but he pulled away, causing me to fall back.

He walked out, went back to his suite. Obviously, he preferred to stand again on the balcony and give the chanting crowd the pleasure of seeing him, than to planting his own seed, than to giving healthy children to his nation.

Alone, I clawed his hat with my nails, stabbing it in and out between my legs until release came.

14 MÄRZ 1938

I sent a car for Mutti and waited for her in the dining room. We were ravenous but had no money. Mutti scribbled a postcard to Oische. At the bottom of the card I added: *Ich bin verrückt.**

The adjutant handed me an envelope containing currency. We

* (I am crazy)

began to eat like swine, as we had been two days with no food. We ate frische Suppe, Schnitzel. The adjutant returned and whispered in my ear: The Kanzler is flying back to Berlin. If you want to go you must leave at once.

I dropped my knife and fork, followed the adjutant.

Mutti called after me, I have no money. What shall I do?

Was I deaf? She sounded like a helpless old woman. I pretended that I hadn't heard. I thought: Mutti, finish eating, order strong coffee, order tarts.

Driving through Vienna to the airfield I saw a line of miserable-looking people. I asked the driver who they were. He told me, They're poor people given soup at noon every day by the city of Vienna. A few of these people were sitting on the curb cupping their hands around steaming cocoa tins.

Before I left I had the adjutant deliver an envelope into Mutti's hand. Inside a small amount of cash and a note: Stay. Enjoy our Vienna.

2 APRIL 1938

The Brown Eminence stands in my way. Behind his back, while I always call him "the Brown Eminence," his *own* wife calls him "the Bull" and repeatedly produces children. The gossip is that she urges her husband: Bear children with your mistresses! Help Germany outpopulate non-Aryan countries!

The Brown Eminence continues to notice that "little Ewe" gives the Kanzler pleasure—though no children, as is the duty of all German women—so he has decided to give his Kanzler *more* pleasure. He knows the pleasure the K. takes in walking up to the tea pavilion on the first level of the Obersalzberg after his meal, so he has arranged the construction of a new teahouse, high up in the Kehlstein, where the eagles fly.

For the Kanzler's repose, he explained, looking at me with childish glee.

Herr B. bragged when he handed me my check, The name Eagle's Nest has been given to the undertaking. This will give him lasting pleasure.

The check he gave me barely pays for my new brooch.

3 APRIL 1938

The Brown Eminence himself climbed the mountain and chose a peak at 1,600 meters. A new road now connects the Berg to the Kehlstein, also a tunnel. An elevator shaft was blasted out of the solid rock.

To get to it, the road circled in hairpin turns, through tunnels. Schutzstaffel sentries stand guarding the huge bronze doors that lead into the tunnel.

I am not permitted to move freely nor to watch the construction. Some days I wait alone so long I feel like I'm an empty valise. A valise that has been turned upside down, the contents spilled. How many bowling balls can I throw? How many times can I comb my hair?

Today I've paced back and forth angrily for hours on end. Still I was not called. Yes, winter is finished, but the false spring lasted such a short time that the frost this morning has blackened the orchards. There will be no fruit in Bavaria this year.

I slept naked, holding my own breasts last night.

4 JUNI 1938

At last I was invited to the Eagle's Nest!

The second door, when opened, revealed an elevator. Inside an upholstered chair and a bench. The walls have mirrors set into polished brass. I could not tell that the elevator moved because it was entirely silent until my eardrums began to hurt. Then, without warning, we were delivered directly inside the Eagle's Nest, seventy meters vertically up through the center of the mountain.

The K.'s face got pale, he appeared anxious. We shall go back down.

No, I want to see it.

Let Herr B., the Brown Eminence, be blamed if something happens to him!

We went into a glassed-in circular chamber. A huge log was burning. About thirty chairs surround the table. The tearoom itself is lined with marble. He started feeling better and showed me rooms made with stone, others with pine and elm paneling. I saw

Salzburg in the distance and clusters of villages. Below the sharp peaks, pastures, forests.

He got impatient and we walked outside. The house seemed to float, until a wall of rock abruptly rose up. He grew animated and launched into monologue: My boyhood friend August Kubizek and I once walked along the Danube, looking down at the river flowing below us. We only wished we could spend our lives in a house of *my* design. What would we do? We would study art. A beautiful woman would keep house for us. All highly intelligent men should have a primitive and stupid woman or a wife as a housekeeper. The house I designed had a tower, a spiral stairway, a vast music room. I believed at the time that I would pay for it by winning a large sum of money in the lottery.

Like an accordion, his talk never reaches the end. He walked a few steps, his back to me.

It was with my boyhood friend that I saw the opera *Rienzi*, standing in the promenade below the royal box. While the trumpets blared the Romans shouted after Cola da Rienzi, 'Heil, Rienzi! Heil, the tribune of the people!'

Herr B. has given you this teahouse. I asked from the heart, What can I give you?

Ach. He didn't turn around.

I was heady from the height. I gushed over, I like your idea of a spiral stairway and I also like the ceremonial stairway in the Berg. I wanted suddenly to bare my soul to him. Can't I be your primitive and stupid wife? Can't I keep house for you?

Come, he told me, uninterested in my opinions, I can scarcely breathe.

19 JUNI 1938

I went to the dentist today, not a pleasant interlude.

There is talk that "Acid Tongue"—Dr. G.—brings young actresses up into the Eagle's Nest. Also talk about the Brown Eminence's mistresses, and worst of all, that the Kanzler visits the Eagle's Nest late at night with female "companions."

The titterers have started calling it the "Love Nest" instead of the "Eagle's Nest." I "die" with these rumors. That he might pinch another nipple.

20 JULI 1938
I have been slimming non-stop and his face fell when I removed my clothes. He complained, When I first met you, you were nice and chubby and now you're thin as a rail.

This is my reward now that my thighs no longer stick together in the heat, and pop when I part my legs.

21 JULI 1938
At lunch I sat silently across from him. There were eight of us at lunch. He ranted the whole time about Herr Chamberlain: If that silly old man comes interfering here again with his umbrella, I'll kick him downstairs.

Then he forgot about Chamberlain. He turned his eyes on me once more. Women are always saying they want to be attractive to their men, but then they go and do the very opposite.

He ate potatoes baked in the oven with raw linseed oil poured over. He offered me a portion, but I turned up my nose at anything that had been "tainted" with raw linseed oil. My feelings were "hurt."

I ate thin slices of roast meat that had been squeezed to get rid of grease, then washed thoroughly so no trace of salt was left. Seeing the meat, he began his familiar harangue to the carnivores, gleefully describing the workings of a slaughterhouse, how live pigs are ground into sausage. He described young girls in rubber boots who work standing in blood up to their ankles.

I must laugh.

As usual, one of us "carnivores" had to leave the table.

He pointed at the departing, pale-faced guest, That couldn't happen to me. I can watch someone pulling up a beet root, collecting eggs.

I pushed my plate away at that point.

How cowardly people are, he remarked, They can't face doing certain horrible things themselves, can't even bear to watch them being done, but they enjoy the benefits without a single pang of conscience.

I could. I thought.

19 AUGUST 1938

I have not seen him for a month. I bought a new musk coat.

So many women I see are pregnant these days, their clothes are dowdy and shapeless. Since make-up is frowned upon, their faces are lackluster too.

I've bought ten lottery tickets. Nieten. Nieten to them all.

Not one bowling partner to be found. I refuse to bowl alone!

29 AUGUST 1938

I cannot bear any longer to wait night after night so Mutti and I have decided to make a voyage together in a ship called the *Milwaukee* to the the North Cape.

Much to do. Much to buy.

2 SEPTEMBER 1938

Mutti was immediately seasick. My cabin, small, but fruit and wine were waiting in a basket, which I sampled and quickly rang for more. The evening meal on the ship—Schnüsch, aal Grün.

I wore my new musk evening coat. It's very soft, very fluffy, has wide sleeves and a little train. It bucks me up.

3 SEPTEMBER 1938

Mutti is feeling better. She has begun a needlepoint of the feet of a unicorn.

After dinner—Fischklopse, Birnen, Bohnen and Speck—I strolled the deck in the cool night air and was noticed by my fellow passengers. In the presence of an appreciator, I swell up inside. I hummed the new hit:

> *At Katrina's with the golden hair,*
> *The boys and girls are dancing there*

Back in my cabin the rolling ship mocks me. Also, my hair has been ruined by the fierce wind. Valerian drops tonight so I can sleep.

I stepped on the scale. When I saw the arrow touch forty-five kilos I vowed to go back onto my diet.

4 SEPTEMBER 1938

Tonight at 10 the purser went to look for me on deck because a call had come through from a high Schutzstaffel. I'm sure the entire ship wondered: What important man is calling the short girl in the musk coat?

His call brought me back to life.

At breakfast much fervent talk about Czech beasts molesting pregnant women in the Sudetenland.

7 SEPTEMBER 1938

We stopped on the way back at North Sea spa for "the cure." Outside a large sign in black letters: *Juden sind hier nicht erlaubt.** I took a seawater inhalation and full body massage. Mutti refused all but a seawater bath with rosemary. Mutti was impressed because Kaiser Wilhelm II and "high society" often visited this spa.

The chambermaid told us about the frequency of suicide in this place. The high winds cause it, she told us with authority. I closed my eyes and headily imagined ending it all.

I rested on a lounge chair, watched schoolboys hiking through the woods on stilts.

8 SEPTEMBER 1938

Wind in my ears the entire day. Felt like ending it all.

1 OKTOBER 1938

He has no time for me these days. Mutti, Mogerl, and I will journey to Italy by train. Much to do.

* (Jews not allowed here)

15 OKTOBER 1938

In Italy it's still so warm that we can sunbathe. And we can also dance. Except for taking pictures, my favorite activity is shopping. I need stockings and underwear. I have not yet found satisfactory underwear since my Jewish-owned shop was smashed.

When we passed a small lingerie shop we entered and Mogerl asked in her limited Italian, Please show my sister your finest Italian silk stockings.

The salesgirl suggested, Don't buy the Italian silk, they're not made well. The best we have to offer are the "Elbee" stockings.

Where are they manufactured?

In Germany.

We'll take twelve pairs, I told Mogerl who translated the order into Italian, ask for a 10 percent discount.

Buying German! My chance to help our cause! A story to tell "Him."

8 NOVEMBER 1938

We're missing a huge scandal that's broken at home. A Jewish refugee has shot one of our ambassadors in Paris. Mogerl's handsome male "friend" and Mutti think that it's political, but Mogerl and I have heard whispers about blackmail, also a homosexual love affair. We long to know the details. We've shocked Mutti by our talk.

We long to return home again.

13 NOVEMBER 1938

When we boarded the overnight train for the return to München, I realized I had increased my luggage threefold. Where will I find the money to pay off these bills?

We had to change trains at Rome but could find no one to help us, so Mutti and I went out onto the platform and Mogerl lifted the luggage out through the window of the compartment one at a time.

I had arranged to have my own compartment. (The older I get the less I can stand sleeping in the same room with another person. I can't bear to listen to another person breathe.) But when the conductor came to look at our tickets he saw that a mistake had been made. He told me, You will have to share this sleeper.

I made a row, stamped my feet. Once again, no one had the slightest idea who I am and naturally I did not sleep one bit so I'm suffering from exhaustion to this moment.

When the train reached the border, customs people knocked at our compartment. Because I had the keys to the luggage I bent down to open the largest valise. The hood of my dressing gown fell over my eyes. This charmed them and to my great relief—as I'm broke—no duty was charged.

Mutti announced: You looked like the grandmother in *Little Red Riding Hood*.

6 FEBRUAR 1939

He has given me a second car for my birthday. It's a prototype of his Volkswagen. It's squat. For now I've shut it up in the garage. Mutti stitched an apron adorned with garlands of flowers for me.

12 FEBRUAR 1939

Where has the time gone? I've barely put pen to paper with so much travel interspersed with so much loneliness. What can I say about my life? I'm another year older and almost never does he have a moment for love anymore. Love has been struck off his schedule. Only my dogs run and jump on me, only the hired girl looks up at me with adoring eyes.

Nor has he given me one piece of jewelry. My birthday came and went with just the ugly car to mark it.

Sat all afternoon with Mogerl drinking colored drinks through long straws as she watched and commented on the "prowess" of the passing men. I'm so despairing that I couldn't really pay attention.

At the restaurant we saw a Jewish-looking man get drunk and slash his own throat with a razor. Lately I've had the same idea myself.

It would serve me well if I could get Mogerl married off to the right man. But Mogerl's reputation is that she is *not overly particular in the matter of men*. At one point the Kanzler wanted her to marry Heinz, the son of my old boss. This didn't work out. Then he chose Fritz D., from his private Schutzstaffel entourage. But Herr D. wasn't interested. I wonder what puts them off? Is it that she gives herself to them so easily? Is it the loud parrot squeal I've heard her make at moments of "release"? Or those "fruity cries"?

24 APRIL 1939

I have been given my own maid at the Berg. Her name is Paula. She's a timid thing with hair like corn husks, which she wears drawn tightly back, her braid is twined around the back of her head like I once wore mine. She is shorter than me, from near Stettin in Pomerania, and was late arriving.

She told me she was sterilized when the new law went into effect. She told me this with a sly smile across her yellow beak. She has no sense of punctuality. I told her I would beat her if she continued to make me wait. And I will, just like the nuns beat me into punctuality.

26 APRIL 1939

I begged but he would not introduce me to the Duchess of Windsor. Nor, despite lamentations, was I invited to socialize with Herr Ciano, Mussolini's handsome and infamous diplomat cum son-in-law.

I am frustrated at every turn. When alone I listen to the hits "Blood-Red Roses" and "Beautiful Gigolo" while gluing photographs into my little book.

The closest I got to Herr Ciano—*le cervo volante**—at the Berchtesgaden was to photograph him through a window with a new telephoto lens. Doctor M. told me that Herr Ciano caught my face in the window and enquired, What is the name of that lovely girl in the window?

Of course, before the night was over, a stern Schutzstaffel presented me with an official order to keep my window closed.

Nor was I included in the official celebration of his fiftieth

* (The flying horse)

birthday. Of course that "adornment," Frau Magda G., appeared with him at the "official" celebration. Like nonentities, Mogerl and I strolled up the splendid new street going by way of the Brandenburg Gate to the Reichskanzlerplatz to view the fluttering flags that line the street.

It got dark, searchlights were turned on to illuminate the event. When we decided to turn back and find a café, we had no chance to push our way through the crowd to the Victory Column and got stuck for hours drinking vermouth while tanks, trucks, cannons rolled by.

I have my heart set on a Persian lamb coat! I'm so sick of my old silver fox I could cry!

9 MAI 1939

Not included once again.

This time I'm left out of the "official" entourage visiting Mussolini in Italy.

10 MAI 1939

Good news. As a consolation he has included me in the "unofficial suite" instead.

Vati refused Mutti permission to go. Instead the proprietor of the Rhin Hotel in Godesberg—a supporter from days gone by—has been invited as my chaperone. What a bore. The group includes her son—another bore—two of the K.'s personal doctors, including Dr. M. and Hanni, who thankfully are always up for a good time.

Paula has much to prepare for me. First, a fresh batch of hair invigorator—a mix of:

1. bay rum
2. alcohol
3. castor oil
4. ammonia

11 MAI 1939

Happily our group has been quartered in the best suite at the Hotel Excelsior in Rome. Barely had I changed out of my traveling clothes when the Italian Secret Police burst into my suite.

They informed us: You may not attend the official parade tomorrow. According to our sources elements unfriendly to the German-Italian *entente* are planning an attempt against the Kanzler's entourage.

This was laughable. Why would any of us be of the slightest interest to dissidents or foreign agents?

As consolation we watched the parade of the fleet from a designated sloop.

13 MAI 1939

I took handfuls of free postcards from every one of the hotels.

> *Dear Mutti and Vati,*
> *We were present at the parade of the fleet, which was very fine. Unfortunately I have caught a cold and my throat is sore. We leave tomorrow for Taormina and not for Capri.*

> *Dear Mutti and Vati,*
> *We went to Capri (the Hotel Quisisana) after all—the journey to Taormina would have been too tiring for me. I've grown thin and very weak.*

27 MAI 1939

I'm happy to be home in my own bed with my "children," Negus and Stasi, lying at my feet. Though the K. is in Berchtesgaden, I have been told to remain here. So to pass the night, I've filled my photo album with snapshots and added notes:

   . . . stroking the ears of a donkey in the narrow streets of Capri.
   . . . climbing the slopes of Vesuvius.
   . . . Capri: We made a tremendous impression on the Italians. I am courted and always referred to as "La bella bionda."

At my audience with the new Pope Pius XII, I wore the traditional black lace veil. What this would have meant to me once is now sadly empty. The photograph of me with the Pope turned out quite pious, just as I once tried but failed to be when the priest would say—*ego te absolvo*—God will eradicate your sins, and your soul will be like the soul of a newly baptized child.

Oh, what would those old nuns say if they could see little Effie keeping company with none other than God on earth?

27 JUNI 1939

The Kanzler has ordered: Fräulein Effie must receive the salute reserved for only the most important dignitaries.

How much pleasure this gives me! Now bodyguards in black and silver uniforms go everywhere I go—a mixed pleasure when Hanni and I want to drink vermouth in the afternoon.

30 JUNI 1939

He has told me: Stop driving by yourself. Take a week off, go to Zürs for a few days, dance with young officers your own age.

Of course I don't "dance with young officers" with my bodyguards not two steps away.

4 JULI 1939

O. has gone to work for one of the K.'s ministers.

Herta has given birth to a beautiful little daughter. Oh that I had experienced childbirth like Herta has!

I'm keeping in shape, weighing less than forty-five kilos. My vigorous exercise has helped me burn calories at a phenomenal rate. Fat stores are burnt. Perhaps a bit of muscle tissue, just enough to keep my muscle and fat from jiggling.

It has been an excellent day of exercise on the parallel bars, I worked on the glide single leg rise mount.

An unusual event in München: First a red light which turned my skin red, then a rainbow of different colors shimmering across the sky. The Northern Lights. An omen?

12 JULI 1939

My menstrual flow has stopped. Why? How? If my legacy is motherhood, I'm sad to say it hasn't happened. I lie naked on the upper balcony at the Berghof listening to the new hit "Bel Ami."

Lying face down I heard the unmistakable sound of his boots. I pretended I was asleep to let him feast his eyes on my naked back and buttocks, but when I heard a little click I could not resist rolling over and saw—his hand shielding his eyes from the sun—that he had taken a photograph of my ripple-free buttocks with a little camera. I parted my legs.

He explained, I want the back view for a reason, *gnädiges Fräulein*. You see, if the photograph falls into the wrong hands, no one will recognize that it is you.

Stasi and Negus, the "hand lickers"—he calls them—sniffed his boots. I closed my eyes again and let him look as long as he liked but he had obviously seen enough and walked inside to answer the telephone.

Where is the half-wit Paula? When I shout at her she becomes even slower. I'm hoarse shouting at her because my dress is not ironed.

22 JULI 1939

I'm ordered to Berlin, though I do not like Berlin at all in the summertime.

27 JULI 1939

At last Herr B. showed me the apartment in the Chancellery in Berlin that is being prepared for my use. Herr B. told me, He has reserved Hindenburg's former bedroom for you. Then he handed me a big check, which I sorely need.

Until now I've been put in a room in the Adlon Hotel on the corner of Wilhelmstrasse and Unter den Linden. I have so often seen the propaganda minister trotting off with one of his mistresses, sex written all over them. The entire country calls him the goat of Babelsberg. He makes no secret of his trysts.

Because the K. has kept his suite at the Kaiserhof, our paths rarely cross. I have been forced to continually hear gossip about his tea-taking—while light music fills the air—in the lounge of the Kaiserhof with socially presentable people. Young, beautiful women are constantly offering flowers to him or begging to touch his hand if only for a moment.

Of course, I cannot be seen with him there.

I'm doubly glad my apartment is almost prepared though each time I go anywhere near the Reich Chancellery, at least 200 people are mutely waiting in the square for even a "glimpse" of him.

28 JULI 1939

What good will Hindenburg's former bedroom do me? He is either traveling, speaking, or in conference. To fill the time here in Berlin, I shop for dresses made by Fräulein Heise, Italian shoes by Ferragamo, French underwear. My bodyguard waits outside the shop for me, his black and silver uniform causing a stir.

And do I get compliments? Not at all. Usually he comments: Women insist upon buying foreign clothes and refuse to believe that German products can be just as good. You want French perfume but who invented *eau de cologne*? We Germans!

After seeing the French underwear, though, he slipped a stack of 100-Mark bills into my purse. I dare not grouse.

10 AUGUST 1939

Still no menstrual flow. I had to get away from so much talk about the crisis in Poland. His prolonged absences have been interminable, so I've arrived in Venice to attend the Venice Film Festival.

People at home are forgetting how to have a good time but not the Italians.

13 AUGUST 1939

The August sun is burning hot. I must go indoors and lie down after lunch.

14 AUGUST 1939

A telegram was brought as I rested from the heat behind closed shutters.

URGENT THAT YOU RETURN HOME AT ONCE! –B.

I could not leave sooner than the overnight train which was filled. The station was frantic but a first-class sleeper was freed after one telephone call.

Through the warm night the train stopped time and again, causing me to have a bilious attack. Finally I saw the scarlet flag with a circle in white bearing a hooked cross in black and knew we'd reached the border. We crossed but delays continued. As dawn came, I saw long troop trains passing.

If war comes, I can't help but think that he'll leave me. I will be made smaller and smaller until I disappear into anonymity. For sure I'll end it all.

I searched for my mirror and realized that I must have left it in the hotel in Venice. Also my lipstick.

17 AUGUST 1939

I have entirely filled this leatherette album. I am twenty-seven years old, a childless spinster who has met and been photographed with the Pope.

E. B.

BOOK III

Berlin, München, Berchtesgaden, Chiemsee

15 SEPTEMBER 1939

With this entry I begin a new account of myself on the pages of this ivory tinted leather album; a gift from Hanni. My initials are embossed in gold.

In these days of our triumphal Blitzkrieg through Poland, we are all in light spirits.

19 SEPTEMBER 1939

I have been instructed to steal into my apartment in the Chancellery through the servants' entrance on the side. Then I must use a rear staircase and never descend into the lower rooms.

Nor am I permitted to walk the long marble polished floor that takes visitors into receptions.

My apartment is not really part of the grand building—newly built—on Vosstrasse. This bothers me, even though Bismarck's portrait remains because the apartment belonged to Hindenburg.

Thick curtains are always drawn across the windows, which makes it quite gloomy. Herr B. has ordered that I must never open the curtains. The servants have also been instructed to keep the curtains closed. So they remain closed night and day, but perhaps it's also a blessing because they keep out the incessant chirp of the sparrows, chatterings of the magpies, the nightingale crescendos that I find quite irritating.

Though there are notices in the newspaper of rationing of textiles, and coal, this doesn't much alarm me. But, my blood goes cold, also rationing of shoes, of soap, of food! What will become of "ME" if I can't buy new shoes?

Perhaps I take too gloomy a view of things. He has promised that the war will be over in two weeks.

Though this dark apartment adjoins the K.'s library and private rooms, my life has become even more solitary because of the war. I've come so far but still long to end it all!

22 SEPTEMBER 1939,

Constantly the newspapers print photographs of "saintly" Emmy G., the wife of the head of the Luftwaffe, calling her "Landesmutter."

I am not permitted to move freely in the official Chancellery at all. If the K. is not with me, my meals are brought directly to my room. I, his "long suffering" shadow, am left alone, the phonograph my only company.

As usual, love has been struck off his schedule.

23 SEPTEMBER 1939

Last night we were together. Käseboullion was carried into the library and my spirits were lifted up until I learned that he'd invited his abominable secretaries to join us.

25 SEPTEMBER 1939

Have returned to München. It's dreadfully dull here.

Herr B. told me just who the young woman was who went to the Englischer Garten and shot herself in the head. Ach. The Englischer Garten is so fragrant in summer with the scent of jasmine that it makes me pine for summer days. People say this woman is tall, has no hips, big breasts. They are trying to keep her name secret.

Of course, I know it's Fräulein M. — the Walküre.

She's in the clinic on Nussbaumstrasse. The wound was in the temple. A tight suicide watch has been necessary in case she tries again.

"He's" in subhuman Poland, at what is called "the front."

26 SEPTEMBER 1939

Because I pity her, I sent flowers to the pathetic girl. White flowers for disappointment.

I spent a dull afternoon with Mutti who has entirely reorganized her homemaking to adjust for the strict rationing system. Imagine—without complaining—she, Vati, and my sister now exist on 2400 grams of bread a week, 500 grams of meat, 270 grams of fat, 62.5 grams of cheese, 100 grams of marmalade, 250 grams of sugar. The final blow—400 grams of coffee substitute.

Mutti jokes that Vati is not the same tyrant without strong coffee.

28 OKTOBER 1939

The doctor allowed Fräulein M.'s friends to visit the clinic. This is what I heard about her: One friend asked, What can we do for you? She begged her, Please bring me a party emblem, the type with the pin in back, I am lost without an emblem.

Her request was fulfilled. Also a photo of the Kanzler was brought for her bedside table. The friends were gathered around her. She reached for the emblem. Rather than stick the pin onto the lapel of her dressing gown, she jammed it into her mouth, and swallowed it.

What I would have given to see that!

Later:

The pin ripped through her esophagus. She was quickly taken by private railway train directly into Switzerland. This is all we talk about in this unpleasant autumn heat.

Oh what drama!

8 NOVEMBER 1939

A blessing. Vati was wounded for the Kanzler's sake! It's so exciting, I can barely write this news!

Vati had gone—as an organization member with the special Green Member's card—to listen to the Kanzler speak at the Münchener Bürgerbräukeller. The K.'s speech to the assembled Old Fighters was unusually short. The K. had departed when a bomb exploded, wounding and killing organization members.

Vati among the wounded! Vati a hero!

11 NOVEMBER 1939

Good news. Vati and Mutti have received an invitation to tea at the Berghof. What joy when respectability comes!

13 NOVEMBER 1939

The day arrived. They looked a dream arriving by special car though the "official" entrance. I'm so thankful that our family has put our differences behind us. If only he had seen the young, radiant Mutti! If only Vati had been one of the K.'s early, "ardent" followers.

Tea was served. I snapped photos with my little camera. Mutti took only one anise-flavored Springerle onto her plate. Seeing this, the K. called the waiter back, and filled her plate with every kind of cake and a handful of cookies. Mutti put her hand up to stop him but he only piled on more cookies and told her, You must eat them all, Frau. They are good for you.

He pointed at his own plate, filled with Tarts, Springerle, Walnusschnitten. My second-helping, Frau.

He ate the tarts one by one, and after a sip of tea, turned his full attention to the cookies which were soon gone. Chocolates next. Then more tea.

Mutti again was mesmerized by his consumption of sweets. Vati never uttered a sound but growled for a glass of beer instead of tea. Later, when the K. had gone to his conference, I confided in Mutti: His stomachache is constant. His insomnia is growing worse. He perceives that his heart beats too fast and too hard. What can I do Mutti?

What did the doctor say?

I showed Mutti the report:

Consultation at the Reich Chancellery. (Kanzler suffering from) a roaring in the ears for several days, with high-pitched metallic sound in the left ear at night. Ears: no abnormalities observed. Hearing: more than 5 meters to each side. Obviously overworked. Preoccupied. Sleeps very little, can't get to sleep. (I recommend) evening strolls before retiring to bed, hot and cold foot baths, mild sedatives. Time off. Always feels better at the Berghof.

Ach! Yes . . . hot and cold foot baths are very good. What can anyone do? Mutti smiled weakly.

What could she, a housewife, add?

I daren't show her my apartment here. It just wouldn't be

right. Respectability hasn't really come. I took her and Vati out onto a balcony to show them the view, melting snow dripped down the back of Vati's only good suit.

1 DEZEMBER 1939

Dr. M. prescribed injections of glucose for the K., which—within seconds of the injections—created a feeling of "well being" in him. Also something added to enrich "virility." The old "meat" smell rose up. My heart expanded.

Let's hope he could at least . . . if only . . .

CHRISTMAS 1939

Mutti baked an entire ham inside a puffed loaf of bread. She told us, This is the first time we can afford such a thing.

30 DEZEMBER 1939

A happy day of tobogganing with Herta's little girl. I found some thrilling, long slides. I squealed with her when we picked up speed. She was terrified. She's so pretty, dressed all in brown and white trim. I pulled the toboggan back up the hill. Then, less afraid, she swooned while we sped back down the slope.

1 MÄRZ 1940

It's normal that he wouldn't take a great interest in me at the moment with all that's going on.

Alone at my villa, Mogerl away with a new "friend." I played with my dogs, photographed them, photographed the villa. I counted my money. Nothing but war news every time I turn on the radio.

28 JUNI 1940

I shan't be included in any of the triumphal festivities.

I sipped Schnaps alone once again with my little hearthrugs. I gave Paula a glass, made her sit down in the sitting room. I said, Tell me the story of your life. She was so scared she spilled half the Schnaps down the front of her uniform. Her fat breasts stuck to the wet fabric, which became transparent. She began to talk of her girlhood on a farm, but my mind was elsewhere.

13 JULI 1940

Paula's Buttermilchsuppe tonight. Sweet and sour at once.

30 JULI 1940

A few drops of menstrual blood, but . . .

12 AUGUST 1940

What good is it that my "cycle" has started again? He's gone back to the cursed front and I'm in my villa for a solitary evening of wine soup because Paula has her night out. I beat an egg in but skimped on the sweet cream.

The radio says that more than a thousand planes have bombed Scotland and England.

I poured the soup over a very slim slice of toast. I am sad as a wet dog.

19 AUGUST 1940

He's back from the front. Three entire days of ringing church bells to celebrate another string of victories. The radio promised that an invasion of England is likely to begin at any moment.

Later:

I'm so happy. He announced that he's taking "ME" for a short visit to Chiemsee. Once more I take pen in hand.

He explained, I have the need to "relax."

Why not, he has conquered most of Europe—one country then another country, etc. He's on his way to enclosing the entire world. Soon there will only be us—the *Herrenvolk*, we the ruling class, and the lowly *Hilfsvolk*, the helping people, to do all our work.

I must:

1. lighten my hair
2. get my nails done
3. get the new shoes that I forgot at the Berg

There is so little time. I dare not drink vermouth tonight.

24 AUGUST 1940

His special Schutzstaffel troop has blocked off an area. He demanded: Patscherl, I insist that you remove your swimming costume.

I did, folded it and placed it beside him in case he wished to touch or smell it while I swam back and forth with athletic strokes.

He stood fully clothed, boots apart, as the afternoon heat haze bleached me to white goose down. When I looked up he held out his arms to "Me," so I rose up from the water, stood in front of him with my tailbone arched to one side. He mounted me, and after pushing into me, we "locked." The penis swelled up, was stuck inside my small vagina.

I threw my head back, nipped at him, squealed ecstatically.

He stood firmly and we remained locked tight for at least twenty minutes with our faces turned away from each other.

Thank you Dr. M. Thank you. Thank you.

Later:

At tea Herr B. once again took a liberty with my name, maliciously called me Fräulein Ewe, which sounds Jewish to everyone, sent titters through the room. I lashed out, I forbid you to take further liberties with my name!

I felt dizzy and turned my back on him. The K. can call me "Veverl" or "Feferl"—Austrian variants of my name—but the Brown Eminence, Herr B., NEVER AGAIN!

18 DEZEMBER 1940

Herr B. had forbidden the singing of "Stille Nacht, Heilige Nacht." How heartless!

Mutti asked me, Will you be with the Kanzler during this Christmas now that we are at war?

I told her, Leave be, Mutti. He had such a horrible Christmas when he was a young boy that he never wants to celebrate Christmas again. His father beat him with thirty-two strokes.

Will you come to us?

No. I saw she was hurt.

She asked, Will you stay and eat with us tonight?

I asked, What are you preparing?

She told me with pride, Raw eel with parsley sauce.

No, I must go.

You once loved the way I prepared eel with parsley . . .

Your memory is faulty Mutti, I always hated eel. Let her be hurt by the truth if she so chooses.

19 DEZEMBER 1940

I've begun making arrangements for "MY" own Christmas.

20 DEZEMBER 1940

I must not sit here and sip vermouth but must begin to shop in earnest because I need to purchase gifts for friends, servants, shop persons who serve "ME." Also, my sisters, parents, and of course, for him. I rack my brain for ways to save money on these gifts.

21 DEZEMBER 1940

Rushed and frantic, I went from stall to stall to buy honey cake, wax angels, gingerbreads until I was entirely broke.

I had to hurry because at 2 I had to pose in the nude for Arno Breker, the great sculptor. Herr Breker has promised that the statue would make "ME" look like one of Leonardo da Vinci's Florentine women.

I told Herr Brecker, removing my clothes, stepping immediately into the pose he has chosen for me, All things considered, I'd prefer to look like Venus!

23 DEZEMBER 1940

Day of the party: I sent token gifts to my favorite shop people. Then I had the servants decorate with red-berried holly and mistletoe while I joyfully wrapped presents and put on the white dress that I wear every Christmas.

In the mirror I studied my pelvis. Because of the intense work on the parallel bars, my pelvis is like a gun-hammer. When my pelvis pulls, the gun cocks.

Finally the party:

One by one my friends—Käthl, Peppo, Georg, Dr. M. and Hanni, Herta, and her husband came. Her husband has been inducted into the army and will shortly report for duty.

When I announced that we would sing "Stille Nacht" a pall fell over the assembled group. Mogerl rushed over, stuck her claws into my shoulder and whispered into my ear, But the party secretary has forbidden it! It's too dangerous! Please Effie.

I told the group, It is not the party secretary who forbids ME, it's I who forbid him. Then I sang with my "sweet" voice:

> *Stille Nacht*
> *Heilige Nacht*

until my friends—who want to stay my friends and receive my favors—had no choice but to join in, and did so with hollow little voices.

Then I distributed their gifts.

CHRISTMAS EVE

I filled my car with more gifts and was driven to the Berg, where I personally supervised decorating the hall with a wreath of Tannenbaum and a tree with candles.

Wearing the white dress again, I had the servants and their families file in and gave each a gift. A special one for Paula who still idolized me even though I've sometimes driven her to tears by demands, mockery at her subhuman chapped face, beatings.

Afterward the children from the entire Obersalzberg gathered. Three roast geese were laid on a table for them. I told them, I give you greetings on Holy Eve.

I may not be "official" by any means, but gifts speak. The children stared at "Me" with awe and admiration. Do they know just who the lady with the gifts is? No. But they can tell—though with no children of her own—she is someone of influence.

3 JANUAR 1941

Let down after Christmas. Bilious attack. When I counted my money, I was shocked to realize that I'd spent my entire savings on Christmas.

Through the night I worried that I have overstepped with Herr B. Have I been in my right mind? Has the "end" come?

Paula saw my angst and made a tureen of Buttermilchsuppe for me.

No call tonight. "The front" has replaced just about everything.

16 JANUAR 1941

Fearful of the rationing in effect, every day I shop for shoes on credit. I'm so worried that I will no longer be able to find beautiful shoes. My new favorite: A pair of crocodile-skin shoes from Madagascar.

Paula served me apricots in powdered marmalade form. When my bread was sliced she added water to the marmalade, which made the concoction swell up, and which was smeared across the bread. Paula stood on her flat feet and studied me as I ate, studied the way my tongue darted into the corner of my mouth to mop up smears of apricot.

19 JANUAR 1941

I heard from Paula that they call me "Miss Crocodile." When she refused to tell me from whom she heard this cut against me, I slapped her so hard across the face, that a gout of vomit came shooting out of her mouth.

She told me it was from Herr B.'s housemaid. I'm not surprised.

I have begun to collect gloves. Also on credit.

12 MÄRZ 1941

Oische returned the diary pages she cut away those years before. I've lost interest in my naive past. Those days of falling on my knees are long gone. I returned the pages to my youthful diary.

Later:

He's in Berlin. I'm feeling agitated. Drank too much, took three sleeping tablets until I found myself in semi-imbecility.

13 MÄRZ 1941

Good news! A check has arrived. Just as my credit was about to be cut off.

Today and every morning Paula drinks the newest concoction a glass of "Aryan skim milk." It's decreamed fresh milk, which non-Aryans aren't allowed any longer to have.

I dare not enquire as to whether or not Paula qualifies to drink it, but it does wonders for her skin. I observed her skin with my dominating eyes, which caused her to lower hers, grip her knuckles until they turned white. Yes, her face is subhuman. A pug nose, flat forehead. But her skin is like cream.

16 MÄRZ 1941

A day of skiing.

Left from the München main station, mingled with other skiers in sweaters and mufflers, skis hoisted over our shoulders. All of us buoyant with . . .

Returned with almost no time to spare and change. Vermouth. A fire. He telephoned from the front on the dot of 10. He is magnanimous with the victories of his army.

He asked, Do you need money?

Yes, I told him, almost hysterical with my good luck. And he didn't shout when I told him how much.

Where are you? I asked but he did not reply to that.

He asked me, Tell me about your day.

And I did. Shopping, tea-taking, cream-topped gateau at the Osteria. But I didn't mention skiing. Then he told me little anecdotes from headquarters—naturally not military matters nor political matters—humorous incidents only: One of my generals dropped a burning cigarette onto my map, a hole burned right through France.

A perfect moment arrived. *du,* your propaganda minister has issued an order that all women must forego cosmetics. I need these cosmetics and hair-waving materials.

I will take care of the matter, Tschapperl.

The Brown Eminence fumes at me, now Acid Tongue will also fume at the Kanzler's "little clerk"! Am I crazy?

While we spoke, I smoked silently.

I have devised something for your beauty, Veverl, once a week take a bath in warm olive oil.

I am having massage.

I forbid it. I'm banning massage, it causes cancer. Ask my doctor his view on massage.

I've started to call Dr. M. "injection quack."

Could Dr. M. poison you?

Without this doctor I would be dead, Feferl.

26 MÄRZ 1941

A special train is being sent to fetch me tomorrow. I'll wear musk fur and will carry Negus and Stasi in my arms.

But which dress? I can't decide.

I turned on my bedside radio hoping for a little light music. Instead, every fifteen minutes blasts of trumpets, smatterings of Lizst preludes announcing "Special bulletins . . . special bulletin . . . victory bulletin . . . victory bulletin."

27 MÄRZ 1941

At the station several big Mercedes were waiting and through the heavy snow I watched the taillights of the car ahead speed up the winding road. When "MY" car stopped at the door, two lamps were lit. The servant greeted me, took my coat and hung it beside his. Negus and Stasi dashing ahead. Quickly I went up the stairway to prepare.

I unpacked his favorite dress: the green wool dress with the fitted top, flared bell skirt, broad leopard-skin belt. The sleeves of the dress hug the lines of my arms, the heart-shaped neckline held by my two gold clips.

I laid the outfit out across my bed, slipped the old blue nightdress embroidered with red roses over my head and waited, but I was not called.

28 MÄRZ 1941

He was again in conference, so I took a long walk in the snowy woods with Herta and her two platinum-haired daughters. Stasi and Negus dashed among the trees looking for rats, weasels, ferrets; the children for squirrels to feed. Negus and Stasi frightened the squirrels away. I took a series of snapshots—Herta, the children, my "hearthrugs," the mountain behind. I also took moving pictures with my 8mm Ciné camera.

I instructed the two children, Breathe the pure mountain air.

Almost at the teahouse, I pointed out to the children the Ach River as it snakes toward the valley. Salzburg is there.

The children saw no Salzburg. It is hidden by the Steinernes Meer Mountains, I told them sweetly, You can take it on faith, it's there.

Stasi and Negus began chasing a white hare. They overran it and bit at its flesh. The rabbit gnashed loudly. Negus held the hare while Stasi tore chunks of fur and red meat from its hindquarters. Then Negus bit into its anus. The hare's eyes were very black, asking, Why? Stasi tore out the intestines. The hare collapsed and died while the dogs stuffed themselves, then regurgitated the small chunks.

The little girls began to cry. I pinched their necks until they stopped. I warned them, Tears make the color of your eyes fade.

When we returned to the Berg the conference had adjourned, but he was resting in his room because shortly was another conference so I threw off my snowy clothes. I bathed, I freshened myself with my favorite perfume—Worth's "Air Bleu"—then restrained my hair, rampant and buzzing with static electricity. But, no call came tonight.

29 MÄRZ 1941

No calls again, so I smoked, took two glasses of vermouth. Eventually a third, and a fourth. Finally I dressed. I feared that again I would not be called, but at 12 the dogs barked to warn me that someone was approaching.

I wanted to time my entrance carefully.

He was surrounded, as usual, by a pack of men in uniforms. When the last of them had climbed down the steps and bent down to enter their official cars, and their lights could no longer be seen on the road, the K. walked back up the steps into the living room where we inner circle had assembled. At "that" second I made my appearance, heralded by the barking and scurrying of my two silky black balls.

Tonight our inner circle:
Henrietta
the dentist and his wife
my sister
Hanni
Dr. M.
Also Herr B., as usual. (Herr B. is still cool with me.)
Herr B.'s brother.

Because of the ferocity of my "hand lickers," Blondi must stay in her cage. The Kanzler kissed my hand. He was deep in thought. I can't ever tell if he's glad to see me.

He greeted each guest.

His valet announced the seating plan, as well as who would escort who into the dining room.

I "secretly" checked to make sure that the floral arrangements were fresh and that the hand-painted white Rosenthal china with the flower pattern matched the napkin in its pochette. If I'd really been hostess, that's what I'd have done.

First the women sat, then the Kanzler, then the men, and immediately—as we were all ravenous after waiting five hours for him—his valet delivered his special meal on a tray and placed it before him. Other orderlies handed round large bowls containing a variety of salads, meat, and potatoes.

His menu: Oatmeal soup, mashed linseed, muesli, fruit juice.

My menu: Vermouth only.

He gulped down food, began a monologue: My dentist says

human teeth are designed for a diet based on fruit. Also vegetables. These two are most suited to the human digestive system.

The dentist nodded in agreement.

He gazed at me. It's proven beyond any possible doubt that non-smokers live much longer than smokers, and that they're much more resistant to disease.

I defended myself, You know I never smoke!

The dentist brazenly added, Cigarette smoke acts as a disinfectant for the mouth. It regularizes the irrigation of the blood vessels.

His voice changed and he began speaking in an angry torrent: I won't hear a word of this. Smoking is one of the most dangerous addictions. I find the smell of cigars and cigarettes absolutely horrible. The smell of tobacco makes women very unattractive. One day I was at a reception in Vienna and was sitting next to the great Viennese actress Maria Holst, a woman of great beauty. She had wonderful chestnut hair, but when I leant toward her, her hair gave off a terrible smell of nicotine.

Mogerl commented, I wouldn't want to live a long life if I couldn't smoke.

He called for second helpings, then cleaned his plate again. He called out, Cook! Come out from the kitchen and taste the "surprises" you have prepared.

The plain-looking cook stood kneading her chapped hands. He demanded, Join me.

And she did.

Konstanze, the new cook, looked at me. I knew that her great terror was that the K. would enter her kitchen unexpectedly and would catch her smoking a cigarette, but her secret was safe with me.

What sweet have you prepared just for me today, Frau, he asked her.

She blushed.

He prodded her.

Apple strudel.

Nice and sweet I hope.

It goes very well with your cumin tea, she replied.

Out of nowhere the colors red and brown alternated in spots before my eyes. No more vermouth!

Later:

Henrietta—now Frau von S.—piped in, Mein Kanzler, when I was in Vienna, I saw a convoy of Jews passing through the streets, being deported. It was a heartrending sight. Those poor creatures looked so miserable. Why do you allow it?

A silence fell on the table following her question. The K. got up and left the room.

Later, at the cinema, the Kanzler returned to watch the film *Vom Winde Verweht** and we were all relieved.

Afterward the dentist suggested: Mein Kanzler, your brief respite from the war must be uplifting. Why not invite our artists to come to you right here or at the front? Have Gieseking, Kempff, Furtwängler come to you.

No, we can play records!

It was the Herr B.'s brother's job to operate the record player and the K.'s to choose the repertoire, which was always the same.

First, he instructed him to play an operetta of Franz Lehar, the *Die Lustige Witwe*, his favorite.

While the records were being located, the K. complained to the group: My entourage certainly isn't very musical. When I'm invited to a gala performance, I have to keep an eye on all the people who accompany me to see that they don't fall asleep. My official photographer almost fell out of the official box during a performance of *Tristan und Isolde*, and I had to wake up my valet and tell him to shake him. Meanwhile, my doctor was snoring behind me. It was horrible. Luckily, when it's *Die Lustige Witwe* nobody goes to sleep because there's so much ballet in it.

Hanni inquired, I thought you didn't like ballet my Kanzler?

In my day the ballet was a visual treat because you could still see pretty bodies with nice round curves. Now all you see are a lot of skeletons jumping about the stage. My propaganda minister is

* (Gone with the Wind)

always trying to drag me along to the ballet and I've been two or three times. I was very disappointed. But at least I don't have to pay now, I'm the Kanzler, I get free tickets.

Then the music began and the K.'s face lit up.

When it was finished he made his next selection, songs by Richard Strauss. After that Hugo Wolf.

I went around with my little 8mm Ciné camera filming the group as they listened.

I was longing for a cigarette. First one, then another, guest tip-toed out of the room. I didn't dare. I could hear their muffled laughter just outside. The K. dozed, Dr. M also slept. I sat beside him sucking a fruit drop.

After Hugo Wolf he played Richard Wagner. This woke the K.

Dr. M. woke too, asked, Mein Kanzler, why do you always want to hear *Die Meistersinger*?

That's just my bad luck, the Kanzler replied. If ever I say I like a particular opera or a certain bit of music, I'm condemned to hearing it all the time. I once mentioned that I thought *Die Meistersinger* was Wagner's finest opera and since then everyone has assumed it's my favorite. I'm fated to hear it again and again.

Finally, the only popular song the K. allowed, "Donkey Serenade." It was 5 o'clock in the morning. The K. called his valet, whispered in his ear and then stood up. Please stay where you are, he ordered the guests. He shook everyone by the hand.

Head bowed, he walked to his first-floor apartment.

I noticed with shame that his shoulders were hunched.

The room was quickly filled with smoke, by me as well. In a low voice I asked Henrietta to stand aside with me. I spoke as though speaking to a four-year-old. I thought it best to correct her: As we all know, Jews aren't Germans anymore, they can't be Germans, they're useless mouths. Some may have written books, some have composed music, but we have been instructed not to read or listen to them anymore. So we don't. It's their misfortune for being born.

Then I put out my cigarette, bid each of the assembled, Good night, and followed the K.'s path.

Hypocrite, Henrietta said under her breath, but loud enough

for me to hear. Effie reads Oscar Wilde, keeps him under her bed-spring. How she has changed, how imperious little Effie has become.

She defiantly raised her voice. Waiter! A Boonenkamp bitters.

I heard Dr. M. call out, Schnaps.

Dr. M. must have thought, Why not drink a little longer with buxom Henrietta, who needless to say will not be invited again to dine with the Kanzler.

Since the war, two Wehrmacht soldiers stand night and day at the ceremonial stairway that leads to the K.'s private office and our bedrooms. I went past them and up to the K.'s private bath and drew the water as he likes it. I dropped in two tablets of pine needles—one at the head of the tub, one at the foot. Then, while the tablets dissolved and spread the aroma of pine through the room, I loosened first the cap of his Drailles Birch-Water hair lotion, and then did the same for his Steckenpferd shaving cream.

He told me bluntly, This is my valet's job.

I turned and left. I heard the door shut, the bolt crunched.

Shortly I took "MY" second Kamille bath of the day, steamed my face with boiling water spiced with eucalyptus and dried parsley boiled down with apple blossoms in sherry wine, then shaved off my excess body hair. Since he had made no overtures, I went into my own room and shut the door. His "primitive woman" was sleeping alone.

I dare not tell Henrietta there's no Oscar Wilde under my bed. Karl May beside my bed only. Quite soon I heard the lock spring shut on his bedroom door. Never did he sleep behind an unlocked door and neither did I. He, for safety's sake, I so that I could remove my make-up and use an excess of Reinigungsmilch.

A long entry, this. It's dawn.

13 MÄRZ 1941

He has again showed amorous interest in me! He watched me tonight while I undressed for my bath. He observed that I was not wearing underclothes.

You're behaving like a whore, he commented as I slipped into the Kamille bath. He added, It must never happen again. You might fall down. How would that look?

Then, he sat beside the tub fully dressed, and observed me closely as if I were a map or a report. He started to whistle a tune he liked. He whistled in a penetrating vibrato.

He marched up and down like a soldier. Only he is allowed to whistle.

That's not right, I told him, This is how it goes. I whistled my way, breaking the rule. He insisted on his way. I bet you that I'm right, I told him.

He narrowed his eyes, not one to ever be wrong.

He got up, left the room, and telephoned his aide-de-camp.

I could hear him: I have made a bet. I heard him whistling the tune both ways. Which is right?

Downstairs the aide-de-camp would be shuffling hundreds of his very favorite records. Quickly the telephone rang with the report.

He walked back in. You're right. But, the composer was wrong. If he'd been as talented as I am, he'd have written my version.

The great joy of being right just once!

Berchtesgaden, Königsee

Silence is the rule at the Berghof. At noon the Kanzler arose. I saw him at lunch. He gave me no sign of recognition. Then, while he worked, I took a two hour walk with Mogerl.

Today the snow was up to our knees. She told me, I can't continue the walk any longer. I am exhausted!

I checked my watch, We have fifteen minutes longer!

So my lazy sister struggled through the snow until exactly two hours were up. Not 121 minutes or 119 minutes. But exactly 120 minutes, which I timed to the minute.

While pulling off my snow boots, Herta brought over a foreign newspaper and showed me an article claiming that the K. is the father of two children. My children! They actually had written my name in the newspaper!

I was happy. A foreign newspaper unfortunately, but at least somewhere my name and face have appeared in print. I also noticed gross lies in the newspaper telling of a great Russian winter offensive. These poor foreigners are being sadly misinformed.

Our newspapers report our magnificent successes on the Russian front. Our Blitzkrieg had brought quick successes in Poland, Norway, the Low Countries, France, the Balkans, and shortly, I have no doubt, Russia, England, the United States, and Canada as well.

Herta quickly threw the illegal newspaper into the fire since it is dangerous to have such a thing. She mewed, Do you know what the K. says when someone asks who you are?

No, I don't know. Tell me.

Herta repeated, He says: She photographs interiors, draperies, windows, vases, and other objects including me.

And witches fly because the Devil makes them weightless, I joked.

Yes. My cameras have become a pleasant diversion. I doubt

anyone outside knows that my nickname is "The Merry Widow" or that I am considered "supercilious"? But I was not joking really. I pulled out a deck of cards.

A game? I asked. When Herta agreed, I dealt her the *Pik** right off the top.

1 FEBRUAR 1943

Herr B. has loosened the purse strings so at last I can have my hair done daily by Bernhard. Why not? When I need waves I use Milla Schellmoses who said about me to Paula, She is often impatient and irritable. She is a perfectionist about her hair but her tips are rather meager.

When these words were repeated to me by Paula, I stopped tipping entirely.

6 FEBRUAR 1943

I've turned thirty-one! Its fitting that the state radio suspended the normal programming for our surrender at Stalingrad and played the solemn music of Bruckner's Seventh Symphony.

His defeat and mine at once.

What is there to say to a spinster? It's fitting that the city is blacked out tonight with nothing but the old moon, dull stars to illuminate us. Here at my little desk, I hear tapping at the window. When I go to look there's nothing there.

I've begun on Mondays and Thursdays to use a night pack of fresh, raw veal on my face. On Sunday I bathe in warm olive oil as he suggested. I'm a slippery "eel" afterward and need Paula to rub away the oily slick from my skin.

Before my bath tonight I worked at my parallel bars. I'm working on movements, trying to make them more fluid and continuous, more ring-like, with no stops between. Today I got stumped by the kick over high bar movement. My legs were supposed to come together as my body rotated backward.

Instead I ended in a muddle.

---

* (Ace of spades)

Thank God I can practice all day tomorrow, and not have to sit in H.'s deadly dull shop ever again.

15 FEBRUAR 1943

New addition to the Berg: From our private rooms the elevator has been cut through 100 meters of sheer rock, an underground bunker is being prepared in case of enemy attack.

I insisted: I must have my own bathroom.

The Brown Eminence demanded: I must have room below ground for my headquarters and also a special dining room.

The K. needs a private dining room, dressing room, bedroom, archive space, study, bathroom, room for his bodyguard.

And a room for Dr. M.

16 FEBRUAR 1943

Herr B. complained: The head of the airforce has more space underground than I do. He confiscated rooms from the defense command and filled them with objects from conquered countries—brass locks, silver candlesticks, pewter plates, jewelry, paintings. The head of the airforce insisted that this tunnel connect to the Kanzler's tunnel.

Herr B. demanded: Leave ten meters of dirt between my tunnel and the Kanzler's.

The K. ordered: Underground kennels must be built for the dogs.

In the end: the K., seventeen rooms; the head of the airforce, ten; Herr B., five; more rooms for the defense command.

And me? Barely more than a very small apartment. I rack my brain for a way to improve my situation.

I gathered several sacks full of food from the kitchen then traded food for shoes in town.

11 MÄRZ 1943

Yesterday was a day of terror that has left me with vertigo. Out of the blue I was roused from my bed. To the shelter, came the order.

Down I went, asking, But why?

Paula kept screaming as I pulled her along. München is being bombed.

Impossible! How could it be?

The rooms in the shelter were not cold, or damp. The polished inlaid floors are covered with heavy rugs. There are wainscotted walls, shiny lacquered doors and door frames. Safes have been built into the rock for valuables but I didn't have time to bring mine. In the distance I heard what sounded like muffled thunder. It was so far away I could not be frightened.

When the "All Clear" sounded we hurried back up into the air only to find it sulphur-yellow and unbreathable.

Later my masseur told me, Your skull is hard as a coconut shell, your jaw is as hard as nails, your neck wouldn't give in a noose. He took cigarettes instead of cash for the massage.

The news is also bad from Berlin, where a monstrous raid has left 160,000 Berliners homeless, an entire suburb is flaming and people in panic are said to be trying to escape lugging bags and furniture. I asked Paula if she wanted to go home. She didn't reply. I took her silence to mean no, that she preferred to stay here with me.

19 MÄRZ 1943

The access roads to the Berg, the entrance to the tunnel to the Eagle's Nest, the surroundings of the house, are now protected by nests of machine guns.

But the Kanzler isn't satisfied. He has ordered that better protection for himself be organized. His tunnel, the elevator, and the Eagle's Nest are all being fitted with poison gas capsules. In danger he would take the elevator to the Eagle's Nest and release the poison gas into the tunnel behind him.

But what about "Me"? Would he take "Me"?

Further, a smoke machine has been designed. When necessary, smoke resembling fog can be released. This would obscure the house even from aircraft. I've heard the head of the airforce boast time and again: If a single enemy manages to appear in the sky over Berlin, then my name is Meyer.

I shouted at Herr B. Why? How?

Oblivious of me he went on with his telephoning.

Sleeping pills tonight to blot out the infernal sounds of insects, frogs, snails, in nocturnal concert. A just cause for semi-imbecility. Paula has crumbled, a pathetic wet-dog look on her face. She asks me, How has it come to this? How? Why? What has been happening beyond our circle? Thank God I'm sterilized, she whispered.

I can't answer her. We all have the same views, beliefs, news, information, and none of us imagined this in our wildest dreams!

19 APRIL 1943

Another bombing has ended. Dust still floats in the air, a vulgar sulphur-yellow fog covers everything. Wardens carried cages with live canaries down into the shelters. I've begun to carry a sack of my jewels and other valuables with me at all times.

I broke the rule. Holding a wet cloth over my face, I left the shelter and went to his workroom, where I otherwise never went. I had never seen his work attire, which was black trousers and field-gray tunic with crossed-over fastenings, a black tie and white shirt. Thank God I hadn't seen it before because I would have stamped my feet and told him how foolish he looked.

I had heard he liked to work in low temperatures. True, the office was freezing. He kept it at eleven degrees. I stood away until he finished reading a document. I knew he'd be angry with me. He wore old-fashioned eyeglasses with steel rims, so secret, I didn't know until that moment that he needed them.

He asked, What is the time? Although he always keeps his gold half-hunter watch in his trouser pocket.

The enemy bombed München, I blurted out, getting hysterical. I demand an explanation. I demand that you marry me. I demand that I be allowed to contribute a healthy child to the nation.

His orbs locked onto mine. It is time for lunch!

I didn't dare to press him. I had shocked myself by my outburst. I was shaking. But he hadn't forbidden me!

He was silent through lunch. So was I.

Afterward he put on his old soft peaked cap, his black trench coat and called to the valet, Bring Blondi.

Blondi's tail was tucked under. Was she afraid of her master? He took his walking stick in one hand, and Blondi's leash into the other, and yanked her. Nietzsche's sister had given him Nietzsche's last walking stick when she was eighty-six. He thumped the stick on the stones. Because the sun was shining, I snapped, Put on your sunglasses. You must protect your sensitive eyes.

Ach, he replied, his first word in an hour, then sank into silence. I did not speak either. I had brought my camera and, finally speaking, tried to persuade him to remove his dirty old peaked cap.

I pleaded, It throws a shadow on your face. Do you want to be remembered with a shadow across your face?

He ignored "ME."

When we arrived at the teahouse, tea was served. Finally his silence ended. He quietly asked, Won't you wear the dress I like so much tonight?

But I wore it for you just last night, du.

My voice was still cool, I refused to give him my sweet voice so easily.

When I like a dress, I want to see it as often as possible. Just when I get used to something pretty, you're wearing something new.

I refused refreshments. He ate hot apple strudel, then biscuits. Cake and petit fours were served to the others, while he ate a second helping. He became morose again, but I was tired of the game. To get his mind off the stupid war I told him in a jolly way, Tonight we're showing *La Jana*. Won't you enjoy it with us?

While the war is on, from now on, I can't.

My chair was beside his. I drank my tea and thought: I must not blame him for the bombs. When I looked up at his face, he was asleep. He was sprawled defenselessly back against the chair. I could study him without fearing his derision and took several snapshots.

He woke and demanded his valet. What time is it?

Five o'clock mein Kanzler, shall I order the car?

Because there was a conference, he drove back to the Berg in a black Volkswagen with leather interior. He sat in front with the driver. The valet sat in the back with Blondi.

I was driven down alone.

Much later:

When our circle was assembled in the drawing room, I told him, Your Blondi is a calf. I was half-mocking, half-affectionate.

Then, I don't know what possessed me—my bladder was full, my dogs were making a racket—I summoned the servant and I demanded, Please remove Blondi from the drawing room.

I braced myself but instead of deriding or punishing me, he sucked his little finger. He nodded when the servant looked to him for instructions. He watched his dejected animal being led away to the kennel.

Then he looked at my dress and switched over to his *süsse Stimme.** I don't understand why you women must always change. If I find a dress especially pretty, then I would prefer to see you always in the dress. You should have to make all your dresses out of the same material and from the same pattern. Hardly have I gotten used to a beautiful dress and you appear in something new.

Of course I'll change it after dinner!

He must have forgotten that he too used to change into gay clothes. I remember the light-blue linen sports coat, the gay yellow tie. The bluish twilight.

After dinner he handed me a box that contained emerald earrings, then asked me with his sweet voice, Veverl, will you allow poor Blondi to join us for half an hour?

What expensive earrings. I loved them.

I didn't say a word but handed Negus to a Schutzstaffel. Then I handed Stasi to a second Schutzstaffel. Please shut them up in my room, I ordered.

Blondi was led back in and laid down at his feet. I asked for a strong drink, triumphant but not daring to gloat.

---

* (sweet voice)

20 APRIL 1943

Herta and I walked to the the Königsee Lake. The day was so pleasant, but neither of us could shake the memory of the bombs falling. We didn't return until evening in time to dress for the Kanzler's birthday party.

Mail had been arriving by the sackful for him; also gifts. In a big pile were:

slippers embroidered with hooked crosses over setting suns

a large handkerchief whose four corners were embroidered
  with his face along with Hindenburg, Bismarck, and Frederick the Great

tarts

cakes

sweets and fruit from all over Germany.

In every shop window—in a gilt frame—a twig and flower garlanded photo of him. Spilling down house fronts, red bunting dotted with white circles offsetting black hooked crosses.

I cannot count the hooked crosses I see in a day: On bed sheets, match books, water glasses, dogs collars.

My gift: A black dressing gown with gray trimmings. And . . . permission that Blondi may accompany him for one entire day while my little "hand lickers" stay in my apartment.

I did wear the dress he requested—his favorite—the sleeveless black silk with the wide bell skirt. The skirt has a tight waist and two broad rose-colored bands running down from the shoulders to form a low square neckline, with two roses in the same color at the corners. On top, a short bolero jacket with very narrow long sleeves.

Evening:

After the "official" festivities, his inner circle as well as three or four people who I didn't know gathered around the great fireplace. Blondi was led into the room and immediately sat down at his feet.

He told the group, You'll be impressed by her intelligence, I've taught her to sit up and beg, also to play "good pupil," sitting on her back legs with her paws resting on the arm of my chair like an attentive schoolgirl. But her party piece is singing. Blondi, sing to us.

In his most coaxing voice—the one he once used before love-making—he told Blondi to stand up and sing.

First, to our amazement, Blondi let out a long howl, then she let out a sharp note. Her song became more and more high-pitched as he encouraged her. When she reached a point that was too shrill, he insisted, Sing lower, Blondi. Like Zarah Leander.

Blondi gave a long moan like a wolf.

Throughout, I sat steeped in self-reproach because I have failed so miserably to turn Stasi and Negus into show dogs too! (Why must I be this way, that I can't enjoy my successes because my failures seem so magnified?) At the end of the performance he held up three fingers and gave Blondi three pieces of cake.

Then the clock struck midnight and the waiters carried in trays filled with glasses of cold champagne. We each took one. He took a glass of very sweet wine. We gathered around him, raised our glasses in a toast and wished him, Long life.

One by one his staff presented their best wishes—the valets, servants, guards, chauffeur, kitchen staff. Everyone was allowed to drink as much as they wanted, which I am paying for this morning.

The K. exhausted the guests with a monologue on automobile engines that went on for FOUR hours. Then he bid us good night and climbed the stairs.

Dazed by the harangue, I smoked one cigarette with Konstanze, then popped a mint onto my tongue. Konstanze picked off a long flaxen hair that clung to the shoulder of my dress. I cringed at the thought that it had been there the entire evening, and no one had pointed it out.

When I joined him in his room, he asked, Aren't you too hot in your clothes? To my great joy since I thought he'd all but forgotten these words.

We gingerly sniffed each other's noses, a faint meaty smell seeped out, his tailbone lifted up and began to wave sideways, but he stopped right there. Instead he switched on the new apparatus that a psychologist had dreamed up to help him overcome his terrible insomnia.

A movie screen had been hung from the ceiling of his bedroom. A color movie of a waterfall was projected. He had been instructed to watch the water go over the falls. He was assured that it would surely put him to asleep. I lay beside him feeling apathetic, my hands crossed over my breasts. We watched the monotony of millions of gallons of falling water until my bladder swelled and I got up and tiptoed from the room.

The usual turning of the door bolt behind me. Perhaps I expect too much? I laid down with my sack of jewels within grabbing distance in case of an air raid. No sooner had I fallen sleep when the telephone rang.

His voice was angry: I think my field marshal sent that psychologist as a practical joke. I have worn a path in the rug between the bed and the bathroom. I have awakened my chauffeur to take us for a drive. Perhaps that will make me sleepy. I would so much enjoy the company of a beautiful woman on the drive.

We sat together in the car as his driver drove the roads high in the mountains at top speed. Like old Mutti and old Vati on an outing. He was gloomy. He'd heard a rumor that a German pedant living in England had found 154,000 errors in German grammar and syntax in his book *Mein Kampf*. Could that be why? But the promise had been kept that by this birthday Germany would be "Jew-free." And so it was. That accomplishment, at least, must please him?

I shan't complain. When I am beside him I wear a beatific expression. It saddens me, though, that I have only two legs and can't run as fast as an animal.

München, Berchtesgaden, Königsee

As I'd been dreading, the order came down.

The entire General Staff is leaving again for the Wolfsschanze in East Prussia on the Kanzler's special train. I feel so desperate.

Vati was away four years during the Great War, and we were forced to live on turnips. I don't think I saw a man up close until he returned.

The departure was set for 9:30 P.M. I sat mutely beside him while he ate a meal of potato purée, two fried eggs, whole meal bread, and drank sparkling Fachinger water. Immediately our entourage left.

He was silent in the car. Between us his painting. He was taking along his prized possession, the painting of Frederick the Great by Anton Graff. Wherever he went now, so did the ornamental circular frame. Frederick wore a perruque and a powder-blue uniform that set off the bright blue of his eyes, which are not unlike the Kanzler's eyes. Also, he carried with him a photograph of his mother and one of his niece but to my knowledge, no mementos of "Me."

I boarded the private carriage along with the valet who held Blondi. I was to accompany the train as far as München where it would continue east without me.

Immediately the train moved into the dark. The moments were running out. We sat on a couch upholstered in shot silk. I ran my hands over the material that had multicolored flowers on a pale beige background. The walls of the carriage were wood panels. The lamps, bronze. The floor, covered in thick carpeting.

I excused myself because of my nerves. My hands needed a good washing. Fortunately there was hot and cold running water, plenty of soap, so I scrubbed myself thoroughly, wrapped the soap in paper and put it deep into my purse.

When I returned he asked me to walk with him into a carriage with red leather seats. It was a conference room with lamps that were brightly lit. I want to crush you, he said, standing with his back to the door, staring at me with bright blue eyes.

I moved into the light facing him, arching the front of my body.

My ears fell back, my blue goose eyes burned with intensity. I was panting. His body weight pressed against me, forcing me down onto the red leather. My hindquarters sought friction with him while his mouth snapped at my throat the entire time.

When the train arrived in München he gave me an envelope. My knees were jelly. I got off the train as his personnel got on. Many men in uniform were boarding: men with hair cropped or shaven, men with sausage-necks, swarms of men surrounding him.

I tore open the envelope and found ten 100-Mark notes. When I had finished counting them, the train had pulled out.

While he has gone back to the front to retake lost ground, proving that he is the greatest conqueror since Napoleon, a car is waiting to drive me to my lonely villa. I know where the train was going because he confided in me this once. He told me: We are going across the whole length of Germany to Mauerwald, in east Prussia near Rastenberg, once a citadel of the Teutonic Knights. He told me, The Wolf's Lair is well named. In summer it's mosquito-ridden. In winter cold mists obscure the trees. Often in the middle of the night I hear the sound of explosions when foxes blow themselves to pieces on mines.

The Wolfsschanze has been a carefully kept secret. Finally, he has confided in me! Now, when the Propaganda Ministry in Berlin announces that he is "in the field" or "at the front" or "traveling," I know he is walking Blondi along a tree-lined lane between minefields.

I am trusted! But to what end? He is gone. Always gone.

1 MAI 1943

Meatless day today. Paula cooked codfish in mustard for Mogerl, and me.

Although the taste was pleasant, it was stone cold when it reached the table. I shouted for Paula. While she crouched and whimpered, I demanded that she serve my food scalding hot.

22 JULI 1943

Played Bimbo with Hanni and Mogerl at Hanni's apartment. Then supper of noodles cooked with dried prunes.

Hanni's white Persian cat kept leaping at me, covering my dark skirt with white hairs. I don't like cats.

Continually, forcibly, I had to push the creature off of me. Finally, Hanni lifted the cat by its hind legs and carried it into another room.

28 JULI 1943

He complained on the telephone, The Wolf's Lair denies me the pleasures of life, painting, music, the presence of beautiful women.

Good, you have no need for beautiful women anymore, I wanted to remind him, but instead I hid my anguish.

He never mentioned that Mussolini had abdicated, and it wasn't until I turned on the radio just now that I heard the news.

2 SEPTEMBER 1943

Hanni is going to Frankfurt University to visit the Institute for Heredity, Biology and Racial Purity to have solvents injected into her scalp, to turn her black hair to blond, and dyes introduced into her eyes to turn them blue. She'll also have the hard spikes on her back removed.

Not a bad idea. She'll fit much better then.

I took her to the old Osteria for Königinsuppe, but the waiter told me that they could no longer get the ingredients because of shortages. A splendid soup, exclaimed the waiter. Yes, I remember it fondly, I replied.

We drank vermouth. Hanni confided: What if the Institute cannot help me? What then?

I could offer no solace.

When we were at the door the waiter rushed over and handed me a sheet with elaborate writing. After the war! he exclaimed and pressed a paper into my hand.

Recipe: Königinsuppe—Queen's soup
4 loaves of white bread
12 carrots
8 turnips
4 bunch parsley
17½ litres rich beef stock
1 kilo ground almonds
finely diced cooked roasted veal
16 hard-boiled egg yolks, sieved
salt
mace
24 slices toasted bread
marrow bones or veal bones

. . . .

Take the loaves of white bread and carefully remove the brown crust, then divide the bread into 16 or 20 pieces, put into kettle; throw in carrots and turnips that have been cut crosswise and whole parsleys as well; then pour in good strong beef stock and boil until the bread is quite used up (dissolved) and the broth is fairly thick; then take crushed almonds, roast veal chopped up very fine, and the yolks of hard-boiled eggs made into a paste, and add these to the broth one by one, each time stirring them all together. Put back on the fire for a little while but the almonds and the rest should be allowed to boil. Next, pass through a fine sieve, so that you are left with a thick white broth. Season with salt and mace. Put back on the fire until ready to serve so that the soup is scalding hot, but do not allow it to boil or it will become curdled and unsightly. Before you pour the soup into the tureen, put in slices of toast. And then you may also add whatever you please—marrow bones or veal bones stuffed with forcemeat or otherwise, or just some forcemeat by itself, either wrapped around a veal bone or molded into the shape desired, smoothed off very fine, lightly scored with the blade of a knife, and baked in a little cake pan, and served up in a bowl. That will make you a splendid soup. 32 servings. This recipe: from 1773, Leipzig.

Top secret: I've applied to the Lebensborn program for permission to bear a child. WITH or WITHOUT his permission!

12 SEPTEMBER 1943

Headache and sleepy all day. Finally I went to see Vati and asked him: Do tell me what is going on? He never tells me anything. Is it true that a quarter of a million of our soldiers surrendered in Tunisia?

Vati averted his smoky blue eyes, shook his gray head, I dare not say anything, especially to you.

13 SEPTEMBER 1943

I went to the head office of Lebensborn in Herzog-Max-strasse near to the cinemas. I've filled in forms and was given an appointment on Ismaningerstrasse next week for an interview.

15 SEPTEMBER 1943

I went to my villa. It's time to inventory my jewelry and furs.

    rings, one big and one small
    bracelet of emeralds surrounded by diamonds
    necklace and brooch of tourmaline
    brooch of emeralds and diamond
    brooch in the shape of a butterfly
    emerald earrings
    a marguerite-shaped brooch of diamonds and rubies
    a solitaire diamond ring
    a diamond brooch
    a ring
    a diamond watch
    a brooch in the form of flowers
    another diamond ring
    jewelry of beryl
    an emerald set consisting of a pin, a bracelet, and a pendant

another ring and earrings   .
a gold bracelet set with sapphires and diamonds
a brooch and a matching necklace

Waves of indecision. What to keep on my person day and night? What to store? What to pack and keep for descents into the shelters?

I soaked in my very hot bath and had to wipe steam off the mirror with a towel in order to see myself.

I thought:

1. thirty valuable pieces of jewelry.
2. a dozen fur coats including a sable coat and a mink, and welled up with emotion.

18 SEPTEMBER 1943

I wore no make-up and borrowed a dress from Herta for my interrogation at Lebensborn. 95 Ismaningerstrasse, an impressive villa surrounded by a very high wall. Inside, a casino. High Schutzstaffel and big blond girls "mix" there. I was taken into an office and questioned for over an hour. An answer is promised in six weeks time. Would I be expected to "mix" with one of these men? Or would they allow me to select a man of my own choosing? The answer to this in its own time.

19 SEPTEMBER 1943

To the Berg to throw a party for my friends. A night of guzzling and drinking. Although Frau B. wasn't well—she'd delivered another new baby, her tenth, and was weak—I insisted that she stay awake as long as the other guests.

Mid-evening I demanded that she get me an after-dinner coffee. She did. Then I demanded that she get me a second cup. The housekeeper said to her, Go to bed, I'll oversee this.

But Frau B. did not dare to disobey "high-hatted Effie" in case her husband would be angry at her. "Saint" that she is, she gave me her sweet smile, and got my second cup of coffee.

8 OKTOBER 1943

I ordered Paula to fetch: fresh violets, which I will scald with boiling milk and use as a skin cream to get rid of crow's-feet! Paula intimated that she had some bit of gossip. I sat her down with a glass of Schnaps. Before she'd even gulped it down, she told me that Frau Magda G. had commented to her housemaid: Fräulein Effie looks frightfully "insignificant" again today.

After lunch I went right to the couturier that Frau G. and I both use—Romatski—and cornered the manager. Who looks better in your clothes, the wife of the propaganda minister, or me? Of course they said it was me.

Feeling vindicated, I shopped for a new piece of jewelry. Also a pair of gloves. When I went to get my hair done but couldn't, I had a fit.

When the telephone rang at 10 o'clock, I burst out. Again the organization has banned the use of electric hair dryers by hairdressers to save electricity. Hairdressers are not permitted to color hair. I could not get my hair done today! These are silly saving measures!

True, said the K. in his resonant voice, Every woman should please her husband with a cared-for appearance when he comes home on leave. She should be able to hide her prematurely gray hair as a result of the events of war. I shall have the order rescinded at once.

I can feel my madness calm down. Thank you, *du*. How is Blondi?

Blondi has become the best-trained animal one could imagine. She is improving her high-jump record. Do you know she stands balanced on a narrow bar for three extra minutes? Ach. Oh yes, I have a new secretary.

I asked with trepidation, What does she look like?

Light hair, blue eyes, round face, pretty face . . .

I dare not get upset. How old?

Twenty-two.

And do you have company when you eat? I asked, my head burning up, fishing because it irks me that he continues to share his meals with his loathsome secretaries. And now a new one who is pretty . . . young. How often have I heard him say, There's nothing more moldable than a young girl?

I eat in complete silence, he explained, What do I care who is sharing my table.

These women visit my bad dreams: Fräulein S. has been with him for decades, always expressing her own views. She works tirelessly, has hormone troubles. I can't stand her. The other vestal, Fräulein W., is quiet with heart trouble and gall bladder ad nauseam. She has short black hair, wears no make-up, takes time off with her eighty-year-old mother. She turns my stomach. Though I can't stand either of them, at least neither is in any way "restful" to the eye.

It's Fräulein D., pretty, slender, with great vitality, who worries me. She has dimples, glistening teeth, and always agrees with him. But of course we all must agree with him. I hate her most of all. That is, almost as much as I despise Frau Magda G. and Frau B., the "perfect" breeders of racially valuable children.

His telephone calls are especially monotonous these days. Why does nothing arouse my interest?

Paula left a bowl of Buttermilchsuppe by my bed. A few spoons of that along with sleeping tablets tonight.

8 NOVEMBER 1943

He will arrive shortly at the Berg! How can I cheer myself up enough to meet him? The Lebensborn officials have refused permission! Despite my impeccable ancestry, the letter explained that I don't meet the strict guideline on "height." I—the mistress of the greatest leader since Napoleon—can do nothing because anytime I ask him for children he says the same thing: I don't want children until after the war. And now, the "official" organization has refused me as well.

10 NOVEMBER 1943

It snowed hard and he still has not come. It's some solace that "refined" Frau Magda G. will be forty-two years old tomorrow. Although she rides a horse and has every social grace, her complexion has grown dull, her tapered fingers are starting to resemble claws. Seven children have taken their toll on her body. Perhaps I'm . . .

24 NOVEMBER 1943

It has snowed for weeks without stopping. The snow has trapped me here at the Berg. No Paula to taunt. No Paula to rub my feet. The workers are shoveling mountains of snow in order to clear even a narrow path to the teahouse for him in case he returns.

Played Bimbo and Tombola with M. until we were exhausted.

30 NOVEMBER 1943

I told him on the telephone, I want to go skiing.

You are forbidden.

But I need to escape the depressing atmosphere, I pleaded, telling him the truth for once.

You could break a foot. It's too dangerous. I forbid it.

12 DEZEMBER 1943

He's irritable and morose on the telephone. I'm depressed and bored to a point of no return. Alone, always alone.

9 JANUAR 1944

Meatless day: They served red cabbage in sauce here at the Berg. Because of air raids the telephones have been out of order all day. Also no water or electricity.

15 JANUAR 1944

A lull in the weather. The roads cleared so that I was able to return home.

INVENTORY OF PAINTINGS:
Landscapes by:
  Fischbach
  Rickelt
  Baskon
  Midgard
  Wax

Bamberger
of Rimini, artist unknown
of Venice, artist unknown
Large paintings by:
   Gradl
   Gallegos
Canvases by:
   Tiedgen
   Hoberg
   Krauss
   Hilbakt
Portraits by:
   Franke
   Popp
   Kauffmann
   Gallegos
   Rosl
   of the K. by Bohnenberger
   of the K. by Knirr
   of me by Bohnenberger

6 FEBRUAR 1944

The less said about my birthday the better. All day, a tapping on my window but when I went to look saw nothing but fiercely swirling snow.

6 MÄRZ 1944

Finally he is back.

The snow has melted down and we walked to the teahouse together. I noticed when he bent to pet Blondi how much gray was in his hair.

I reproached him, *Du*, you are so bent over. Can't you straighten up?

He explained, That comes from carrying such heavy keys in my pocket. He added with sarcasm, This way I fit better with you. You wear high heels, Fräulein Effie, so you are taller. I bend over a little, and so we fit together very well.

Sensitive about my petite size, I burst out: I am not short. I am 1.63 meters, like Napoleon.

How do you know that? he asked, glared at me.

Every educated person knows it.

So where were you educated? he mocked, *Schadenfreude** as usual, his favorite form of fun.

Of course he's right. Though I'm blond and blue eyed, and my family can probably prove its Aryan ancestry as far back as 1750, I don't qualify to bear a child for the organization.

Yes, sacred is every mother of good blood, which doesn't mean me. Or pathetic half-wit Paula either.

8 MÄRZ 1944

Not only is he stooped and gray but his waist is thickening. Like "Me" he has fear that he will put on weight. Any time he puts on weight he takes a powerful laxative followed by opium to quiet the stomach. Then immediately he takes another type of medicine—one he keeps secret—in order to purge any germs that might be accumulating in his body.

My method: starvation, vigorous exercise, ordinary laxatives.

10 MÄRZ 1944

He is gone again.

Had a bilious attack.

20 MÄRZ 1944

Air raids all the time on München. No longer can I see the sky. Nor can the sun get through the black smoke.

22 MÄRZ 1944

At 12 Wasserburgerstrasse an underground shelter has finally been completed. He designed it himself to suit me and included both a ventilator, air pump, and an armored door leading to an underground passage of reinforced concrete. Also, a radio and a

---

* (Malignant delight)

telephone. I can almost leap from my parallel bars in the garden into the shelter.

Good news: I've reached near perfection with the single leg stem rise movement, my movement of the moment.

26 MÄRZ 1944

I trimmed Negus so his coal-black coat ends in uniform length. Then I brushed his hair to keep it lively, to remove dead hair. He was so docile, so happy to be groomed. I took both his ears into my hands and held his head still, called him by name, and looked into his eyes.

I heard the bell and pushed the heavy drapes aside. A priest whose left sleeve was empty stood outside in the downpour. Answer the door, I shouted to Mogerl who was resting upstairs.

He shook rain off his hat.

Not on the carpets, Mogerl snapped at him.

He told her, I am the Reverend Father Liebisch, I am Bavarian. I was sent by Mother Palmeria.

I dropped Negus onto the floor and patted his bottom.

Mother Palmeria needs your help, the priest said. Perhaps you remember that Mother Palmeria was the principal of the school in Maria-Medingen where you were a student? You see Dr. Hans Wölfel of Bamberg has been arrested. He is a relative of Mother Palmeria.

M. asked, Who arrested him?

The Geheime Staatspolizei.

On what charge?

Defeatism.

She saw the Reverend Father out the door, and returned to the sitting room. She sat across from me, looking at me with begging eyes.

I take it you want me to intercede? I asked, cleaning hair from the dog brush.

Yes. Why not?

And for every lunatic? Every Pole, Gypsy, red, Jew, Slav? Every alcoholic? Every contragenic? Tell Paula to dry the carpet and tell her I'm not eating tonight.

27 MÄRZ 1944

I read in Mogerl's diary:

I no longer recognize my sister, Effie. She has become arrogant, tyrannical, and lacking in tact toward her family. Living with the great of this earth makes one selfish, even cruel. She distributes her old dress like a queen.

I had to laugh at this. Biting the hand that . . . the dress had only been worn twice. I had, in point of fact, just answered a plea from Oische for financial help with an offer of 10 Mark a month! I'd written to Oische: *I cannot ask the Kanzler for anything for my family. It just isn't done.*

And I shan't. The 10 Mark were out of my own pocket.

I'm so short of funds, I continue to trade bacon from the larder for shoes, eggs for silk stockings, butter for bits of jewelry. Do they think I'm made of money?

2 APRIL 1944

Today a note arrived for Mogerl from Mother Palmeria again begging for intercession. I asked Herr B. about the matter. He snarled, Dr. Hans Wölfel had already been found guilty of defeatism.

I asked, Can anything be done?

No. Wölfel was condemned to death. He was beheaded in the courtyard of the prison in Brandenburg.

3 APRIL 1944

Waffen-Schutzstaffel General Hermann F. was drunk last night quite late. He declared, I am a coward.

He is the liaison officer between the head of the Schutzstaffel and the K. Herr B. is his great drinking friend. I have watched him these last weeks "mixing" with the women at Berchtesgaden. He's a former jockey, illiterate but a "cocksman." He demanded that I join him for oysters, which I've never tasted.

They are "alive" in half-shells, like boneless frogs, but smelly and slimy. Dr. M. swept up the oysters I didn't eat, and stuffed them into his mouth. With his mouth full he questioned General F: But you have been decorated with the Knight's Cross, with oak leaves, too high a distinction for a coward. We've heard that you accomplished an important mission in the KZ at Theresienstadt.

Yes, the general bragged, sucking up an oyster from its shell, I supervise physicians who do medical experiments on prisoners like amputating shoulders and arms, sealing glass into wounds to study battlefield wounds. All very interesting to see.

Dr. M. asked him why he'd gotten the Knight's Cross.

The general bragged, Because mercilessness is generously rewarded. You see in Slovakia subhumans were buried alive in large graves, some were thrown into fires, bayoneted, starved, others tortured or suffocated . . . I was in charge!

After oysters, General F. handed me a bottle of forbidden good French perfume—*Je Reviens*. Later he got even drunker and I heard him call Mogerl a "stupid goose."

I don't seem to care a twit anymore if I hear this kind of talk about my sister.

Later he seduced the same "stupid goose."

11 APRIL 1944

Before I left the Berg I filled my car with:

potatoes
butter
flour
pumpernickel
sugar

Paula had asked for caraway seeds and Bratwurst. I found no lemon juice for Paula's Buttermilchsuppe.

4 MAI 1944

Important news! The Kanzler has arranged a match between General F. and Mogerl. He is a cad, but I can make good use of this match. It will legitimize my position. If my sister is married to a general—I can:

1. Be presented everywhere! Finally!
2. Be seen in public!
3. Travel with official personage!

I must encourage this "match." Also, General F. has a great ability to get hold of things that no one can get anymore. Out of nowhere he gets his hands on perfumes and furs and he has been generous to me, which he won't regret.

12 MAI 1944
Looked through my piles of snapshots. Alas, I get no comfort anymore from memories . . . just jewels, furs, shoes, gloves.

15 MAI 1944
I told the K.: I want the wedding to be very beautiful, elaborate, as though it were mine. I would like the reception to take place up at the Kehlstein.

5 JUNI 1944
The civil wedding was solemnized at Salzburg Town Hall. The party secretary and head of the Schutzstaffel stood as witnesses. I gloated as Margareta Franziska Bertha and Hans Georg Otto Hermann were legally wed.

I am now legitimate! I can barely contain myself.

For the world to see, we journeyed by special car back to Obersalzberg. The cortège wound up the road to the tunnel entry. Then the wedding party entered through the gilded elevator door. The Kanzler refused to sit in the red plush chair in front of the Venetian mirror. He muttered against my hair, The cable might break, might be cut.

Toasts were made at the great hearth at the center of the marbled tearoom. The band struck up. To everyone's surprise—as I had *begged* the Kanzler—dancing was allowed. The K. stared out of the great Gothic windows at the summit of Kehlstein, which was shrouded in heavy mist. I excused myself, grabbed my new brother-in-law by the arm and pinched until he led me in the first dance. More champagne! I shouted to the waiters because at last I can demand as much of everything as I please!

The armaments minister insisted on dragging me off to the side. He told me, The Kanzler's hair has turned gray, his hands tremble, his hearing is going, hundreds of bombers have been destroying our fuel plants in eastern and central Germany.

As soon as this minister left, I was again whirling and drinking champagne. Yes, I was dancing. For the first time I was dancing in public with official personages! Out of breath, I stood off to the side and took a glass of champagne. Immediately his secretary, Fräulein S., cornered me and began to whisper. The Kanzler is only a shadow of his former self.

She gave me such a plaintive look, but I didn't dare say what was on my mind, dare to gloat: Did she think I didn't notice? Did *I* put him into the world of politics? Did *I* insist on making war across six continents and on all the oceans? What do these people expect ME to do? I'm flattered yes. I brushed her off too.

The Kanzler retired early. I danced on until the bride and groom left for their honeymoon at a castle in Austria, which the Kanzler had given Gruppenführer F. as an appanage.

I danced more, guzzled more. I, the mistress of the greatest man in the world, got so lightheaded and couldn't stop hiccupping when Herr B., very drunk, was carried away by two men. My most favorite dancing partner: Heini Handschuhmacher. His eyes glow with white light.

Heini and I danced together till dawn when the news filtered through that that an enemy invasion had landed in France. At this the musicians packed up their instruments and departed leaving Heini and me alone on the dance floor.

Though I hated to see the evening end, Heini kissed my hand and bid me good night because he had to drive back into München.

7 JUNI 1944

Before I awoke, the K. and his staff left to go back to the front. Just now I heard his voice on the radio. He was screaming: Let them come! Within nine hours we will throw them back into the sea!

Here at the Berg I can see a red reflection in the sky over München in the distance. He has left strict orders that I not go to München during any air raid.

8 JUNI 1944

A telephone call came from München. Dear Heini Handschuhmacher, the handsome, young actor—my dancing partner—has
been killed in an air raid! I insisted to Herta, Please accompany
me to München to the funeral.

But we have been forbidden.

I'm afraid I must insist. He'll never know that we went. And I
called for my car.

10 JUNI 1944

I've never seen anything like what we saw in München. The funeral was a shambles.

This evening I waited for his call. When it finally came we had
a terrible connection. I had to shout into the telephone, *du*, you
would not believe the devastation . . . dead . . . injured. How?
Why?

He screamed: I vow to pay the scoundrels back a hundredfold.
Vergeltungswaffen are in the air as we speak! After a long silence
he added, I forbid you to go to München again!

And no answers to my questions. But no censure for going
against his orders either. Can this be? Can he have forgiven me?

20 JULI 1944

A hot day. Herta and I went for a swim in the Königsee. The gossip today: Magda G. Is she having a mental breakdown? Is it simply pain in her face from an inflamed trigeminal nerve? She's a patient at the Weisser Hirsch Sanatorium in Dresden at this
moment. I can't say I'm sorry for her.

While Herta burrowed in the stones on the shore, I dozed for a
while lying on a raft and let the sun bake into my cold fingers and
neck. From where I was, I could see a young boy on the beach
walking on his hands. I looked across and saw an official car approaching on the road that leads from the Berghof to Königsee, so
I dived back into the Königsee.

With long, perfect strokes I swam ashore and the chauffeur
handed me a note in a sealed envelope, which I tore open. A terri-

ble premonition prickled my ears: There was an attempt on the Kanzler's life, but he wants you to know that he is all right.

I left Herta and was driven quickly back to Berghof.

First vermouth. Then I began to telephone East Prussia but couldn't get a call through. The telephone failed time and again. As I waited, I looked in the mirror and saw that I had lain too long in the sun. Looking more closely, I saw that pale freckles had appeared on my collarbone and on the back of my hands; on all exposed skin. My heart jumped into my mouth. Quickly I drank up the vermouth and filled the glass with urine. Then I called, Paula, bring vinegar, salt.

When she did, I mixed a tablespoon of vinegar and a pinch of salt with the urine. Standing with her thighs apart, her palm clutching the washcloth, Paula helped me apply the mix to the freckled area every half hour. Then with a fresh cloth she washed it off with plain cold water. I was so grateful for such a thorough scrub that afterward I held out my arms to her. When she rose up from her knees I stroked her twisted corn-colored hair. She began to speak, but my mind was elsewhere, waiting for news that he is dead or alive.

I can't help but think that he's dead. Or, he's seriously wounded. If he is dead what will become of "ME"? I flail around the villa because I can do nothing but wait for him to telephone. Paula knelt down and rubbed the soles of my feet for hours on end to calm me down.

14 AUGUST 1944

Again tonight the film.

After the attempt on his life he ordered that the execution of the conspirators be filmed. Although he refuses to visit bombed cities, the wounded in hospitals, and lowers the shades in his train window when passing "unpleasant" devastation, he makes "ME" watch this film with him over and over again since he returned to the Berg.

He ordered the executioner to perform the rites in a special, a cruel way. He explained: Death occurs in hanging when the neck is broken. As the men were being hanged, I ordered that they be pulled up on the rope and slowly strangled.

The film shows that as they hang in the sling, their trousers were pulled down by the Schutzstaffel, their genitals exposed. He wants me to watch again from beginning to end, though—all things considered—I had other ideas for this evening like watching the German film *Eine Motterliebe*,* which is so naive and sentimental that it makes us all roar with laughter. I so would rather forget the misery being foisted on us by our enemies.

During our viewing last night he drank tea and I had a small glass of vermouth having promised myself to drink only one. It is ever curious the effect of violent death on the private parts of a man. I should be repelled but I am not. I want him to see how hardened I am, that I am like him, and not the bleeding heart I once was.

15 AUGUST 1944

Last night he presented me with the bloodstained, burnt uniform he was wearing when the assassination attempt failed. I am deeply touched. A beautiful moment.

16 AUGUST 1944

Since the explosion, his hands shake, especially his left. His ears hurt. Dr. M. says the tympanic membranes on both sides are broken. His stomach keeps cramping up, so Dr. M. has been giving him additional injections and leeches are being brought.

17 AUGUST 1944

Without anesthetic—at his own request—he had the edges of the tympani cauterized today.

Still pale from shock, he took me by the hand and led me to the reception room to gaze at Adolf Ziegler's portrait of his niece that hung in the most honored place. He stood in silence while I suppressed the disdain I felt for her ever-young mocking face.

* (*A Mother's Love*)

Then he walked over to the painting by Feuerbach called "Nana" above the mantelpiece.

He muttered, "Nana" looks so marvelous. Her hands are luminous.

If only I could keep these artists names straight. And the nude sculpture of me? The great Arno Breker still has not completed his commission.

21 AUGUST 1944

He made time for me today! He took me for a walk!

The gate was closed. In the old days the crowd made a human wall around the last gate. Then, when he walked, the gates would be opened and the crowds would rush to follow in his path; hysterical women would pick up stones he'd trodden on as souvenirs. It's a pity, that was before the war. Now there is no one to be seen except some filthy, subhuman Russian prisoners in rags who are building new fortifications around Obersalzberg. I took snapshots with my little camera.

24 AUGUST 1944

Another walk.

He began a monologue on our walk with Blondi. I don't know what brought it on because he so rarely speaks to me about important subjects: I have absolutely no time for the Church. The Christian faith is a hypocritical institution which corrupts men. My religion is the laws of nature and blood. My dogma goes with the laws of nature and blood.

I wished he'd sniff "Me" instead.

I've had no time anymore for naive sacraments, holy water, holy pictures, crucifixions, confessions. Childish toys from my naive past.

I agree, *du*.

He continued: Science hasn't yet established the roots of the human species, the only thing that is certain—there was a sudden fire in his eyes and he made a grand sweep with his right hand, then pounded on a tree—is that we are the highest stage of development in mammals, having begun as reptiles and ended up as man. We're a link in the chain of creation. We're children of nature and the laws that govern all living creatures apply to us too. Anything that is ill-adapted to life, or not strong enough, gets eliminated. It's only man himself—now he was yelling and his lungs were expanded—and especially the Church, that has decided artificially to prolong the lives of the weak, the misfits, and those who are inferior.

You are my church, *du.* Happily you are eliminating all those "useless mouths."

He stroked my hand, One of these days I'll have only two friends left. Yes, you, Fräulein Effie, and my loyal Blondi.

If words can penetrate my needy place, these have. His voice was so lively, but suddenly it turned to a croak.

He confided, I have a polyp on my vocal cord and need an operation.

29 AUGUST 1944

Again I no longer know where the telephone calls are coming from: Adlerhorst, the field headquarters in the west in the Taunus Mountains. East Prussia, the Wolfsschanze. He doesn't say.

31 AUGUST 1944

Daily enemy bombs have been falling on all of Germany! The sirens wail. Whole squadrons of aircraft cross Austria into Bavaria. Who would have ever, *ever* imagined? Even Vati, who was against him, never imagined this. When the machines that make artificial fog are put into action at the Berg, the house is wrapped in a thick cloud.

I dare not get gloomy so I made a party last night. Hilarious time was had by all. I am paying the price today with dehydration and red threads in my eyeballs. My thoughts are repeats.

5 SEPTEMBER 1944

Earlier and earlier in the day now, the sirens. I quickly grab jewels and furs, and then down the sixty-five steps to the air raid shelter. He has promised me: The Luftwaffe's new weapons will make the enemy pay a hundred times over for what they've done to us! He raised his voice even higher, Not a single bomb will fall on the Berghof!

6 SEPTEMBER 1944

And, as he promised, it has not. The Berghof is so far unscathed. Everything he says by telephone he yells. Thank God, after fifteen years, I know he is not yelling at me. My thoughts: The new secretary.

7 SEPTEMBER 1944

Attended a small party. Hilarious.

8 SEPTEMBER 1944

In a private ceremony in Breslau, O. has married. She's in Breslau with her new husband whom none of us know a thing about. Just when we all thought that she too would be an old maid. Oische's an *Ehefrau** instead!

Now I am the "spinster," but I shan't lose hope.

* (wife)

München

Even the K., since his return, no longer goes down the sixty-five steps into the shelters unless the anti-aircraft flak has begun. Instead he stands by the entrance and watches like a guard dog to make sure none of us leaves the bunker before the sirens have stopped. I am the particular object of his surveillance.

Today after the sirens began, Mogerl went down into the shelter, but when she found no one there, she came back up the steps to where the K. stood. When he saw her, he shook his finger and said, Don't be so rash, young lady. Go straight back down into the shelter, rejoin Fräulein Effie. The alert isn't over yet.

Mogerl went down again without saying a word. Of course she didn't tell him that I wasn't there. It's getting too hard to lug furs and jewels up and down night and day. Let them blow me up with my treasures. Let my treasures—along with bits and pieces of my bones—rain down on Bavaria like hail stones.

Later:

Two nights running he showed the film of the Army officers at Plötzensee Prison; the meat hook on the ceiling with running nooses made of wire, around the hooks, around the necks. I watched them pulled slowly up. Each man strangled. Those private, blunt parts. I don't bat an eye nor feel an iota of pity for even the handsome ones.

After using leeches, I also had blood drawn by Dr. M. The Kanzler and I gazed at the test tubes. He began a harangue: Blood is the cement of civilization. You know that blood soup was popular in ancient times. All too familiar.

He stopped speaking when Dr. M. counted out ten drops of Cardiazol and Coramine for his endema. Immediately he became stimulated and began to speak about blood again: When I've finished, even Moloch, the idol of blood, will be pale.

Yes, the test tubes, little chalices holding our blood, our very own consecrated wine. Along my arm, streaks of blood, ending at my wrist. Finally another injection for "virility." I watched his eyes, the great joy I feel when we are together. The meaty smell. Immediately after Dr. M. left the room, I began to pant.

Beside him I am a small mammal. He reached around me, his lupine arms crushed and squeezed me. His tongue painted my entire face, wet my eyes and nose. But his stabs did not enter "Me." I murmured, cried out. Eventually he dismounted and put his nose against my nose. I was still panting, my whole face sticky. He jabbed at me again, but his blunt efforts were unruly, too jerky, completely missing me.

He became morose once more, combed his hair in the usual way and without an amorous word went to his conference.

I need to do more work on the parallel bars. My pelvis has a slightly rubbery feel. But first a bath. Yes, I thought, scrubbing my face, *he wants to undress me himself. His strong hands make me "quite crazy," but he can't really undress me because he simply is not skillful enough.*

23 SEPTEMBER 1944

He has gone back to the front. Our amorous forays have been at cross purposes.

I've invited the gang but doubt very much I'll be able to join in.

Paula's attempt to feed us has gone awry. We're missing too many ingredients, so her Pichelsteiner stew had no flavor except paprika and no smell except cabbage.

24 SEPTEMBER 1944

Frau T.'s male Alsatian, Harras, was invited to mate with Blondi, to "marry" Blondi off, he called it. His call was early. Yes, *du*.

He complained, The dogs won't comply. Blondi was muzzled and put into a sling. Dear Blondi.

And me? I've never been mated!

25 SEPTEMBER 1944

More anguish about Blondi on the telephone today. My exercises had to wait. He told me, The man in charge of the kennels has dashed my hopes. Though the entire country obeys his every command, Blondi won't comply.

I'm so sorry, *du*.

He continued, The man in charge is encouraging me to mate Bella, or perhaps Muck. Do you know that Bella knows exactly what time it is?

I didn't know that. I've never met Bella or Muck, two of his "intelligent" Alsations.

Ach. Bella the magnificent! Muck, another of my specimens. She's fine. But Blondi, Blondi. Ach! Blondi learns everything, follows me like a shadow, is courageous, faithful, attentive.

After the call, my exercises.

Now my muscles ache from too much work on my parallels. I have the skin and heart of a thirty-year-old but the shape of a seventeen-year-old.

26 SEPTEMBER 1944

Frau J., his new "young" secretary, came to see me today. She was in München visiting her mother. She told me that her husband was killed on the Eastern front. Then she leaned in. She kneaded her pink paws and spoke in an intimate way, The Kanzler is taking an unbelievable number of drugs.

Somehow she must know about my relationship with him. But how? Yes, up close, she is pretty, though her behind sticks out like a duck. I do not like her on sight. I replied, Of course I more than anyone know this. I stared just above her egg-shaped head.

She went on: He takes Dr. M.'s "anti-gas" pills by the handful. His valet gives him five different pills either before or after meals. The first pill to stimulate the appetite; the second to stimulate digestion; the third to stop flatulence.

Ach. Let her see she is not my equal. I lit a cigarette.

His doctor is prescribing twenty-eight different drugs for the Kanzler.

She looked longingly at my cigarette.

Yes, she is very pretty. Yes, I see also she slightly resembles me but is tall with dull eyes, a girlie smile. She is about to go back to the Wolfsschanze in East Prussia.

I explained, My sister is already pregnant with the general's child. Perhaps you can keep an eye on her husband for me? Now I gave her my girlie smile. I assured her, One day things will be better. A cigarette?

Yes, she replied, and I gave her the entire packet.

Later:

At this point in my gymnastic development I can go no further on my own. To enhance my training, I have asked the organization to provide me with a private trainer. The organization has recommended a gymnast who has trained young girls in clubs across Bavaria. She is Frau Hochschmidt, and I admired the tilt of her tailbone on sight. She's a model of health and fitness. She was wearing a blue skirt, brown blouse with a white collar. She's about twenty, tall, has deep blue lidless eyes. She has qualified to bear children to give to the Lebensborn and has given one to them. She quickly got down to business, established the intensity of my perceived exertion, heart rate, etc.

While she critically observed, I demonstrated my crotch circle movement on the parallel bars until we were interrupted by a telephone call. The young secretary told me: He cannot get out of bed!

In my supercilious voice I told her, I cannot speak to you now. I will ring you back when I can.

I got back onto the bars and grasped the low bar with a reverse grip. I extended one leg between my hands and the other behind the bar in a stride position. With my head up and my arms straight, I lifted my body away from the bar. I lifted my front leg and leaned forward to start the rotation around the low bar while keeping my body "stretched." The bar stayed between my legs near my crotch but started to slip.

Frau Hochschmidt shouted at me, Not your knees!

Quickly my hands slid around the bar to return on top where my grip tightened to stop my forward momentum. I began to lighten up at this point in the exercise then I returned to starting position to conclude the movement.

I couldn't see from the look on her face whether or not I had done well. I perceived myself almost perfect in this position. But was I? Frau Hochschmidt told me: I am satisfied with your poise so I'll speed up your training. Then she worked on my resistance using a towel which she held while I pulled.

She told me, Your triceps need strengthening.

She attached two kilo weights to my ankles with buckles and instructed me: Kneel on all fours. Now lower your body to your elbows, kick one leg out behind, lower it, strengthen it. Now bend. Do this eight times a day.

I will.

And, if you'd like to stretch your muscles, wear the weights, and hang upside down like a monkey.

What I'd really like is to "stretch" my entire length. Increase my height . . .

It's as easily said as done.

Was she serious? I gripped her wrists. Locked eyes. Is it? I asked.

Yes, yes. She assured me. Just attach the weights, hang like a monkey. She spoke seriously, I guarantee you'll become taller.

I felt as though I'd known her all my life, that she was my true "sister." I invited her inside. What fun we had, a vermouth, stories of her adventures on the gymnastic "front" since age twelve.

27 SEPTEMBER 1944

We call his personal bodyguard "the gorilla" because of his walnut-shaped head and fists the size of tree-trunks. His skin is as shiny as patent leather, tufts of hair fill his ears. He telephoned me: He won't see anyone, has told us staff, From now on I will take my meals alone.

I fear that growing old will render me shamefully inferior too. His weakness makes me fear that I too am threatened with dissolution.

The bodyguard continued, He is completely apathetic. We don't know what to do. He isn't even interested in the situation on the Eastern front.

How strange, such an "intimate" telephone call. Perhaps I've misjudged the use the new secretary might be. I decided to telephone her. In my *süsse Stimme* I asked her, Tell me what has happened?

Her words poured out: He summoned his secretaries to his bunker bedroom, which is more like a cell than the abode of a Supreme Commander. She stopped to catch her breath, then continued. His room contains a wooden kennel for Blondi so there was very little room left over for him.

I can't believe that he was sharing his room with Blondi. Who else came to the bedroom, Traudl?

Two secretaries, Herr Albert B., the aide-de-camp, the Ambassador H. was shown in.

I asked, How was the Kanzler dressed?

He was wearing a thick gray wool dressing gown, a cravat, a pair of very ordinary black shoes, a simple soldier's shoes.

I'm abashed. No doubt that under the dressing gown hung a long white shirt that might have been issued by the Wehrmacht. The cuffs would be unbuttoned because they were too tight. The dead white skin of his arms exposed. A "scene" only I had seen until now. They could all now see why he never wore Lederhosen or a bathing suit.

I probed, And what did he speak about?

Just polite talk. He asked me, Tell about your day. I replied, I typed reports from all over Germany, the tally of the bombing raids, the extermination figures from far and wide. He listened to news of my mundane day. He was prostrate, irritable.

Perhaps I've misjudged her? As time goes on she seems to be a good sort. And my brother-in-law? I ask her.

She squeaked, To be frank, the general has a mistress. Everyone knows her, she's a Berlin actress with flaming red hair who had, she hesitated.

I demanded, Had what.

. . . a child with him. Though he does not provide for her or the child at all.

I couldn't believe my ears. When do you see him?

I see him in nocturnal drinking with the party secretary. I hear loud toasts to Bruderschaft. They swallow drinks in one gulp with linked arms. Then she lowered her voice, He beds women while wearing his Knight's Cross with swords and oak leaves.

29 SEPTEMBER 1944

I was dripping from my fervent exercise. I had hung upside down for over an hour. When I came inside the "hearthrugs" were cowering. Paula was on her knees scrubbing the piddlings they'd made on the rugs. Her breath came in pants, her orbs were narrowed in concentration. Her black wings hung limply at her side. I went down on my haunches and sniffed the rugs to see if the odor remained.

Good news! he shouted into the telephone, Blondi has finally been mated. Remember this date! 29 September. The father is a greyhound belonging to one of my soldiers!

He went on and on, then he rang off. When I looked across the room I saw Paula gazing across at me, pawing the ground, carrying a tray with my dinner. I motioned for her to bring it to me. I noticed that her hair had been cut and tinted an amber color. I couldn't help but laugh.

30 SEPTEMBER 1944

Every night I listen to the radio for news of air raids. My suitcases and bags, which are full of shoes, jewels, and furs, are ready for descents into the cellar. To pass the time after I've attached the weights and hung like a monkey, I often take snapshots of my "hearthrugs." Almost daily, the whole of Berchtesgaden is wrapped in an artificial smoke screen. I shout, Paula, Champagne! Schnaps! Musik!

13 OKTOBER 1944

He had the polyp on his vocal cord removed. It's a pity. I shan't talk on the telephone to him, so I spend even longer hours working on the new position, the single leg squat through arms position, without fear that I'll miss his telephone call.

15 OKTOBER 1944

Frau Hochschmidt got caught in an air raid and missed our session but I was diligent in practicing the position. When I finished, my heart was singing.

19 OKTOBER 1944

They're bombing München again!

Sleeping tablets. State of semi-imbecility. Fear for Mutti and Vati's safety.

8 NOVEMBER 1944

An order: Go to the Berg immediately.

11 NOVEMBER 1944

I disobeyed his orders, drove myself to München taking the back roads. First I checked that Mutti and Vati were unharmed. They are shaky, trying to put on a front of bravery. Then, I set out for my villa. I have so many possessions of value there.

Trying to reach the villa I saw a building explode with a roar. Smoke and flames shot out. Immediately the adjoining building collapsed. Debris of all kinds flew up into the sky, a woman's body fell to the sidewalk, a woman about Mutti's age, no longer with the slightest appeal. I didn't look back. A pity.

Sections of München are blazing. I dare not shop for gloves.

I made it home and discovered that my villa has been damaged in one of the recent bombings. Why didn't Paula tell me? Filthy workers in rags from nearby Dachau were already making repairs.

These slave laborers had yellow faces, and one of them looked at me as if I owed him something, had left an account unsettled. He had obviously lived among filth for quite some time. His feverish eyes made me look away, but—insulted by his eyes—my hackles rose, I returned his stare.

My own eyes bore against his. Am I to blame if he is racially inferior? He would not break his gaze so I did first with a shrug, but immediately I looked back realizing that I had been looking into the eyes of Paul, the handsome waiter from the Carlton who I used to confide to about my girlish problems. He certainly wasn't young nor handsome any longer. More like a human skeleton. Thank God I'd dropped him long ago.

12 NOVEMBER 1944

I've run out of writing paper but found sheets belonging to Mogerl. Looking around my villa at everything I own, I noticed that except for the doll with golden braids and the music box which plays *Ach, du lieber Augustin*, nothing remains of my life before him. No longer are there prayer books, holy pictures, little crucifixes from convent years tossed carelessly onto my bedside table like they were when I was growing up.

I crossed out M.'s name on the stationary, wrote my own name across the top, in capital letters. On this I'll write my will and beneficiaries. When I finish, I'll leave it for safekeeping with Herta.

Other lists to write:

1. dresses, shoes, gloves
2. documents

CHRISTMAS NIGHT 1944

I took a look at my sister's diary and saw that she had written: *Had a nightmare in which I saw my sister on a pyre, smiling but surrounded by rats. Then a wall of flame hid her from sight.* When I tried to sleep without sleeping tablets, I woke. Paula heard my tossing and brought hot buttermilk, sugar, cinnamon, nutmeg, and hot brandy whisked together so hard it was frothy. I patted the foot of my bed, got her to sit down while I drank just as enemy planes began bombing the town. She was so frightened that she buried her face between my breasts. It took all my strength to unstick her face and push her off the bed. She's so frightened that she doesn't know what she's doing. And me? I no longer fear anything.

Later:

I have catalogued my entire estate. I'm awed.

My Christmas has been ruined by these air alerts. When I finally get a call through, I ordered his secretary, See that a small

Christmas tree is put in his bunker and that candles are placed on it. And, I asked, What about my brother-in-law?

She lowered her voice: One night a guard surprised him in bed with one of the chambermaids. She whispered more, but our connection went bad.

München, Berchtesgaden, Berlin

30 DEZEMBER 1944
Our nightly telephone calls have not resumed since the polyp on his vocal cords was removed.

5 JANUAR 1945
He spent Christmas in Adlerhorst headquarters lunching with his secretaries, taking tea with the generals. I am in a never ending state of under stimulation, alone, bored, uncaressed. I hung upside down for well over two hours.

I've fired Paula. She was late once too often! Also the rationed Harz cheese she bought smells vile!

7 JANUAR 1945
A heavy bombing raid today in München. Blood-red sky. The explosions lit up the whole town. Railway lines have been damaged and the telephone is not working. Streets are filled with desperate people who dig interminably into still smoking ruins that once were their homes. Mutti and Vati, so far, are unharmed.

12 JANUAR 1945
I have just received word that he's coming to Berlin; that he has ordered me to meet him. I must get to Berlin in time to meet his train but am all at sea without Paula to help me. What a fool I was to fire her.

I have invited Monalisa Hochschmidt to follow me to Berlin, to continue my training.

13 JANUAR 1945
In Berlin the clock on the Kaiser Wilhelm Memorial Church has frozen at 7:30. In spite of our ordeal there are streetwalkers who wear boots and carry umbrellas. They walk brazenly to and fro—pubic bone first—catching soldiers' eyes. I noticed an inscription

in chalk on the blackened walls of a bombed building: *Mein Engelein, wo bleibst Du? Ich bin in grosser Sorge. Dein Fritz.** Below, also in chalk, was an answer, *Befinden sich in Potsdam.*† I've run out of cigarettes and was forced to borrow a vile Drummer from my bodyguard.

As the Kanzler's train pulled into Berlin, I felt suddenly timid. I saw that his shades were lowered to avoid viewing the scenes of devastation. I quickly sucked a menthol tablet, was escorted aboard. His face has acquired a gray hue, his hands shake. He tried to make light, It is better that my hands shake then my head. His voice was hard to hear.

I smiled lavishly as much as I could. As he talked I could only see one thing. His eyes are yellow.

He muttered, You are the only one who cares. He began stroking my hand. Had I heard right?

When we arrived at the Reich Chancellery he went directly to his second-floor private quarters so I went to my apartment, shut the heavy drapes, and waited. A glass or two of vermouth, my heart pounding. Had I heard right?

Later:

I noticed that he shuffles when he walks. He ordered, This time you will stay with me.

Had I heard right? Is it possible that I'd heard those words come from his mouth? If only . . . at last.

Then he said, Tschapperl, I've never been so certain of victory as now.

I am enormously assured. I asked for vermouth to celebrate. My heart expanding.

17 JANUAR 1945

I took a nap. I dreamed I saw a cardinal in his robes who undressed me, caressed the most sensitive places, made love to me

---

* (My little angel, where are you? I worry greatly. Yours, Fritz)
† (Staying in Potsdam)

Greek-style. When I gathered up my clothes, he reproached me for too much love of gaiety.

I just woke with a bilious attack.

He is in conference.

Frau Hochschmidt was due to arrive, but has not, so I began without her. I need routine and am working painstakingly on the front lying cast to squat position on my parallels. I finished in a squat on the low bar on the balls of my feet.

Alas, a kink in my calf, and I had to stop. Just then Frau Hochschmidt swooped down. She insisted that—despite the pain—I buckle on two kilo weights and do leg lifts, then hang.

Later:

I'm still experiencing pain in my calf. I summoned the hairdresser, had my hair done. Then I walked Stasi and Negus in the Tiergarten where they went their separate ways, smelling and watering their special spots, balancing on hind legs, cocking legs in the air. A few drops here. A few there.

Evening:

He's in conference.

I summoned the dressmaker. The ambitious woman told me, My workrooms have been bombed, but I've found other work space. I'm at the Kaiserhof Hotel, which may collapse at any moment.

I ordered three new dresses though I'm low on cash.

The stupid "broom girls"—the half-breeds—continue to sweep the streets ten or more hours a day but still the streets are dirty.

19 JANUAR 1945

The telegram arrived: *Forced to flee from Breslau.*–Oische.

25 JANUAR 1945

This January has been quite cold, too cold to go out early, so I sent an official car at dawn to Schlesien Bahnhof.

The driver told my big sister that a room was reserved at the Adlon Hotel and took her there. Shortly I telephoned. My voice vibrant: I'm so sorry not to be able to put you up at the Chancellery, but it's full of generals and we're rather short of space. Naturally you're dining with me this evening.

Another car was sent that brought Oische here to the Chancellery. I wore a new dress for her.

We ate in the library and drank yellow malmsey wine. The silver dishes were brought by white-gloved valets. After eating, I offered her a cigarette and vermouth. Her hand was shaking so much I had to light it for her.

She told me, I've been separated from my husband.

Irritated, I asked, Why isn't your husband in the army?

She began to cry, I've nothing left to wear, my furniture is all destroyed. One small cloth suitcase is all that I have left of my possessions.

Haughtily, I reminded her, That could have been avoided if you'd moved in with me to Wiedermeyerstrasse when I asked you. I guarantee that you'd have acquired more substantial possessions!

She scratched her cheeks with her fingernails. I'd made my point. With reassurance, with my *süsse Stimme*, Don't worry Oische, in a fortnight's time you'll be back home in Breslau.

She looked at me like I was crazy, her small pointed teeth biting into her knuckles. I assured her, I have this from a reliable source, you've nothing to fear.

As I sprayed the room with French perfume to cover the smell of smoke and popped a mint in my mouth, she began to shout at "ME": Wake up, Breslau is lost, Silesia is lost, Germany is lost. Don't you know that thousands of people are choking the snowy roads, fleeing from the enemy who is ravaging us, carrying off everything we own? Your Kanzler is a fiend, he's dragging you into the abyss with him and all of us along with you.

I jumped up, flung open the window, How dare you! It's against the law to speak like that! I gasped for air, and I sank into a chair.

Then I blacked out.

6 FEBRUAR 1945

My thirty-third birthday! The guests this evening are:

> pregnant Mogerl and her husband who has brought delicacies, earrings, good whiskey.
>
> the Brown Eminence,
>
> Dr. and Frau M.
>
> mein K.

The K. gave permission for dancing! Between dances he whispered in my ear, but I couldn't understand what he was saying. When he went to take a telephone call, Herr B. asked me to dance. I noticed that two buttons of his jacket had popped, a shirt button as well, that the skin on his stomach was pink and wrinkled. His feet turned out when he danced. He whispered in my ear, The Kanzler is in a radiant mood!

Herr B. also was in one, and pulled me close in his sucking way, but quickly I rotated dancing partners to avoid his clutches. The K. surprisingly stayed on. Dawn was coming. For once I left first, got into bed, but heard what sounded like a coin tapping against the windowpane and have yet to sleep a wink.

7 FEBRUAR 1945

He has ordered me: I am sending you to the Berghof.

I cried out: But you said we would stay together!

*Der Kanzler ist in uns und wir in ihm!** At Easter I will join you. I forbid you to come back to Berlin. Of course I would not lie to you.

He ordered Herr B. to accompany my sister, Frau Hochschmidt, and me to the "vegetable train." The "vegetable train" will be leaving after midnight. I've decided to take important possessions: photo albums, diaries, some jewelry, several furs, as many shoes as I can. Also food, cigarettes, and staples. It is simply too much so I've left some of my treasures with my brother-in-law for safekeeping.

I sent a telegram to Paula: Meet me in München. All is forgiven.

---

* (The Leader is within each of us and each of us is within him!)

8 FEBRUAR 1945

We got off in München, which was black with people. Paula met me with a newly sterilized young girl with long pigtails named Charlotta. We piled everything into Charlotta's strong arms then I clasped Paula tightly by the elbow while we pushed through the crowds. When I looked back Charlotta was nowhere in sight. Ach, I signaled Paula. While Frau Hochschmidt and my sister waited impatiently, Paula dashed off to find Charlotta and pulled her roughly through the crowd. Because the packages were so heavy the girl began to whimper. Paula slapped the girl so hard that twists of thick saliva shot out of her mouth all over Paula's coat. Immediately the girl gripped her sad breasts, slunk down like a puppy-dog in submission.

There were lines in front of all the shops, in front of the shelters. Nothing but lines of dirty people clutching rubbish. When we got to my villa, my dogs were overjoyed, ran everywhere, jumped on me. Overly excited, Negus soiled my dress and though it hurt me to do it, I pressed his nose into it. Quickly I pulled off my dress and threw it into the fireplace.

First Hochschmidt and I threw a medicine ball back and forth, side to side, above our heads to one another. Then we visited my parallel bars. She crouched on her haunches to watch me, the afternoon sunlight causing her to make a shade with her hand.

Again and again I circled backward around the low bar, released it, and came to a front support position, which immediately made me circle backward . . . released . . . circled.

She called out, I think the stretching is paying off, you appear taller.

I was heady when I dismounted and roamed the walled space of my enclosed garden where he and I had sniffed and bitten and bared our teeth. Could I grow tall enough to qualify for child bearing? Nature called and I squatted down spreading my knees like a funnel as the forceful river gushed into the earth, pooling and frothing like squeezed lemon juice, pooling at the roots of a tree but gradually soaking into the cold earth, leaving only froth and uremic, brown bubbles. I looked up into the sky and saw starving brown birds flying straight down to drink from the froth.

At the Isar, Monalisa and I went our separate ways. She turned right to visit her mother, and I walked through rubble-strewn streets with butter, flour, bacon, for Herta and her children.

My old friend Herta got tongue-tied when I was about to leave. She was teary, threw her arms around me. I told her, I will meet you at the Berg in a few days and we will go boating. The bombers will not bother us there.

Then I took my diamond watch to be repaired. First thing tomorrow, a visit to Mutti and Vati.

9 FEBRUAR 1945

Today when I shouted, Paula, there was no reply so I went into her little room and discovered that without permission she was sharing her bed with Charlotta and Charlotta's dirty bundles. I told her that Charlotta had to go. She begged me to let Charlotta stay. She said that Charlotta had been bombed out, had no home, and since she'd been sterilized was not feeling well. I noticed that Charlotta had an open sore at the corner of her mouth, was flicking her tongue into the raw place. I told Paula I needed to think, and when I turned away the old sly smile was smeared across Paula's yellow beak.

11 FEBRUAR 1945

Terrible air raid. Paula and her protégé got so hysterical that I forbade them from joining me in my shelter. From now on they must use the public shelter instead. I just can't have it!

16 FEBRUAR 1945

I've made arrangements for a second birthday party at my villa on Wasserburgerstrasse. Käthl, Peppo, Georg, my sister. My new "sister" Hochschmidt. During the party, as my assembled guests stood with glasses raised, the chauffeur made a presentation: The Kanzler's gift.

I tore off the wrappings and dangled it for all to see as they gasped. It's a pendant of topaz in a setting of diamonds. I put it on at once.

I couldn't help thinking: A diamond protects against poison. A diamond ends nightmares. A surge of happiness! An impulse! A resolution!

I announced to the assembled, I will not take refuge at the Obersalzberg. I'm going to return to Berlin.

Mogerl snapped at me, That's jumping into the lion's mouth. The others tried to dissuade me, but I crossed my arms, lifted up my shoulders, and told them, Death matters little to me. Although he has forbidden me to return, nothing can stop me from my "fate."

I shivered with the flood of joy I felt at my courage.

Mogerl dutifully asked, Shall I accompany you? But I knew she didn't really mean it.

Frau Hochschmidt will follow after me. Won't you Monalisa?

Then I sat down and ate everything in sight.

17 FEBRUAR 1945

White and trembling, Paula asked just now, Is it true that you're returning to Berlin?

I told the dear little half-wit, Yes, it's true.

You are not going to Obersalzberg?

No.

After morning toilet, I snapped at Mogerl, Please take these scissors and give me a little haircut.

She was surprised. I explained, They say a thick mane of hair will result if a pregnant woman cuts your hair. I hugged a squirming Stasi against my breasts as Mogerl—my *Kolibri**—snipped a few hairs. I'll press them here.

I've made arrangements for Paula to take Stasi to Obersalzberg. Two dogs are too much to carry to Berlin when there is so much else to lug. Negus will accompany me to Berlin. I told Paula, Charlotta may stay!

* (hummingbird)

She seemed too despondent to care. She mumbled, I know this is the end.

I assured her, Things will get better.

She mumbled, I do not want to live in a Germany without you. I started to laugh but suddenly, stopped.

Later:

I filled the car with eggs, bacon, and flour and went to see Mutti and Vati. I will be going on to the Obersalzberg, I lied.

Vati predicted: Even the Angel Aloysius returns to München at Carnival time.

Standing in the kitchen, Mutti beat eggs, milk, and salt on her faithful board. She kneaded in flour I'd brought until the dough was stiff.

Then I pitched in, rolling the dough into round rolls. When I tried cutting the slices, the knife stuck and pulled the dough apart. Mutti took the knife, and skillfully cut the roll into even slices. Then she fluffed and separated the noodles, dropping them one by one into the boiling milk on top of a spirit lamp.

For a moment we were mortally happy. We once baked gingerbread men together for Christmas like this when Vati was away on the front during the Great War. Now, like then, there was dough under my nails. I asked Mutti, Remember the gingerbread men we baked together?

Of course I remember, Mutti said bravely, A stay on the Obersalzberg will cheer you up. It will be nice and quiet after Berlin.

She insisted that I sit down at the table with her and Vati for pickled beets and the homemade noodles cooked in milk into which—because of me—she'd added bread cubes browned in the last of their oil ration. At the center of the table, a clutch of bright yellow coltsfoot that she'd set out to cheer us. But these common weeds insulted rather than cheered me.

This very meal had always been our Good Friday supper, but who knew where we'd all be when Good Friday comes? While I ate my second plateful, I looked closely at her face, looked for my face in hers, so relieved that now I'd never have to say goodbye to my good looks since . . . What courage Mutti has had to leave her good looks behind.

How I pine inside since I said farewell to Mutti and Vati. How we tried to hide the fear of this separation.

> *Pfefferkuchenmänner* (Mutti's Ginger Men)
> Ingredients:
> *honey*
> *sugar*
> *flour*
> *baking powder*
> *whole almonds*
> *candied lemon peel minced*
> *ground cinnamon*
> *ground cardamom*
> *as much ground clove and black pepper*
>   *as will fit on the point of a knife*
> *egg*
> *confectioners' sugar*
> *lemon juice*
> *hot water*
> *cutter shaped like a man*
> *Brush men with glaze, almond halves*
>   *as eyes, nose, buttons.*

24 FEBRUAR 1945

My Daimler-Benz cabriolet—the coupe type with two seats—had been garaged along with the squat Volkswagen since the start of the war. I commandeered Waffen-Schutzstaffel Officer Walter G. to do the driving.

It will not be easy to get to Berlin, he told me. Also it would be best to paint it the dark gray of most Wehrmacht vehicles.

I telephoned Herr B. to demand paint.

25 FEBRUAR 1945

This evening when I returned to the villa I found Paula and Charlotta slumped over, dead at my kitchen table. A chalky liquid in two glasses.

There was no dinner left, no note either. But of course Paula didn't know how to write. At first tears welled up in my eyes. The little pygmy. But then I thought, How selfish of her. How could she do this to ME just now? How?

1 MÄRZ 1945

I stuffed the car with my valuables. As we left München, heavy bombers had begun to bomb the city again. Negus barked, yelped and tried to jump out of the window. Approaching Leipzig, two Mustangs made a strafing attack on my car. A tire exploded. Officer G. drove on three tires under a viaduct while I sat stone-faced.

When the Mustangs had flown on, Officer G. changed the tire with the spare. I urged him to drive on. I could tell he thought me quite crazy, but he didn't dare contradict me, and drove again. Following behind an army truck on the main highway, we managed to go as far as Dessau.

Later:

The army truck ahead of us was blown up by a low-flying P-38. As a result of the explosion, Negus had diarrhea on the floor of the car. Officer G. insisted that we detour into the woods and wait until dark though I protested.

He threw military papers over the mess on the floor. I couldn't sleep. I smoked and paced back and forth on ground-frost between brown trees in a rage that this common officer had dared disobey "Me." He'll regret it. Thank God, I will never get trapped in the spider web of old age!

2 MÄRZ 1945

When it was dark we resumed our trip. About ten miles from Zossen, passing through a town, we heard bombers. Officer G. stopped the car, shouted, Get out and run for the shelter! I opened the door and, refusing to be bullied, walked regally down the street to a public shelter clutching Negus. I heard the bombs exploding to the west.

Inside, the shelter shook, lights flickered and went out. A clutch of townsfolk moaned with terror. Officer G. had given me a little pocket torch, which buzzed like a bee when I pressed the bottom to light it. When the light finally went on, I was covered in plaster dust, my hair a sight. I couldn't stop the perspiration or leap-froggings of my heart muscle. Then the room shuddered again, and I heard another explosion much closer. Negus went berserk.

I regained my composure. Hummed *"Tout ira très, Madame la Marquise"* as I left the shelter. I insisted, Take me the rest of the way, Officer! He didn't dare refuse. I had won. I needed a bath, food. Negus too.

3 MÄRZ 1945

What a shock to enter Berlin. Bombs had fallen up and down Tauntzienstrasse, most of the shops were smashed. Everything smelled of gas. So many buildings on the verge of collapse, whole streets cordoned off with signs saying: *"Achtung! Minen!"* We were able to reach the Reich Chancellery by the road through the gateway of the old Zossen Palace.

Tree trunks were scattered, bomb craters filled with gray water, sandbags piled all along the avenue. Rolls of wire, trams turned on their sides and filled with stones. The soldiers we saw were pale teenage boys. A handsome young Wehrmacht private was hanging from a lamppost. He was dead. Tied to his legs, a large card that had written on it: *Verrater. Ich lieb mein Volk im Stich.** Everywhere, homeless Germans wandered as though they were in a fog.

I went directly to the K.'s study in his private quarters. With him, his damnable secretaries, also his valet, and Frau G. The Kanzler was seated on a sofa with blue and white patterns. When I entered the room, he stared at me, then bracing his trembling hands on the sofa, pulled himself to his feet. He kissed "Me" directly on the lips with a long tongued kiss, and ears cocked. I could have crowed. No one has ever seen him behave so in public, seen him acknowledge me. Then he made a show of scolding me for risking my life to reach him, but tears had sprung to his jet-rimmed, still yellow eyes. Yes. It's true.

---

* (Traitor. I deserted my people.)

When I had gone to my room to freshen up he said to Frau G.—
and she told me just now in an unusual moment of cordiality—
I'm so proud of Fräulein Effie. What devotion! I've known her for a
very long time, but do you know that it was years before she allowed
me to pay for so much as a taxi fare.

Though he stretches the truth, I'm flattered.

Later:

We sat on the sofa listening to records like *Die Lustige Witwe*, sniffing old photo albums, eating cookies. Fraught as we both were, we
tried to make love. He smeared me with Vaseline. I made an effort
to steady his flank but tremors interfered and he was unable to
perforate.

I crouched down upon him demanding, panting, licking his
face and hands because I want one last union with him so terribly,
and perhaps it isn't to be.

6 MÄRZ 1945

I've been taking walks in the park with Frau J., the young secretary. I plied her: Perhaps you know more about the state of the
war? What is really going on? What happened?

She confided: Over and over he repeats, The decisive battle will
be won in Berlin.

Breaking the law I asked, What does he dictate to you?

What I type, doesn't tell me anything. Forgive me, but I know
as little as you do. But, she lowered her voice, there are rumors
that the Americans have crossed the Rhine over the bridge at
Remagen. Also that the Russians are about to cross the Oder
River, encircling Vienna.

The penalty for such "defeatism" is death. I'm impressed that
she was willing to speak to me this way. I know nothing of this. A
big nothing. Can these rumors be true?

7 MÄRZ 1945

The secretary and I walked to the nearby grounds of the zoo with
our little dogs, my Negus, her little fox terrier, Foxl. Walking
through the aquarium, we saw that the filthy water had seeped

into the tanks. Reptiles and snakes were swimming in the bottom of the tanks. Snow was on the ground. We saw people gathering bits of wood, searching under smashed trees for a few broken branches to feed their stoves. Women our age had made a long line, passing bricks from one to the other.

We watched them, then walked into a wooded area. For a few moments we threw snowballs for our dogs to chase. Foxl ran, Negus ran even faster. The gloom left. We threw snowballs at each other and mine broke against her hand, which she held up to protect her face. I felt kindly toward her. Then Negus returned but not Foxl. She called out, Foxl!

I took Negus into my arms. I dare not tell her my suspicion that Foxl was already simmering in a soup pot. I walked back clutching Negus away from my coat, as he had gotten wet and dirty in the awful snow, and I do not want him dirtying me.

Later:

Frau J. just came and squeaked almost inaudibly: I searched but did not find Foxl. My obedient, faithful animal. How can I live without the joy he gives me? Her maudlin mood annoyed me.

We shared an aperitif, bonded by devotion to our little creatures, but this is where any closeness ends.

11 MÄRZ 1945

While he worked in his study, I went to the garden where the valet had set up my parallel bars. First I hung upside down in the chill for two hours. Then, to warm up, my normal exercise. Because the dismount is the last move the judges see, Hochschmidt told me that it should be as impressive as possible, with good form, good presentation.

As in the mount, it is important to control and maintain the dismount without falling. I began by assuming a straddle stand with the arches of my feet on the low bar facing the high bar. One hand was in a regular grip on the low bar, the other hand was in a regular grip on the high bar. I piked at my hips then released the high bar hand to regrasp the low bar in a regular grip. Both my hands were in a position between my straddled legs. I kept my legs straight and pushed my feet against the low bar while pulling with straight arms to create equal stress. I pressed my buttocks back and downward, maintaining equal "push-pull" with my legs and arms.

I circled backward as the siren began to shriek. I circled three-fourths of the way around the low bar leading with my buttocks; then I relaxed my feet, pushed them upward and outward, joining my legs at the top of the arc while controlling my hips. The explosions came but I refused to lose my concentration. After all, everyone knows that only the athletically disciplined person will be the citizen of the future! I methodically released my hands from the low bar to allow my body to arch up, out, and then with the utmost concentration, to land. I ended standing regally with my back to the low bar while all around me was fire, deafening noise, smoke. I had dismounted with total control and perfection. I would have bet my diamond watch that I was taller. I felt taller.

Alas, no Frau Hochschmidt to see the control I had achieved.

12 MÄRZ 1945

After my bath, I walked Negus in the winter garden beside the pond, and into the greenhouse on the other side. The floodlights were already lit, as dark comes so early. I noticed that he was watching me from behind the gray curtains on the window that overlooks the garden.

I spend twenty marvelous minutes aware of his eyes on the back of my neck.

14 MÄRZ 1945

He summoned me to his study. I walked beneath the concrete eagle perched on the hooked cross above the door with Schutz-staffel standing guard on either side. The vast room is decorated with hooked cross reliefs. I stopped on the carpet. He sat in his black chair facing the window, his back to the door. His left leg was jerking back and forth like a ticking clock. On the desk: A pen-and-ink stand, a blotter, a telephone, a bell, two paperweights. Of course *Frederick the Great* in its circular gilt frame hung over the desk of solid oak.

He stood up and turned toward ME, his hands trembling, his walk was wobbly. I was repelled by the stoop of his shoulders because it made him look so short. He pinched my hands until I yelped in pain. He told me: In 1921 I had my first Alsatian. I was busy and gave him away. But he ran back to me. From then on I have been devoted to that breed, Veverl. Tschapperl. Blondi will shortly give birth!

24 MÄRZ 1945

Parts of the Chancellery have been destroyed. The Red Army continually shells the city. The joke is that the fires in Berlin are being put out with skim milk and beer since it seems that there's almost no water left to fight the fires.

*Die Gross Entscheidung!**

28 MÄRZ 1945

Orders from the K. were delivered to my room: Move down into the underground Kanzlerbunker. He has given the main bunker over to high ranking mothers and children of Berlin, all sixty rooms. Water stagnates in some passages but people fill the rooms. A section has been given to the Chancellery staff, it also has padlocked storerooms filled with tobacco, canned foods, liquor, chocolate, bacon, medical supplies—enough to withstand a year's siege. Vermouth galore, thank God. His personal bunker is situated under the site of Hindenburg's old Chancellery. I must . . . must . . . must . . . but I don't know what.

29 MÄRZ 1945

Four servants carried my clothes, jewels, furs, and effects through a gallery that opened onto the garden. I counted thirty-seven steps down. Then down again, this time a circular staircase. Thirteen steps down. I thought: The spiral stairway of his youthful fancy has come to pass. All that is missing is the tower, the vast music room.

The adjutant assured me, The Kanzler's bunker is the safest

* (The Final Decision)

place in Berlin. He is protected by two meters of earth and five and a half meters of concrete. Twenty rooms are on either side of this corridor.

The adjutant walked with me down the corridor faced with wood paneling and decorated with Italian paintings in gilt frames. These underground rooms are brilliantly, though glaringly, lighted. Schutzstaffel guards stand at the entrance.

Dr. M. came toward me, These are the Kanzler's living quarters. He took me inside the Kanzler's rooms through a waiting room, then a living room. I heard the Kanzler's voice calling, Doctor! and followed the doctor into the sleeping room where mein K. was lying covered in swollen leeches.

For high blood pressure, Dr. M. explained, making small grunts as he removed leeches that were engorged with blood.

The K. was gleeful, he teased me. I am going to make a pudding of my blood. Why not? You have such a fondness for meat.

The living room is small and narrow, not unlike the shape of a prison cell. The sofa, a small table, three chairs. I'm surprised that the sofa is so shabby. Two people can sit comfortably on it, and three uncomfortably. Frederick the Great, of course, over the desk. A portrait of his mother, on the desk.

Another room divided into a lavatory, a kennel for very pregnant Blondi. Seeing her protrusion gave me a pang of jealousy. Why was Blondi bearing a child for him and not me?

No parallel bars. A cause for panic! I must not panic.

31 MÄRZ 1945

We had lunch together with the secretaries—vegetable soup, corn, jellied omelets. I cannot help but resent these pathetic women, so much less composed than I.

After lunch he napped while I unpacked my things. My room is small and cold but carpeted. There is ventilation in the ceiling that provides a kind of air circulation. When I turn it off, I suffocate. When I leave it on, it makes a ferocious noise. A dressing room adjoins my bedroom and sitting room, both accessible by inside doors to his study.

I have been given a servant, Liesl. A simple girl but clean, a breeder of children for the cause, not like my poor sterilized Paula.

5 APRIL 1945
Afternoon (but I lose all track of time here in bright artificial light):

He has gone upstairs into the park to decorate young men with Iron Crosses. He has been a new man since he learned that the warmonger Roosevelt has died. In the mirror I see that my pelvis is still rock hard, a cocked gun-hammer. I can fire it at will.

20 APRIL 1945
Evening:

His birthday: The secretaries and I sat cramped in the small study. I noticed that Frau J.'s clothes were not fresh. I needn't worry about my own, as Liesl has done miracles with them. Fräulein W. and Fräulein D. both asked, Do you intend to leave Berlin?

He replied, No. If I did, I would feel like a lama turning an empty prayer wheel.

He will turn fifty-six at midnight. I dare not be gloomy.

Night:

I presented him with a new portrait in a jeweled silver frame. He admired it but put it aside when the wife of one of his generals gave him a painting of his mother. This he immediately hung on the study wall. My feelings were bruised by this brush off.

Gifts had been arriving at the Chancellery. Some were brought into the bunker. (Since no one in Germany but me, his circle, and senior generals knew where he is, gifts have also been sent to the Berg.) Then General R. took me aside. You alone have influence on him. If you tell him you want to seek refuge, he'll do it for you. My eyes blazed into the eyes of the general. I wanted to say, "Me" whose birthday gift lies tossed under a pile of cushions with hooked crosses. But I forced a smile.

That night my brother-in-law visited my room. He threw an army officer's uniform on the ground, spat on it, and trampled it underfoot. From his briefcase he removed two souvenirs from the KZ. A bleached human skull and a pair of gloves made from the skin of a prisoner. I have no room nor interest in a bulky, bleached skull of no value. I did accept the gloves. Then he proposed: Fräulein Effie, perhaps you'll share my bed?

I sent him away, took sleeping tablets, but I can't sleep at all down here.

Later:

I cannot sleep.

21 APRIL 1945

Today Dr. M. arrived to give the K. his daily injections. First the K. growled, then he leapt to his feet and pointed to the door. Doctor, leave my room at once. You want to drug me so you can forcibly take me away from Berlin. But I'm not going.

Dr. M. was shaking. The Kanzler screamed, I order you to take the next airplane out of Berlin.

I was shaking too, shocked to see him turn full circle against such a loyal friend, but steadied myself by imagining that I am an andiron, that I can support even burning logs.

I gave some of my jewelry, furs, and effects with instructions to Dr. M. to take to München. Also some coffee for Hanni, riddled with infections from her treatments in Frankfurt. I bid him farewell. Tottering on his feet, Dr. M. climbed up the steps with a bundle of my valuables under his arm.

Under Berlin

Vermouth and Leberkäse all morning. (I don't know morning from night anymore.) Today he went without any injections or pills, and I wore a magnificent new dress of silver-blue brocade. After tea he went back to his map room. Determined to fight the gloom, I announced, I want to celebrate!

I led several of us up the steps into the old living room on the first floor of the Kanzler's apartment. Much has been destroyed on all sides, but this room is still intact. Most of the good furniture has been taken down to the bunker, but the large round table remains and Liesl laid it out for a party. Frau J. lugged up her gramophone, but lamented, I have only one record.

Champagne was poured for Reichsleiter B., for the secretaries, for "Me." The record began to play. *Blutrote Rosen Erzäblen dir vom Glück.** Harmonious music, a good omen. Discordant music, trouble and unruly children. As though competing with the music, the sound of artillery grew louder. Every explosion set the windows trembling. Then the telephone rang with no caller on the other end. The others began to straggle back down to the bunker, but I danced to the record until finally there was no longer a dancing partner.

Later:

So wide awake, I ached for a workout on my parallels. I can feel my spine shrinking, my hopes of motherhood shrinking with it. I dare not guzzle myself into semi-imbecility.

He called me in. We watched as Blondi yelped, then lifted her tail away from her rump. A brown sack was expelled from under her

* (Blood Red Roses Tell You of Happiness)

tail. She turned her nose and, using her sharp teeth, pulled out and severed the brown sack. She chewed up the afterbirth and dropped the dark brown sack near her teats. She panted, then dropped another protrusion from under her tail.

When there were four brown rat-like beings that had been licked with her long tongue, her tail finally fell back. The K. picked up the fat one. He held it up to the light, his voice was jubilant: I name you Wolf. I pointed my 8mm Ciné camera, but in that garish light, I put it down. I used my still camera instead, taking several snapshots of the gooey brown sausages.

Later:

I have been given a pistol and have begun to practice in the courtyard of the Ministry of Foreign Affairs. Bullets and explosions have torn away at the lawns. Great limbs have been ripped from trees. Along the wall are *Panzerfäusten** in orderly piles. I shoot accurately and only wish my targets were our enemy instead of flocks of starlings and dirty sparrows.

Later:

After shooting practice, I crept into the park through the broken walls of the Chancellery garden to my parallel bars to work just a little on dismounts, but the bars have either been removed or stolen.

I saw children covered with lice. I remember as a young child having my hair treated for lice—how it burnt. Then my braid was twined 'round the back of my head. I'm desperate at the thought that after so much work on my parallel bars to keep in condition, my musculature has already begun to sag.

Later:

I was sitting near him. He called Fräulein S. and Fräulein W. into his sitting room. It is time to leave, he told them. You can take two suitcases. You'll fly at dawn.

* (wooden-handled grenades)

Then he called in Frau J., also Konstanze, the cook, and spoke to all of them. To my horror, he included me in the group. He told us: It is best that you women go to the Obersalzberg immediately. There will be aircraft leaving at dawn. It's the end.

I broke away from among the group of women, walked to his side. I took both his hands in mine, pinched them and, totally composed, spoke as though speaking to a sad child. But you know very well I'm staying with you. Why are you trying to send me away?

He leaned forward once again, kissed me on the forehead, pressed his nose against my head. Then, from where they stood frozen, the two secretaries and the cook told him, We will also stay here.

Back in my room I wrote to Mogerl.

Dear Mogerl,
It's still chilly, look after yourself. I rang up last night, just imagine, the dressmaker is demanding 30 Mark for my blue blouse, she's completely crazy. How can she have the face to charge 30 Mark for such a trifle?

Later:

I went up for a walk in the Tiergarten. The fire bombs have scorched off the leaves from trees, and no longer do the swans glide along the lakes. Paula and Charlotta had eaten one, so must have other hungry Germans. I exude superior composure even gayness. I'm mortally happy.

I've returned to my sitting room to write letters.

Dear Little Herta,
When I rang you up, the connection was so bad that I wasn't able to express these best wishes by word of mouth. I wish you a quick and happy reunion with your E., which I'm sure must be your dearest thought and desire.

My whole life is spent in the bunker. As you can imagine, we're terribly short of sleep. But I'm so happy, especially at this moment, at being near HIM. Not a day passes without my being ordered to take refuge at the Berghof, but so far I've always won. Besides it's now im-

possible to go through the front lines with a car. But when everything has resolved itself, there will certainly be the possibility of us all seeing each other again. The secretaries and I have taken up pistol shooting and have become such champions that no man dares accept a challenge from us.

Where are Käthl, Georg and Peppo, and how is Mogerl? Please write quickly and at once. Forgive me the style of this letter, which is not up to scratch, but I'm in a hurry as usual. With my fondest regards to everybody.

Ever yours,
Effie

I studied the photograph of Blondi and her puppies. Then took up my pen again and drew an "arrow" pointing to the the runt in the litter.

P.S. The photo is for Mogerl. One of the sausages (puppies) is destined for her. Would you please tell Frau Mittelstrasser that the Austrian chamber-maid, by orders from above, must be given leave to go home. But only for a limited time. I imagine a fortnight at the most.

24 APRIL 1945

At dawn I heard the sound of bullfrogs in the plumbing. The pilot's plane took off from the emergency airstrip close to the Brandenburg Gate. It carried those who were leaving to a waiting aircraft at Gatow. *Guten flug!**

Later:

He told me: If we're captured, we'll be put in cages and hung up in the Moscow Zoo.

Later:

While he has disappeared again into the conference room, Frau J. and I took Negus into the park. I would not believe it was suddenly springtime.

* (have a good flight)

Minute shoots have burst out on the half-burnt trees, birds have come from somewhere and sing as though nothing has changed. Crocuses and snowdrops have also shot up through the rubble and grass.

A beautiful bronze statuette, a naiad, lay in the rubble and grass, a goddess. I must have it. Close by a headless, limbless female torso. Marble perhaps? Negus ran exuberantly, sniffing and marked the rubble, also marking a damaged hedge of blossoming forsythia with little drops and squirts. We two girls sat down on rubble, and I lit a cigarette. Frau J. squeaked, May I have one?

I struck a match for her.

The air raid siren began to howl, so from my pillbox I took a menthol tablet for my breath, and we rushed toward the door but Negus was disobedient and scampered into the rubble just when a grenade exploded so near to me that I felt hot air across my face. It took me no more than an instant to come to the realization that stupid Negus has been blown to bits. How stupid he was to go there.

The K. was sitting on a long bench in the corridor with puppies on his lap. He stood up and patted the wood for me to sit next to him. Tell me, *du*, I asked, putting on a radiant face, Do you know the bronze statuette in the park? It's absolutely enchanting. It would fit perfectly in my garden, near the pond, beside my parallels. Would you buy it for me?

He held my hands, Mein Kind, it's probably state property, so I can't buy it and put it in a private garden.

Yes, I replied, But you could make an exception if you succeed in beating back the Russians and freeing Berlin.

He laughed: The logic of women. Then he kissed my hand, scraping my skin with his coarse mustache.

I brushed red and black chalk dust from his uniform. Look! You can't wear this coat any more. It's a mess. You mustn't try to be like old Fritz in everything. You walk around looking as though you have no one to care for you.

But it's my working coat. Do you expect me to wear an apron when I'm bending over maps and using colored pencils?

Later:

Together we went up to ground level with Blondi. He took me over to the bunker in the Voss Strasse where a large model of the City of Linz was erected in one of the rooms. He pointed to the museum, I have gathered priceless art treasures. We have Rubens, Rembrandts, Tintorettos, Holbeins, Frans Hals packed in crates in deep salt mines.

Blondi was restless, straining to leave. The thought of stupid Negus made me angry but didn't shake my strong resolution.

. . . Also Dürer, Breugel, Vermeer, Goya—nearly 10,000 paintings are packed in crates. Some are in Thuerntal Castle near Kremsmuenster, also in King Ludwig's Castle of Neuschwanstein at Füssen and even in tunnels of the salt mines east of Salzburg.

Blondi's tail had drooped. I held back the news that my "hearthrug" was no more. I looked at Blondi with new maternal interest.

Later:

Frau Magda G. and her six children just arrived and have taken over Dr. M.'s empty rooms. Frau G. looks a sight. Her salivary glands have suppurated, her cheeks are swollen. She's in terrible pain. Frau J. was made responsible for the five little girls and one little boy—Helga, Holde, Hilde, Heidi, Hedda, and Helmut—and took them to choose toys from among presents left over from his recent birthday. Magda proclaimed, I will be faithful unto death, and fastened the gold emblem between her breasts.

But she seemed on the verge of collapse. Above us the air raid sirens howled again, the telephone continued to ring for no reason.

Later:

At lunch he told our little group, At all costs, I must not be taken prisoner. My body must be burned and so well hidden that no one will ever find any remains.

He looked at me when he spoke. The safest way is to put the barrel of a revolver in your mouth and pull the trigger. The skull is shattered in pieces and death is instantaneous.

I was shocked. I exclaimed, I want to be a beautiful corpse. I'm going to take poison. From the pocket of my dress I brought out a small capsule in a yellow copper casing, which I've had for five years. I asked, But will it hurt? I am willing to die courageously, but I want it to be painless.

He instructed, Death by cyanide poisoning doesn't hurt.

Fräulein S. whispered something to Fräulein W., who spoke for all of them, May we each have a capsule?

After lunch the K. went to each secretary and gave her a capsule. He murmured as he did so, I am sorry I can't offer you a better farewell present. Their eyes were moist, their dignity flew out the window.

Later:

Telephones ring constantly. The diesel engines make humming sounds. The overhead lights flicker while I work on cataloguing my remaining jewelry, furs, and shoes.

Later:

I instructed Liesl to give me a manicure and pedicure. Her hands are so jittery that she made a mess on my toenails, which I had to repair myself.

Later:

The K. attended military conferences in the afternoon and also at midnight. Since none of us can bare to be alone anymore, we sat in the little kitchen and drank Schnaps and Bier.

I went upstairs occasionally to smoke, then sucked on a fruit drop, taking in the desolation. I saw hungry and homeless Berliners searching through the rubble-strewn streets along the Unter den Linden for scraps of wood, and bits of food. Our soldiers were barricaded behind tree trunks and sandbags and are fighting for their Kanzler. All of Germany is wondering: Where is he? How would they feel if they knew he was right below their very feet in the center of Berlin? With little Effie.

Later:

We sat at the table in the little kitchen. Waiting.

25 APRIL 1945

Today he gathered together documents and papers from the cabinets of his study. He called his valet and told him, Burn them! The valet carried the stacks of paper up the stairs to the Reich Chancellery garden, burned them by handfuls. When he returned, he was given the order to perform the same duty in München, and then to go and do the same at Berchtesgaden.

Later:

Frau J. knocked furiously on my door. She was in a frightful state. I gave her schnapps, What happened?

She described the following: The Kanzler was at the daily war conference. When he was told that a particular general had disobeyed an order, he began to breathe very heavily. At the same time his head jerked as though he was having a fit, then he stalked back and forth in the conference room, raving and screaming and began to swing his right arm madly. After ten or twelve minutes he stood stock still, his jaw dropped, his mouth hung open. He was frozen. Then he walked out of the room. His generals are calling it a mental collapse. She looked at me with round sapphire eyes.

I sucked my cheeks in. I told her to leave the room. What did she expect me to do?

> *My dear little Herta,*
> *These are the very last lines and therefore the last sign of life from me. I don't dare write to Mogerl; you must explain all this to her with due consideration for her state. I'm sending you my jewelry to be distributed according to my will, which is in the Wasserburgerstrasse. I hope that with this jewelry you'll be able to keep your heads out of water anyway for a time. We're fighting here to the bitter end, but I'm afraid this end is drawing dangerously near. I can't describe to you how much I'm suffering personally on the K.'s account.*
> *Forgive me if this letter is a little incoherent, but the propaganda minister's six children are in the next room making an infernal racket.*

What else should I write you? I can't understand how all this happened, it's enough to make one lose one's faith in God!

The man is waiting to take this letter.

You have my most affectionate and kindly thoughts, my faithful friend! Say hello to Mutti and Vati; they should go to München or Traunstein. Regards to all the friends. I shall die as I lived. It's no burden. You know that. With fondest love and kisses,

> *Yours,*
>
> *Effie*

P.S. Keep this letter to yourself, until you hear of our fate. I know this is asking a lot of you, but you're brave. Perhaps everything will still turn out happily, but he has lost faith, and as for us, we're hoping in vain.

Berlin

My dear little sister,

How sad I am that you're going to receive such a letter from me. But it's inevitable. Every day, every hour, the end may be upon us, and I must therefore use this last opportunity to tell you what remains to be done. The Kanzler has lost all hope of a happy outcome of the conflict. But all of us here, myself included, still believe that while there's life, there's hope. So I beg of you, hold your head high and don't despair. But naturally we're not going to let ourselves be captured alive. The faithful Liesl refuses to abandon me. I've proposed several times that she could leave. I should like to give her my gold watch, but unfortunately I've bequeathed it to M. I want to wear the gold bracelet with the green stone until the end. My diamond watch is unfortunately being repaired. I'll write the exact address at the bottom of the letter. Maybe you'll be lucky and manage to retrieve it. I want it to go to you, because you've always admired it. The diamond bracelet and topaz pendant, His gift for my last birthday, are also for you. I hope my wishes will be respected by the others.

In addition, I must ask you to attend to the following things: Destroy all my private correspondence and above all the business papers. I owe the Heise firm the enclosed bill. There may be other requests but not for more than 1,500 Mark. I don't know what you propose to do with the films and albums. At all events, please only destroy everything at the last moment.

I'm sending you at the same time the wherewithal for food and cigarettes. Give some coffee to Käthl and the L.'s too. Give the L.'s some of the cans from my cellar. The tobacco is for Vati. The chocolate for Mutti. There's chocolate and tobacco at the Berg. Get them to give you some.

    I hope Dr. M. delivered the jewelry to you. It would be terrible if something had happened. Now, my dear little sister, I wish you lots and lots of happiness. And don't forget that you'll certainly see Hermann again.

    With most affectionate greetings and a kiss from your sister,
    Effie

P.S. The watchmaker's address: Schutzstaffel Unterscharf. Stegemann Schutzstaffel Lager Oranienburg evacuated to Kyritz.

Under Berlin

The news just came that the Berg was bombed! The local inhabitants rushed in and started pillaging. I'm furious. After all we have done for them!

I'm doing everything I can to get:

1. news of my possessions
2. news of Stasi

It's hopeless to get lines out. All I can glean is that Stasi ran away during the bombing. I went into my room to nap but my eyes wouldn't close.

Later:

I joined the K. at 4 o'clock for cups of chocolate and cakes with Dr. G.'s children. He's subdued, but himself again. He was called to the telephone. While he was gone, Waffen-Schutzstaffel Orderly Hermann Grossman and Waffen-Schutzstaffel Orderly Bussie—who had been joined by their fiancées in the bunker—clicked their heels and begged "Me" for a minute of my time.

One said, As it appears that we are going to die defending Berlin, we would like to marry our girlfriends.

I asked, Why tell me?

We tried to see the Kanzler, but he was too busy to see us. Could *you* ask him if he would give permission for us to marry in the bunker?

They were asking me for help! I replied, I will speak to the Kanzler. Wait here.

I left but returned shortly. The Kanzler is delighted to give his permission.

If I were an oyster I'd have made a little pearl today.

Afternoon:

There has been a double wedding attended by "Me" and the Kanzler together. Because one of the brides had been shot on the way
to the bunker, she lay stretched out on a stretcher during the ceremony. Because of the close quarters, I heard a waiter tell Fräulein
G., while pointing out the K. and I, They seem deeply moved by
the wedding.

The flippant secretary whispered so loudly that I heard her
reply, If Effie ever thought the Kanzler would marry her, she
knows better now. Time has run out.

Her voice carried across the room, everybody must have heard,
but I kept my head high.

Later:

I was just called to the phone. My brother-in-law told me: Effie,
I'm safe here in Berlin West. Don't worry, the jewelry you gave me
to deliver is safe also. Listen to me. You must leave the Kanzler. In
a few hours it will be too late to escape from Berlin. Don't be stupid. It's a matter of life and death. I'm going to join Mogerl, a father must be near his child.

I shouted over the bad connection, I have no intention of leaving. My bed is made, Hermann. But the line was dead.

The K. was standing at the door when I looked up. He seemed
to know who I was talking to. He told me, The Geheime Staatspolizei has discovered that he keeps an apartment near the Kur-
füstendamm.

I turned white as a rabbit.

27 APRIL 1945

He brought me into his map room. On the maps, silhouettes of
boats, airplanes markers. He told me to listen as the Schutzstaffel
gave this report: A gray Mercedes followed by a military car full of
police arrived at 5 P.M. outside the general's apartment. They entered and found him in civilian clothes, with suitcases packed and
with a small Hungarian lady, the wife of a diplomat, and a child.

The woman spoke in French, said, I am rich. We hope to start a new life together in Switzerland.

The Kanzler picked up the telephone: Arrest him and shoot him if he tries to escape.

But my sister is having his baby!

Two hours later:

My brother-in-law was just escorted, in uniform, into the study. He'd lost all his composure, was a gibbering idiot. When I rose to leave the room, the K. told me to stay, so I sat back down. You are a coward, the K. bellowed, his cheeks mottled red.

He ripped Hermann's epaulettes and his Knight's Cross off and tossed them onto the floor. I spoke out, He's young. His wife is expecting a baby, the only one in my family.

But then the arresting Schutzstaffel opened the suitcases. I sat aghast while a soldier counted:

1. 217 pieces of silver,
2. a diamond watch,
3. two chronometers, (one Universal, one Omega,)
4. an international watch,
5. another watch chronometer,
6. two pairs of gold and diamond cufflinks,
7. several bracelets,
8. fifty Swiss gold pieces,
9. 105,725 Mark,
10. 3,186 Swiss francs.

I reached in and picked up the diamond watch that I had put in for repair. How did you get my diamond watch? This is mine. This was meant for Herta.

The K. screamed in a fury, He's a traitor. There must be no mercy.

I had gone rock hard too. The K. was right all along, there is nothing more pathetic than kindness. You are right Kanzler, I told him. Family considerations no longer count, and I looked right into my brother-in-law's handsome monkey face with scorn.

My brother-in-law called, Effie, lovely sweet demure Effie.

Before my eye I saw a strong man grovel until he was removed. When the door closed behind I asked, What will they do to him?

He'll be taken to the grounds of the Ministry of Foreign Affairs and shot.

Among the spring flowers, I thought. Among the remains of my pet.

Later:

Frau Magda G. drank quantities of Martell brandy while Frau J., in a hyper-nervous state, looked after her children. She read stories to them and played forfeits. These rather fretful children were ready for bed. They were all wearing flannel nightgowns decorated with intertwined red roses and blue flowers.

I squeezed into the crowded room. Holde told us: The wicked bandits are trying to destroy everything but Uncle Adolf will get on his white horse and give them the lesson they deserve.

Hilde and Hedda added, We are making a big journey. Mutti and Vati have promised an excursion to the beach in Pomerania.

Helga, the eldest, with walnut eyes told me, The journey is not true.

Tell her about Wieland the Smith, demanded Hilde. By "her" she meant "Me."

Helga talked expressively: Uncle Adolf told us this story. It is set in a mythological Iceland, where Wieland and his brothers are fishing on a lake called Wolf Lake. In the background are flaming volcanoes, icy glaciers, also huge rocks. Suddenly three *Walküre* in shining helmets and wearing white robes over their armor float out of the clouds.

I recalled these white cloaks in *Lohengrin* when I, at seventeen, had gone with him to the opera.

After Wieland the Smith was lamed by his king, he avenged himself. He raped the king's daughter and killed her two brothers. Then, he drank out of their skulls before flying away on wings he had hammered out in his smithy.

I recalled gliding easily on skis, then lying in a chalet that had canary yellow walls and ceilings; listening to the brown woodpeckers.

The two little ones had been excited by the skull drinking, they looked at me for approval. I was too wrapped up with my own concerns to do anything but pat their silky heads.

As I was leaving, Fräulein D. squeezed into their room. Her eyes were red-rimmed. She sang "Brahm's Lullaby."

Tomorrow, if such is His will
The Lord will wake you once more . . .
I tiptoed away for a whiskey.

Later:

I cannot sleep without a workout on the parallel bars. I mulled over the perfect routine:

1. mount
2. eight to ten movements
3. dismount, predominantly swinging moves
   facing both directions
4. moments of nonsupport as well as support.

No matter how much I'd practiced, how much I'd defied gravity, I'd never felt completely free of the apparatus. During the course of all my routines, I varied my tempos with pauses followed by movements, ring upon ring, of strength. I have somersaulted and done twisting and turning combinations, but the support positions had always predominated for me. I could give the impression of a flowing pattern of movements but never a free body swing. Nonetheless, a real "amateur" gymnast was what I had become with my years of discipline and toil.

Later:

Still cannot sleep. Much worry over Mutti and Vati.

28 APRIL 1945

This afternoon when I walked back down the corridor, a crowd of people had arrived in the Kanzlerbunker. A line had formed, reaching right down the corridor. He was moving slowly along it, holding out his hand to each person, looking at them without seeing them.

Frau J. asked me, Has the time come? She seemed ready for dictation or death, whichever came first. She was like a cat on hot bricks.

I didn't reply. I was then handed a note by an orderly. I took it in with me to the K.'s workroom. Frau J. was also just walking in and took up her dictation book. The note was from Hermann Grossman. I read it out loud to the K: If I am killed in battle now I will die happy because I was permitted to marry my sweetheart and the Kanzler congratulated me personally.

The K. didn't look up as I read it. Finishing, I clutched the note to my throat, muttered, I'm so happy for them!

I couldn't help it. I *was* happy. His ears pricked forward as he got to his feet. Frau J. followed him with her eyes. He walked over to me, leaned down, and whispered into my ear.

I must have appeared shocked at his words. He pinched and patted my shoulder then walked toward the map room gesturing for his young secretary to follow him.

In triumph I stood up. I announced to her when she was half-way out the door: Tonight you will certainly cry! Tailbone curling down, I walked into my room to assemble my wardrobe.

Later:

Just now, also a wedding. A kitchen maid married a driver. As soon as we congratulated the young couple, someone produced an accordion, another produced a violin. The newlyweds danced and ground against each other while the walls trembled and the windows rattled. Then the violin player stopped, lowered his bow to the ground, while the accordion swelled up like a balloon.

Frau J. returned. Her robin's-egg-blue eyes brightened as she read aloud to me from her stenographer's book: He dictated this: *Although during my years of struggle I believed I could not take the responsibility of marriage, I have now decided at the end of my life's journey to marry the young woman who, after many years of true friendship, came of her own free will to this city when it was already almost completely under siege in order to share my fate. At her own desire she will go to her death with me as my wife. This will compensate us for what we both lost through my work in the service of my people.*

I put down my head, and peeled back my lips to show my teeth. So! Has time run out? I gloated and poured vermouth into two large glasses.

Later:

I worked on my face. Liesl walked in and out in an irritating way. She ironed my dress. She has tortoise-like hands. I complained out loud: Oh why didn't I bring the brocade dress that belonged to my grandmother. Oh why isn't Paula here? I could have cried. Oh that Mutti and Vati could be with me now!

Liesl tried to help me wash and set my hair, but she was too clumsy. My children need me, she begged, may I leave when I've finished my work with you tonight?

I told her, No. It is more important that you stay here with me.

My Wedding!

The valet laid out the table in the anteroom beside the K.'s study with a tablecloth with the Kanzler's initials, silver dinner service, champagne.

A few minutes after midnight, I made my entrance. I was wearing a long gown of black silk taffeta with a very full skirt and a high neck. I also wore:

1. my gold bracelet set with the original tourmalines from so long ago
2. my diamond watch
3. my topaz pendant and gold clip, pinned to my hair

He was not there.

After a ten minute wait, tempering my *Schwärmerei**, I went to get him. He was giving reams of dictation to Frau J. still in rumpled uniform. He was saying: Destroy all amenities of civilization, all industrial plants, gas, water, electric, telephone systems must be smashed. All essential to life must be destroyed, all ration card

* (gushing enthusiasm)

records, registry and bank records, food suppliers destroyed, farms burned down, cattle killed. Destroy all works of art, monuments, palaces, churches, opera houses, theatres, castles leveled, every footbridge destroyed, every stalk of wheat.

When he saw me, he broke off his dictation.

I told him, The justice of the peace and senior organization functionary have arrived.

He explained, Frau J., I will return shortly, and left his secretary sitting at the desk.

We joined the others in the small map room where a table for the signing of documents and a few seats had been lined up.

I stood with Herr B. as my witness. Dr. G. acted as his witness. A two page document was prepared from my identity card with birthplace of parents, parents' names already filled in. The justice asked, And what about the Aryan origins of each of you? And hereditary diseases?

Need he have asked?

The Geheime Staatspolizei provided two gold rings, slightly too large. We were each asked to sign the document. I nearly signed my maiden name but crossed it out and wrote his name.

Muscles quivered up and down my flank. He gave me his arm and walked with me into the corridor to receive congratulations from his staff. Then we walked to his study where the *Hochzeits-mahl** was laid out—sweets, champagne. The secretaries, Colonel von B., the cook offered congratulations.

Baring his teeth, Dr. G. explained, My wife's nerves are very bad tonight. Her salivary glands have suppurated. She sends her congratulations.

I gloated over his words. The valet poured champagne.

Our witnesses stood together, then raised up glasses toward us. Even the K. drank a few sips of sweet Tokay wine and toasted: My wife!

When he said it, I pictured the statue of Venus in the park. The torso was limbless, headless, dazzling white, naked to the waist.

* (wedding meal)

He then made a little speech: My wish has always been to return to Linz, my hometown, and settle down with Effie for the life of an average citizen.

Though I tried to concentrate I got lost in my own mind, in which a calliope played many dreamy notes—false and true notes—and when I returned to his speech he was concluding, . . . Now it appears that I will not need such a place.

Immediately he showed signs of impatience and departed to rejoin his secretary so that he could continue giving dictation. I didn't mind. I let my head roll back, I ordered the waiter to bring champagne and cakes to the secretary who had missed the wedding in order to finish the typing. Over and over I played "Red Roses" while artillery and bombs exploded above.

Later:

I returned to my room. Liesl had laid out my blue silk Italian nightdress. I put it on though my thoughts went to the old blue nightdress embroidered with red roses, which I'd inadvertently left in München. I sat on the bed, the bed was high so my feet didn't touch the floor. I waited for him to return.

He did at 4 o'clock. He kneeled in front of me and I stretched my head forward. I licked his hand, laid my head lightly on . . .

29 APRIL 1945

He woke. His valet brought his breakfast: porridge oats, grated apple, nuts, lemon juice, wheat germ soaked in milk, a slice of cake, and a cup of chocolate. He ate. Then dressed and left the room. Liesl brought my coffee, my porridge oats. I was giddy, hungry too.

What time is it?

After eleven, *gnädig*, Fräulein.

Gnädiges Frau, Fräulein! She turned red as if slapped.

Liesl dear, when I'm no longer with you, I want you to go to see my friend Herta in München. Give her my wedding ring and this nightdress.

I gave her one of my rings—a semi-precious stone. Take this

ring in memory of me. It was meant for my devoted housemaid Paula, but Paula took her own life.

Liesl began to weep. For you Frau, she uttered, and handed me two small devotional cards. The first, the child Jesus with yellow curls wearing a pink gown. Mary was dressed in blue. The second, Christ on the cross being tortured with a crochet hook.

I couldn't hold back a smile. Had I once been that naive too? Help me dress now, I want to look my best.

Later:

I joined the Kanzler at the table. I poured tea for him. He pushed a dispatch over for me to read: *Benito Mussolini is dead. Captured by Italian partisans as he attempted to escape into Switzerland from Northern Italy, he was taken before a tribunal and sentenced to death. In the village of Dongo the sentence was executed by partisans, who machine gunned him in the back. His mistress Clara Petacci, was also captured and killed with il Duce. Their bodies were subject to public degradation. After being dragged through the streets, they were hung head downward in the public square where thousands spat at and reviled the corpses.*

Spat! For the first time I experienced hesitation. The tea spilled across his lap. I grabbed a towel and tried to wipe his wet lap. He brushed my hand away. Konstanze brought boiled eggs, a plate of potatoes in their jackets, curd cheese. A maid sprinkled powdered vermicide along the edges of the room. Bring the new doctor, he ordered.

Dr. Ludwig S., the new bunker surgeon, was brought. Would my dog Blondi respond to the cyanide the same as a human? he asked.

Yes, mein Kanzler.

I asked, And will I?

Ja, guadige Frau.

How do I know it will work? His voice was peevish. Bring Blondi!

Blondi was walked in, fixed her trusting gaze on her master, her ears erect. Dr. S. pulled apart her long snout and lower jaw, broke a capsule in her mouth using tongs. Blondi rolled her jet-rimmed, amber eyes. Her tail drooped, paste-like feces shot out from under her tail. She made a disgusting sound then keeled over.

His bodyguard brought the box with her four puppies. He lifted Blondi up and dropped her in with them. The babies pressed against Blondi's teats as the bodyguard carried the box up into the garden in order to kill the pups.

Quickly my husband ate the potato, then the eggs, then he went inside to continue dictation while I called: Vermouth!

I raised my bare throat up in order to drink down my vermouth.

Later:

I went to bed at 2 singing "Tea for Two."

When his dictation was finished at 3 o'clock, he returned and got into bed with me. I made a tiny sound of welcome, like mewling birds do.

30 APRIL 1945

Traudl told me at breakfast about her late night journey into the main shelter. She described the following: An erotic fever has taken possession of everybody, everywhere, even on a dentist's chair, I saw bodies locked lasciviously. The men and women had discarded all modesty and were freely exposing their private parts. The Schutzstaffel went out on "whore" patrols. People were stuffing themselves on rolls and caviar . . .

I was fascinated. I demanded, Come with me.

I led Frau J. into my room. I took from the cupboard my fine silver fox coat. Traudl, take my fur coat as a memory. I stroked my initials—E. B.—embroidered on the lining, intertwined in the shape of a four-leaf clover and lifted the coat into her arms.

She took it and I added, Say hello to München, to Bavaria, and once again began singing, "Tea for Two":

Two for tea,
me for you,
you for me.
Can't you see,
how happy we would be? Let her remember me this way!

1:30 P.M.:

The secretaries and the cook ate lunch. I drank tea, ate cold meat, bread, butter. My husband joined us and had a dish of spaghetti.

Later:

I went back to have my hair washed and waved.

I needed to pinch my cheeks for color. Mutti used to pinch me this way to keep me still and also to make me yield to her wishes.

I walked on his arm wearing his favorite black dress with pink roses at either side and a low square neckline. The dress was tight around the waist but I no longer cared if I had started on an ungainly path. On my wrist, the platinum wristwatch studded with diamonds. I smiled until my jaw ached, and stood beside my husband when he ordered the pilot: You must make sure that our bodies are burned.

The Kanzler handed the pilot *Frederick the Great,* by Anton Graff. This cost 34,000 Mark in 1934. Many of my paintings are more valuable, but I'm fond of that one. I don't want it to be lost. He looked one last time at *Frederick the Great,* and whispered: Beside him, I'm just muck.

Later:

I went back to have my hair combed once more. I folded my blue silk Italian nightdress, then I removed my wedding ring and placed it inside the fold in the nightdress.

Now:

His bodyguard carried a machine gun across his shoulder. He went from room to room in the bunker. He bared his teeth and announced: Come! The Kanzler wants to bid farewell in the corridor.

My husband and I came out into the corridor. The secretaries and the cook stood there. Over my dress I had tossed a little coat with long sleeves. I'd changed into brown suede Italian shoes with modern wedge heels—evening shoes—sandal form. In my hair, one last embellishment, the gold clip.

My husband offered his hand to his staff one by one but was looking through, not seeing anyone. To each person he muttered, but no one could make out the words. I followed close behind him, silently. To Frau J., smelling her soiled dress, I whispered, Wear my fur coat. I always like well-dressed people!

Coming down the corridor just then—almost running, wearing a leopard-skin belt—I saw Frau Hochschmidt and heard her trumpeting cry. When she reached me I kissed her straight on the lips.

My husband took my arm, opened the door. There was the sound of the tap running. He led me toward the study, but just before the heavy iron door closed, I turned back to look at Monalisa with gimlet eyes and waved at her.

Then the door closed behind me. The telephone rang. The lights dimmed and flickered.

While my husband methodically combed his hair in his unique way, I changed into my blue polka-dot dress. Then my husband took up his pistol, but his hand shook so badly he could not control it. He told me: Frau, a shot fired with the muzzle pushed against my skull will produce a gaseous recoil. It will leave a large hole at the point of entry and pull portions of my brain out with it. It won't do.

He handed me the pistol. He ordered, Frau, shoot two inches from my skull.

I watched with amazement. Without a further word or farewell, my husband clamped his teeth against the lethal dose of cyanide. He moved his teeth in grinding action, then covered his scrotum with folded hands. Immediately bits of sinewy fur and spittle welled up at the corners of his mouth. He put his head down, half-closed his smoky, yellow eyes as his brindled gray hair fell across his eyes. How easy it looked.

Following his orders, without a sentimental lapse and with a rock steady hand, I shot my husband through the left temple two inches away. Then I removed his mother's painting from the wall, propped it against his chest. I replaced it with my photo in the pretty, jeweled silver frame.

I slipped off my expensive brown Italian shoes, tucked my feet beneath me as I liked to do when listening to phonograph records, and prepared to bite into my poison capsule by arching my throat.

I looked at the large wedding ring on his hand which cupped his scrotum. I looked at mine, also too large. I know he had truly been in happy repose those many times sprawled out asleep next to me after tea. One last time I smoothed my hair, straightened the gold clip, the necklace.

Quickly I will put these last memories together with these notebooks, all wrapped in an orderly way, into his brown pillow-slip. I'll scrawl a note to Hochschmidt, and will set the package beside me. Then, end it.

Here ends this accounting of my life. I'm thirty-three years old, a widow. I . . . we . . . Farewell!

E. H.

END

AUTHOR'S NOTE

This is a thick soup of speculation as its author lived an insular life. It makes no claim to chronological or historical accuracy. Its morally reprehensible, soulless ingredients are reconstituted from various reputed primary historical materials—letters, interviews, anecdotes, studies, memoirs, diaries, including Eva Braun's diary fragment from 1935, her twenty-three photograph albums held in the National Archives in Washington, the Musmanno Archives, the Public Information Department of the Pentagon, and from a bountiful supply of secondary source works. My thanks to the authors of the factual foundations and other sources of information and inspiration onto which this fiction is grafted: J. R. Ackerley, Ruth Andreas-Friedrich, Robert B. Asprey, Ian Beckett, Alan Bullock, James Bunting, Roger Caras, Norman Corwin, J. V. Denenberg, Alfred Döblin, Bella Fromm, Pierre Galante and Eugene Silianoff, Richard Grunberger, Nerin E. Gun, Ernst "Putzi" Hanfstaengl, Robert Harris, Glenn B. Infield, Regina Jais, Traudl Junge, John Keegan, W. R. Koehler, Claudia Koonz, Walter Langer, R. D. Lawrence, Gottfried Leske, Heinz Linge, Hans Lunge, Golo Mann, Monika Mann, Thomas Mann, John T. Marvin, Werner Maser, Donald M. McKale, Hans-Otto Meissner, Ib Melchior, Richard Overy and Andrew Wheatcroft, Robert Payne, Peter Padfield, Gerald L. Posner, Richard M. Reslak, Cornelius Ryan, Horst Scharfenberg, W. Schwarzwäller, William L. Shirer, Howard K. Smith, W. D. Snodgrass, Louis L. Snyder, Albert Speer, H. Trevor-Roper, Marie "Missie" Vassiltchekov, Betty Watson, Christa Wolf, Erik Zimen, the grocers, from whom I have shopped. Sections written in italics are actual quotes.

This soup can be left simmering over a low fire.